THE RETIRED ASSASSIN'S GUIDE TO ORCHID HUNTING

RETIRED ASSASSIN'S GUIDE
BOOK 2

NAOMI KUTTNER

Author's Note

This book is set in New Zealand and will show you a glimpse of life and culture there. British spelling is used throughout the book. Enjoy!

ISBN: 978-1-991430-04-5

"In the middle of the journey of our life, I found myself in a dark wood, for the straight way was lost."

— Opening line of *Inferno*, Canto I, by Dante Alighieri, 1321 AD

PROLOGUE

In which the stage is set.

It was nine o'clock on a Thursday morning in the seaside town of Te Kohe, New Zealand. Outside, the sun shone brightly, the bees buzzed, and the birds busied themselves about the garden.

Inside, Dante sat cross-legged on the floor. A black cat with three white socks lounged in his lap. On the coffee table in front of him, a pair of military-grade night vision goggles sat on a lint-free cloth.

His cleaning kit lay open next to them, complete with cotton swabs, microfibre cloths, lens cleaning fluid, and a set of tiny screwdrivers.

Dante found the task of keeping his gear in top condition relaxing. His old MI6 trainer had often told him that 'fortune favours the prepared mind.'

In Dante's experience, fortune also favoured the man with superior firepower, meticulously maintained surveillance gear, and a fortified position on the high ground.

At this moment, he was working on the well-maintained surveillance piece of this equation. The cat rolled over, revealing a snow white belly. On autopilot, he stroked its tummy, and it began to purr.

Dante was filled with a feeling he couldn't quite name — a strange mixture of contentment and restlessness. It was like homesickness for a place he'd never been.

He wondered if that were even possible, and if so, could Te Kohe be that place?

The eyepiece he'd been unscrewing fell open. The tiny screw dangled magnetically from his screwdriver, and Dante deposited it carefully on the white cloth.

Feelings came and went like the weather. Right now, he had a job to do.

In Dante's back garden, his gardener and friend, Charlie, pruned and weeded. It was his favourite time of day to be out, before the sun grew too harsh, and the dew was still to be found in the shadowed hollows of the land.

Right now, he was contemplating a patch of begonias living in the shade of a weeping willow.

"That tree's on its last legs," said Mrs Davison, hands on hips. She looked up at the tree with a disappointed turn to her mouth.

"This heatwave's been too much for it," said Charlie. "Also, it's getting on."

"As are all of us," said Mrs Davison.

"Well..." Charlie stuck his tongue in his cheek while he thought of something tactful to say.

He could see the begonias through Mrs Davison's translucent form and the wide brim of her ghostly sunhat. She hadn't aged a day since her death from a heart attack one year ago.

"Metaphorically speaking, that is," said Mrs Davison, her eyes twinkling. "Tell me, Charlie, what do you think you'll want to plant in its place?"

A few streets over, Eleanor held the phone to her ear and listened as two voices spoke in tense tones on a heavily encrypted channel.

"How do I know you'll send the payment after I hand over the artwork? I need further sureties." The voice was gravelly, with a Balkan accent.

Unseen by the speakers, Eleanor made a face. It was hard work brokering illegal art deals between unscrupulous customers. They all had trust issues — for good reason.

"Gentlemen," she said, "we've reached a place I like to call 'the breaking point.' To put it bluntly, we cannot make a deal if there's no trust."

A few beats of uneasy silence followed.

Eleanor smiled brightly, knowing that it would come through in her voice. "To break the deadlock, I propose we engineer a situation of mutually assured loss."

"And how would that work?" The second voice had an aristocratic British drawl.

"I'm so glad you asked," said Eleanor. "The art goes into a sealed vault; the payment into a locked crypto wallet. They are released only when both parties input their unique keys within a 24-hour window. If the payment is withheld, or the art removed by the seller..." she shrugged. "Mutually assured loss. The crypto wallet is locked forever, and a remote-activated mechanism incinerates the art in the vault. You both lose. Trust the process, and you don't have to trust each other."

There was a tense silence.

"Fine," rumbled the first voice. "I accept."

Curious, Eleanor waited for the second operator to make their play.

Outside, the warm summer air of Te Kohe sang with rhythms of beetles, birds, and growing things. Above it all, the sky stretched, wide and vast as the ocean it mirrored.

And on the horizon, unnoticed by the busy inhabitants, storm clouds gathered, darkening the future with the promise of rain.

1

In which Dante grapples with moral ambiguity.

Dante drew the blinds, checked the room for any details that might identify his location, and sat at his desk in his front parlour. It was time for a weekly Thursday meeting he'd attended without fail for the last six months.

Under the desk, his fingers wrapped around the handle of his Glock 17. He let out a slow breath, chasing the inner calm his therapist had said this would bring. His fingers tightened around the stippled grip of the gun, the polymer plastic cool against his palm.

The cat butted its head against his calf, and Dante's pulse slowed. His focus drew inwards to a single point as his shoulders relaxed. It was time.

Dante keyed the connection, and the screen of his computer flared to life. Looking back at him were four faces: John, Aubrey, Jasmine, and Frankie. Four retired assassins, four members of Assassins Anonymous, four killers doing their level best to keep their days homicide free.

Dante found that some days this came more easily than others.

"Hello," said Dante. "My name is Dante, and I am an assassin."

The group chorused through their greetings, but Dante couldn't help noticing a missing face: Caleb. He had been Jasmine's sponsor, and Dante wondered what had happened. His speculation was cut short by John getting down to business.

"I'm sure you've all noticed that Caleb is missing," said John.

There were nods of agreement around the group.

John laced his fingers together. "I'm still piecing together the picture. At this point, it looks like Caleb encountered some interested parties from past contracts."

Frankie pursed his lips in a silent whistle, Jasmine looked sympathetic, and Aubrey winced. Dante took this to mean that the family of someone Caleb had killed had come seeking vengeance.

"Caleb has gone off grid for the time being," said John. "He'll rejoin us when he's ready, I imagine. However, he will have to start his count of homicide-free days again."

"That's rough," said Aubrey, his thick black eyebrows drawing together.

"People can be so judgmental," said Jasmine.

"A guy's gotta do what a guy's gotta do," said Frankie. He held up his hands in a placating gesture. "I get that we're turning over new leaves and all. But what if it was just him or you? Just the two of you, and no one would ever know."

John steepled his fingers. "No one would know? You would know. And he would know."

"But he'd be dead," said Frankie.

John's eyes were calm. "That is the core of our work here. Who are you, when no one else is watching? What would you do if you knew you could get away with it?"

Frankie, the ex-hitman, wrinkled his forehead. "I done a lot of things and got away with it. I mean, there's all those people I whacked."

"Is this, like, one of those philosophical things?" asked Jasmine, her blue eyes wide and innocent.

"Like the trolley car problem," said Aubrey. "Where you have to decide whether to push a fat guy onto the tracks or kill three people."

"Hey man, I'm being serious here," said Frankie. "If you was like Caleb — facing a guy with a gun, and it was you or him? Because I'm not getting iced just because I'm trying some different stuff. I mean, I've kept to the code the last few months, but if it was him or me..." His voice trailed off, and the other ex-assassins looked thoughtful.

"That is the ultimate test of principles," said John. "Most people live their whole lives and never have to make this choice. But now," he opened one hand, as if holding the dilemma in his palm, "when you have committed to not killing others, you may be faced with this impasse."

"I'm no peacenik," grumbled Frankie. "I can manage not to kill anyone Monday through to Sunday. Business as usual. But if someone comes at me packing heat, all bets are off."

"I would push the fat guy onto the tracks," said Aubrey. "The math adds up."

Frankie shook his head. "What is it with you and this fat guy? He someone you had a hit on, back in the day?"

"I'm not ready to hang up my Beretta yet," said Jasmine. "I mean, I'm not planning to use it," she spread her mauve nails, admiring their sparkle, "but it pays to be prepared."

"It's like that story of the frog and the scorpion," said Aubrey. "We're trying our best, but I don't know if any of us can really change. If it came down to the wire, I'd make sure I was the last one standing."

"What about you, Dante?" asked John. "Have you considered what might happen if old enemies came to call?"

Dante thought about this. The talk of trolley cars and scorpions felt like a distraction. But absolutes like 'him or me' he understood very well. In the past, he'd always made sure it was him. "I don't know," he said at last. "If they threatened my..." he hesitated, the word strange on his lips, "... friends, then I might need to take steps."

The other ex-assassins nodded.

"Fair point," said Aubrey.

"Does the code really want us to be sitting ducks?" asked Jasmine. "Seems a bit extreme."

"The AA five step path is not easy," said John. "We all meet challenges along the way. That's why we're all here to support one another."

The talk wound through various topics for the next half hour, until John's eyes flicked down to the time on his computer. "We will end this meeting with the invocation."

Dante turned the question over in his mind as they intoned the closing prayer of Assassins Anonymous.

"May Life grant me the serenity,
To accept that not all things are solved by violence,

Dante had never left a target alive during his many missions around the globe. He'd never missed.

That sometimes the right thing to do is walk away.

But the people he'd killed presumably had relatives. People who might, perhaps, be moved to vengeance.

Allow me to tolerate this world with all its flaws,
And never seek to improve it,
By removing from it,
Those whom I deem unworthy of life.

And then there was his old employer. His handlers had been bureaucrats at heart. But sometimes they needed to make a ledger balance, and that might require removing a small impediment, such as a retired assassin living in the Antipodes.

Dante was a wanted man in many countries, but he'd always been excessively careful. Most places, no one had any idea he'd been there.

May I possess the wisdom to know,

That burying the bodies,
In a place they'll never be found,

But you never knew.

And leaving no witnesses,
Is not the same as living a life of peace."

There were, after all, no certainties in life.

Except death.

"Thank you all, and see you next week. Keep to the code," said John.

Dante cut the connection and stared into the blank screen. His head and shoulders made a dark silhouette, reflected in the black mirror of his laptop.

If it were between him and an armed assailant, what would Dante do to stop him?

In Dante's experience, in that kind of situation, training and tight-focused adrenaline took over. Bodies wanted to live, even if the people inhabiting them held lofty ideals.

If it were between him and me, Dante suspected the 'him' would end up dead, and Dante would face the lesser cost of squaring this moral deficit at the next AA meeting.

That outcome, he could live with.

2

Which raises the question of fate, and whether it can be altered.

On Friday morning, Charlie stood in Dante's kitchen with a view both of the stormy sky outside and his friend's folded arms and fierce scowl.

"I'm not going to see anyone. And I don't like doctors." Dante's voice was flat.

Charlie shifted from foot to foot. He'd been working his way up to having this conversation for a while, and it was not going well.

"He's not, like, a medical doctor or anything," said Charlie. "Professor Carroll is a naturopath. I think. Actually, I'm not sure why everyone calls him the professor. He knows a lot about plants, and he makes natural remedies from them. And he has the best orchid collection in Te Kohe."

This did not appear to have the effect Charlie was hoping for. Dante's stance remained unmoved, but his gaze shifted into the thousand-mile stare Charlie had seen too often over the last few weeks. Since his friend was six foot two and built like a street fighter, it was hard not to get worried when Dante's grey eyes fixed on the middle distance, and he went somewhere else.

"He can give you something to help you sleep better."

"I don't take medications," said Dante. "Especially not ones that might slow my reaction time."

Charlie racked his brains for something that would change Dante's mind. What would his friend Eleanor say? She'd lived a long and interesting life and was good at tricky conversations.

"It'd be good for you to meet the neighbours," he said.

"I've met my neighbours," said Dante. "They all came round when the corpse plant bloomed. One visit every seven years is enough."

"But Professor Carroll didn't come round. He was abroad, and he only just got back."

"Which house is he in?"

"Well..." Charlie thought about how to couch this. "If we went over your fence and onto the track in the reserve behind your property, and then we walked for about twenty minutes, we'd reach his place."

"That doesn't sound like a neighbour to me."

"There're no houses in between your place and his. So technically, he is your neighbour. A next-door-with-a-few-acres-of-forest-in-between neighbour."

Dante considered this piece of information. "Does he know about cats?"

"He might do," said Charlie, hoping he did. "He knows an awful lot about a lot of things. What's up with your cat?"

"It's getting fat," said Dante.

"The professor might be able to help," said Charlie cautiously.

"Ok." Dante began stowing their tea cups in the dishwasher.

"Ok?" said Charlie.

"Ok. Let's go."

The last rain flurries cleared as Charlie and Dante headed up the narrow dirt track that led deep into the forested foothills behind Te Kohe. The path was slippery with both mud and tree leaves.

Occasionally, a gust of wind would shake the trees above and dump water down the back of Charlie's neck.

There was, in fact, a road that led to Professor Carroll's house, but it was unsealed, winding, and prone to landslides. It was faster to climb the steep track behind Dante's house until they reached the clearing.

Dante was silent as they slogged uphill. Saying nothing was normal for him, but Charlie was impressed at how silently the ex-assassin moved. Even when he stopped to listen, he couldn't hear Dante's footsteps.

As the track grew even steeper and they had to grab onto branches and tree roots to climb, there was no sound of huffing or even heavy breathing. Dante looked as serene as if he'd just strolled down the corridor for a cup of tea, while sweat trickled down Charlie's neck.

Charlie was fairly sure they could trek for the rest of the day before Dante asked how far they had to go. But after fifteen minutes of climbing, the path levelled out, and they reached the final stretch — a trail that meandered through a stand of kauri trees.

Kauris were among Charlie's favourite native trees, and he took time to tell Dante about them as they walked — how they could live for more than a thousand years, how the giants among them had trunks more than thirty feet across, and how whole ecosystems lived in their branches.

"And kauri gum can be carved into beautiful sculptures—" Charlie broke off as a lanky figure rounded the bend and strode towards them, cane raised in greeting, or possibly as a threat. "Hi, Professor."

The man stopped short and glared at them through thick-lensed glasses. He had broad shoulders, only slightly bent with age, and a weathered, strong-featured face. Tufts of white hair stuck up in an unruly thatch on top of his head, giving him a wild, windblown look. His manner changed as he recognised Charlie.

"Ha! Sorry, lad. I thought you were that old busybody, come back to badger me with questions. Who's this?"

"This is Dante," said Charlie carefully.

"'In the middle of the journey of our life, I found myself in a dark wood, for the straight way was lost,'" Carroll recited in a rolling baritone, and the hair rose on the back of Dante's neck.

"What's that from?" asked Charlie.

"Dante's Inferno," said Carroll, with a genial smile. "I'm Professor August Carroll." He thrust out a square-fingered hand, and Dante shook it.

"Pleased to meet you," said Dante.

"Is this a social call, or are you after something specific?" asked Carroll.

"If it's not a bother," said Charlie. "My friend Dante wants to sleep better."

"You do, do you?" Carroll's eyes sparked with curiosity as he looked Dante up and down. "I imagine a fit, strong man like you would have no problem with sleep. Must be something up here, then." He tapped his temple. "That can affect even the healthiest specimens. Well, come on!"

With that, he spun on his heel and marched back up the path, leaving Dante and Charlie trailing in his wake.

"Don't mind that," said Charlie in a low voice. "He's ninety-three, and he says he lost his filter years ago."

"But not my hearing," said Carroll. "Don't make apologies for me, lad. I think your friend prefers when people speak their mind. Saves time."

They rounded the corner and came upon a clearing where an old settler bungalow nestled back into the New Zealand bush.

Sunlight broke through the storm clouds and lit the house in sepia tones as they walked up the weathered wooden steps and onto the front porch.

"Welcome to my humble abode," said Carroll, and waved them inside.

The first impression Dante had was that he'd stumbled into an alchemist's den. They were in a moderately sized room with shelves on every wall. Filling every shelf were bottles, and filling every bottle were oddly coloured liquids with plants, seed pods, and even insects floating inside. Bunches of dried herbs hung from the ceiling, and the central work table was crowded with cutting boards, mortars and pestles, and various other mixing implements.

“Tea?” asked Carroll.

Dante was about to say ‘no’ when he remembered what his therapist had told him about declining hospitality. ‘Not everyone is trying to drug or poison you, Dante. Sometimes, a cup of tea is just a cup of tea.’

“Yes, thank you,” he said at the same time as Charlie nodded enthusiastically.

“Professor Carroll makes the best tea. Brewed with herbs from his own garden.”

“Thank you, lad. This boy,” Carroll nodded towards Charlie, “is a good boy. Always helping out, never too busy to listen to an old man.”

Privately, Dante agreed. Charlie was twenty, but his auburn curls, rosy cheeks and genuine air of goodness made him seem younger. He would need his own protection detail if he ever visited any of the places Dante had operated. He shuddered at the thought of Charlie, blithely tripping through warlord fiefs and gun smugglers’ dens, complimenting them on their healthy poppy plantations and well-sharpened machetes.

“Now, why have you come here?” Carroll shot a finger skywards. “I remember. A brew to stop nightmares.”

Dante had said nothing of the sort, but he kept quiet, studying the bottles for signs they might be dangerous.

While Carroll whisked around the room, pulling various bottles and jars from the shelves, Charlie sidled up to Dante.

“See?” he murmured. “This will sort you out just fine.”

“I’m not taking anything that will compromise my ability to defend myself,” Dante muttered.

“Oh, you don’t have to worry about that,” said Carroll from the other side of the room. His tufted white head was bent as he examined a row of small bottles filled with suspicious brown liquids. "I would never do something so crude. The remedy I'm designing will lift your spirits. After that, sleep comes naturally."

Dante wasn't convinced his spirits needed lifting. He was probably going through what his fellow AA members called 'the six month slump.' Meaning if he didn't kill anyone soon, he might just have to do something drastic, like enter a no-holds-barred cage fighting tournament, or go to Mumbai to compete in the 'wall of death' car races.

"I know what would take your mind off whatever's bothering you," said Charlie enthusiastically.

"What?" Dante's mind was far away, contemplating the 'wall of death.' He didn't know whether driving a car at top speed around a cylindrical wall thirty feet in the air, only staying in the air by centrifugal force, would help his ennui. But it might.

"We could grow some New Zealand orchids in your greenhouse. Something interesting, like a Greenhood orchid."

"A Greenhood orchid. Sure," said Dante.

Carroll set several bottles of varying sizes on the table and took an empty bottle and a cork stopper from a chest of drawers under the table.

Dante remembered his earlier conversation with Charlie. "Professor, do you know much about cats?"

Carroll's bright eyes met his. "I know that cats prefer to be left to their own devices. What's the matter with yours?"

"It's getting fat," said Dante.

Carroll pulled up a chair and sat at the table. "You don't mind? I do my best thinking when I'm off my feet. If I were you, I'd feed your cat a bit less and see what happens."

This seemed like sensible advice. Dante nodded and took a cautious sip of his tea.

"While I mix this up," said Carroll, "I want you to tell me about the upcoming Orchid Symposium."

Charlie beamed. "Isn't it amazing? Coming to our very own town."

Carroll grunted. To Dante, he looked less than pleased. "Yes, yes, it's a great honour and all that. But who is coming? They'll all be staying at your mother's hotel, yes? Have you seen the guest list?"

Charlie bit his lip. "I've been helping out, so yes, I know a few names, but is it ok for me to tell them? Isn't that confidential?"

Carroll waved a hand. "I'll see them soon enough at the conference. Indulge a curious old man."

"You'd have seen the speakers' list," said Charlie.

"Oh yes. The speakers are the usual suspects. Edmonds, Tyburn, Fiorelli. I've seen their schtick a hundred times before. But is there anyone new? An unusual guest? A well-known collector?"

"If someone's really famous," said Dante, "they would use an alias when booking a hotel."

"Pshaw," said Carroll, "no one is that famous in the orchid world, though they like to think they are. Ours is a small and close-knit garden. Though it has some tangled roots that are best left undisturbed."

Dante's attention was piqued. "Do you mean orchid smuggling?"

Carroll's face split into a toothy smile. "Dante from the Inferno, that's a good guess. Charlie, thank you for bringing your friend. I like him."

"Are you worried someone might try to steal your orchids?" Charlie's eyes were round. "You have some pretty rare plants here."

"I might be." The old man's gaze was keen. "So tell me, who's on your mother's guest list?"

Charlie swallowed, then said hesitantly, "Well, there are quite a few. The hotel is completely booked out. There was a Roebuck," the old man made no reaction, "and a Thorogood, a Christie, a Derringer, and a Fairfax. I remember that because his booking reference said 'Lord Fairfax.'"

"Jeremiah Fairfax?"

"No, Martin."

"Ah. The younger brother." Carroll turned to Dante. "The Fairfaxes are an old, aristocratic English family. Practically royalty when it comes to plant collection — they've been at it since the 1700s. Anyone else?"

"Let me think," said Charlie. "There was a guy with a foreign name, French maybe?"

Carroll sucked in a breath through his teeth. "A French name like Lucier?"

"That's it!" Charlie's face broke into a grin, which slipped when he saw Carroll's face. "Are you ok?"

"Of course!" Carroll's mouth twisted in a smile. "Just reminiscing. When you're my age, it happens a lot. Now, we make the remedy."

The next few minutes passed in silence, with Carroll measuring, muttering, and titrating drops of liquid from his assembled potions.

At last, the concoction was ready, and Carroll pressed the small bottle into Dante's hands. "For you, my friend. May it bring you deep, dreamless sleep and sweet awakenings."

"Thank you," said Dante. He wasn't sure he would ever take the medicine. Maybe once he'd installed some extra safeguards on the front door and bulletproof glass in the main bedroom window. Maybe.

"Are you worried about your orchids?" asked Charlie. "Because I could stay over during the conference if it would help."

"Charlie," said Carroll, "I have lived a long life, and I have learned many things. One of them is this: sometimes the steps you take to avoid something are the very thing that brings it to your door. Don't you worry. I'll be fine."

3

In which murder is discussed. Over tea.

Dante did not want to spend his afternoon making polite conversation, or any conversation at all. He'd only agreed to come because Eleanor had said it would be a good opportunity to practise being a civilian. As she was one of the few people who knew his former occupation, her advice was valid.

Also, Andrea, the local veterinarian, might be there. Dante hadn't seen her since the corpse plant had bloomed in his back garden, and he wanted to see her again, without turning it into an event.

Now, he and Eleanor were seated at a long table in the back garden of Marjorie Everton, Te Kohe's resident socialite and orchid grower. Eleanor was wearing an elegant linen pantsuit that matched her white-blond hair. Her alleged sixty years sat lightly on her as she smiled and made easy conversation with the other guests.

Also present were various members of the Te Kohe Botanical Society and two trophy guests — both important speakers at the Orchid Symposium that would start that evening.

Andrea didn't appear to be there, so Dante studied the guests of honour. There was a glamorous black-haired lady in a red dress with perfectly made-up features, wide dark eyes, and a sharp chin.

Next to her was a man in his fifties with cool grey eyes and an ascetic's high cheekbones.

Dante toyed with the cake in front of him and eyed his tea with scepticism. The last time he'd attended a garden party, he'd been the guest of a Colombian drug lord on the occasion of his daughter's quinceañera.

A rival agent had seen the celebration as an opportunity to attack. The event had not ended well for the drug lord or the rival agent. Dante and the quinceañera debutante had taken cover behind a steel catering trolley that had careened towards them in the ensuing action. It had been carrying a tres leches cake that, even upended over the two of them, had been delicious.

"It's such an honour to have you here," said Marjorie, holding up a glass of sparkling wine. "To Dr Isabella Fiorelli and Marcel Lucier."

"The honour is all ours," said Dr Fiorelli.

Dante checked the garden for unseen watchers. He didn't like being surrounded by dense, semi-tropical foliage, full of hiding places and opportunities for ambush.

"Your garden is ingenious," said Marcel Lucier with a slight smile. "The English cottage garden out front, and this jungle paradise hidden in the back. Perhaps we can see your greenhouse later?"

Marjorie's chest ballooned with barely contained pride. "You would be most welcome. In fact, I was wondering if Dr Fiorelli would do me the honour of dividing my prize Gastrodia cunninghamii."

"Oh, yes?" Fiorelli raised one contoured eyebrow.

"It is my stud orchid," said Marjorie, "and I was wondering if you could divide it after we finish tea. I've been delaying the operation until your arrival. I would so appreciate your skill and expertise in this matter."

"Oh. Yes." Fiorelli gave a smile that was there for one second and then gone the next. "I would love to."

"Tell me, Dr Fiorelli," said Lucier, "I'm curious — why did you decide to speak at this Symposium? I thought you were booked to go to Holland."

"There was a change of plan," said Fiorelli with a slight shake of her head. "I didn't know you paid such close attention to my movements."

"As a minor player in the orchid collecting game," said Lucier, "I like to keep track of the key people. Your scientific research could be a game changer."

"Well, that is a compliment indeed," said Fiorelli, with another of her lightning-fast smiles. "It is not usual to see a woman succeed in this field, yes?"

Lucier raised his teacup in silent acknowledgement. His grey eyes studied Fiorelli, and Dante studied him in turn.

The orchid collector reminded him of Ahmed 'One-time' Jaziri — a man he used to buy weapons from in Tunisia. The 'one-time' was because if people crossed him, they only did it once. It was hard to cross someone twice if you were drifting gently out to sea on the Mediterranean currents and extremely dead.

"How deadly is orchid collecting?" he asked Eleanor quietly.

Her eyes crinkled in appreciation. "Let's find out." She raised her voice. "Monsieur Lucier, I was wondering, how dangerous is the game of orchid collecting?"

Lucier shifted his steel grey eyes to Eleanor. "It depends," he said.

"On what?" asked Eleanor.

"On whether you have been struck by the orchidelirium," he replied.

A collective sigh ran around the table, and Dante was reminded of the feeling of shared longing in his Assassins Anonymous group.

"Orchidelirium?" Eleanor tried the word out. "I've never heard of it."

"Then you must be newly arrived in the world of orchids," said Lucier. "It can afflict anyone at any time. No one is immune to its pull. Not once the orchids sink their roots into your soul."

Eleanor gave a tiny 'ah' of understanding. "It's the yearning to obtain those orchids which are most rare, most unique?"

"More than that," said Lucier. "When orchidelirium strikes, you must have the object of your desire — by any means possible." His cool gaze flicked over to Fiorelli, then back to Eleanor. "It is well known in our world and must be guarded against."

"Is there an Orchidelirium Anonymous support group?" asked Dante.

Lucier's full lips curled in a secretive smile. "There should be. If there was, I'm sure my brother would have been part of it. And you, Doctor? Would you ever admit to being struck by orchidelirium?"

"I am a scientist," said Fiorelli. "I live in the realm of the intellect and the facts. We scientists do not let our passions get away from us."

"But surely passion is the reason you entered this field in the first place?" said Lucier.

Fiorelli shook her head, causing her silver jewellery to flash in the sun. "I am excited by the research and the scientific discovery. Not the collector's obsession."

"Research?" asked Eleanor.

"Doctor Fiorelli has been working on bringing back extinct orchids through DNA extraction," said Marcel Lucier. "Exciting times." His face didn't betray even a hint of excitement at this pronouncement.

"Yes, my work is groundbreaking," said Fiorelli. "It will change the game — especially for collectors and sellers of rare orchids." She carved off a small mouthful from the rich slice of cake in front of her.

"Isn't Professor Carroll a researcher, too?" Eleanor asked innocently.

Fiorelli's smile flashed as she speared her piece of cake with a small fork. "Ah, yes, your local, ah, academic. As I understand it, he is more of a naturist."

"Someone who prefers nudity?" asked Eleanor, her brow wrinkled in puzzlement.

Lucier's lip twitched. He asked Fiorelli a quick question in French, and she replied in the same language. "Ah," Lucier, turning to Eleanor. "I believe Dr Fiorelli meant a naturalist."

"Yes, yes, that is what I mean," said Fiorelli, waving one hand impatiently. "Someone who believes in leaving nature to its own devices. But without scientific insight, we control nothing."

Dante felt like there was some hidden code being passed back and forth in the conversation, but he wasn't getting it. Eleanor seemed happy to play along, but Dante preferred the direct approach.

"Would you kill someone," he said to Lucier, "to get the rarest orchid in the world?"

Eleanor appeared to choke on her tea. Lucier stiffened, and Fiorelli swung her beautifully made-up face in his direction.

"What a strange question," said the Italian.

Lucier slowly relaxed and tapped a finger on his plate. "I wouldn't kill someone for an orchid — even the rarest one. But that wouldn't rule out every other method of getting what I wanted."

"How about you, Dr Fiorelli?" asked Eleanor.

"Such a dramatic turn of topics." Fiorelli's red-painted lips curved upwards. "Of course, no, I would never. One must have principles, even when chasing perfection."

"Perhaps," said Marjorie Everton, a little breathlessly, "we could change the subject? To something a little lighter?"

"By all means," said Lucier pleasantly.

"I was wondering if the Doctor," she gestured at Fiorelli, "would like to visit my greenhouse now, and perform the delicate operation of splitting my prize stud orchid?"

"With pleasure." Fiorelli speared another small piece of cake and popped it into her mouth.

"Hello, there," came an English voice so cultured it had to have been bred for generations. "So sorry I'm late." A youngish man with classic good looks appeared at the gate to the back garden.

"Lord Fairfax!" exclaimed Marjorie, as the other guests turned to see the newcomer. "You're not late at all. We were just about to go through to the greenhouse, but you can start on tea instead if you prefer."

"Gosh, no," said Fairfax, leaning on the gate. "I'm always up for some orchid action."

Dante evaluated the newest guest. Perfectly coiffured blond hair, golden tan, tailored suit, and patent leather shoes.

"Hi, everyone," said Fairfax, waving good-naturedly. "Introductions to come, I'm sure. Dr Fiorelli, Mr Lucier, what a pleasure."

"If you'd all follow me," said Marjorie, "the greenhouse is in the front garden."

The small crowd of guests duly trooped through the wooden gate that led into the front garden.

"This garden feels like home away from home," said Fairfax in delight. "Alliums, peonies, foxgloves, and is that chamomile? Just like my nan's. She always made tea with her own herbs."

Fiorelli, walking in her high heels just in front of Dante, tripped slightly. He caught her under her elbow to steady her, and she smiled back at him.

"Grazie, grazie." She stepped forward as Marjorie motioned her towards the greenhouse.

"The rest of you will have to wait outside, I'm afraid," said Marjorie, smiling in satisfaction as Fiorelli, Fairfax, and Lucier entered. Eleanor winked at Dante and slipped in behind Lucier. With a shrug, Dante did the same.

Marjorie, still holding the greenhouse door, looked up at him, opened her mouth to say something, and then shut it.

Inside the greenhouse, the air was warm and humid, like one of the Central American countries where a man of Dante's description was wanted, dead or alive. Orchids grew in neat rows, their glossy green leaves framing brightly coloured blooms.

In pride of place at the front of the greenhouse was a single orchid plant on a stand. To Dante's untrained eye, it was a fairly ordinary white flower, but the guests all oohed and aahed appreciatively.

Marjorie squeezed past Dante to get to the front of the space. "I have a pair of gloves purchased especially for the occasion." She held out a pair of bright green gardening gloves like a judge presenting the Palme d'Or.

"Ah." Fiorelli made no move to take the gloves. "I am so sorry; I cannot accept these. I have the latex allergy."

"Oh." Marjorie's face fell. "I don't have any leather gloves."

"But," said Fiorelli, flashing a smile, "it is no matter. It is a common hazard when one deals with orchids that one might need gloves. So I have brought my own." She opened her handbag and took out a pair of delicate olive-green leather gloves.

Marjorie clasped her hands together like a two-year-old in a sweet factory. "That's wonderful. Please." She waved towards a space on the bench where another plant pot, a small trowel and some potting mix had been placed.

Fiorelli pulled her gloves on and lifted the prize orchid off its plinth. With one swift motion, she pulled it from its pot. Dante felt strangely sympathetic to the plight of the plant — its roots suddenly exposed to the eyes of strangers.

"The splitting of an orchid is a delicate procedure," said Fiorelli. It was as if she were on a lecture podium, addressing an unseen audience. "It is the surest way to clone a plant — especially a prize breeding stud like this one. With seeds, you never know quite how the plant will turn out. When you split the plant, you keep all the characteristics of the original." With quick fingers, she selected two pseudobulbs and tugged them gently apart. They gave, and the orchid slowly divided into two plants.

Again, Dante felt a pang of sympathy. He had felt like this at times — pulled between two lives.

"We separate the plant so that each leaf stem has its pseudobulb — like this — and can continue to live." Fiorelli sliced down with the trowel, then laid the two halves of the plant on the bench, her green gloved hands arranging the pallid roots. "It is one form of cloning. Of course, with my new DNA methods, we can achieve perfection."

"Nicely done," said Fairfax in his BBC radio voice.

"A true maestro," said Lucier. His eyes narrowed as his gaze flicked between Fairfax and Fiorelli. "I wonder, did you ever cross paths with my brother? He had some theories on orchid cloning."

Fairfax opened his mouth to reply, but was interrupted by Fiorelli.

"Ecco," she said, placing each plant into a pot and gently tamping down the roots. "It is done."

"That was simply marvellous," gushed Marjorie. "I shall treasure this day."

"Prego," said Fiorelli. "Your stud orchid is a fine plant. It is my pleasure to help."

Her face glowing with satisfaction, Marjorie ushered all her guests into the back garden, where more tea was brewing. As they returned to their seats, Fiorelli made elaborate apologies, citing another engagement.

"Perhaps the good Signor Fairfax can take my chair? Then there will be no gap in the seating."

"With pleasure," said Fairfax, gallantly opening the gate for the departing Fiorelli.

Marcel Lucier watched her go, face expressionless, before turning back to the conversation.

Eleanor caught Dante's eye. She looked meaningfully at her watch, which showed twenty past three, and inclined her head towards the gate. It was time to make an unobtrusive exit.

4

In which Eleanor encounters a past nemesis.

The Orchid Symposium was being held at an eclectic group of buildings known in Te Kohe as 'The Local Bughouse.'

This was not entirely fair, as bugs were not especially welcome there. But the name had emerged at some point hidden in the mists of time, and it had stuck.

The Bughouse's official function was the Te Kohe Town Hall, but it was so much more than that. The town hall was a glorious stone mansion built in the mid-1800s, where the local governor had once resided with his family and servants.

The building was later converted into a theatre, and then a cinema where silent black and white movies were shown, followed by colour classics like 'The Wizard of Oz' and 'Gone with the Wind.'

Finally, in the seventies, an astonishingly ugly wing had been added. It was in every way unsympathetic to the existing building and so had immediately won several architectural awards. This wing housed the golf clubhouse and the various activities of local community groups.

The Bughouse sat on a hill overlooking Te Kohe town and the rolling golf course that ran along the cliffs on the northern side of town.

Throughout the year, sheep grazed the course, keeping the grass down and fertilising as they went. In honour of the Symposium, the sheep had been herded to the front nine holes of the course, leaving the fairways nearest the Bughouse sheep-free.

Eleanor wondered again why the Symposium was being held here in Te Kohe. There were many bigger and more accessible venues. While the Te Kohe Botanical Society was as vociferous a group as you could hope to find in a small town, she doubted they held much sway in the larger orchid society of New Zealand.

Still, it was an occasion. And as someone who sometimes missed the bustle of events and Things To Go To, Eleanor had signed up as a guest. She was looking forward to seeing what happened when a bunch of people who were nuts about a small flowering plant all got together.

It was the opening Friday evening of the Symposium. Eleanor shed her summer trench coat as she stepped inside the Bughouse and passed it to a waiting staff member. She held Dante's arm as she walked in stately fashion into the main room.

Polished concrete floors, high vaulted wooden ceilings, and miles of glass greeted her eyes. The architect must have gotten the brief: 'Whatever you do, make sure the view hits visitors over the head wherever they look.'

"How... colourful," she murmured, taking in the scene.

It seemed orchidists loved to dress in bright shirts covered in rainforest foliage, with the occasional toucan making the colours even louder.

"Dante, could you escort me to the bar? I feel in need of a bourbon to kick start the evening."

There was a small crowd around the bar, but Dante manoeuvred expertly through them, seeming to anticipate exactly when someone would shift position and create an opening for them to slide through. Finally, there was just one person in front of them, wearing a linen jacket and a light blue shirt. His outline seemed vaguely familiar. As Eleanor stepped up to the bar, she realised why.

"Inspector Avery," said Eleanor, "what a surprise."

Dante's gaze swung round to skewer the police inspector, and one arm came protectively over Eleanor's shoulder.

"I'd say the same of you," said Avery, his eyes flicking down to Dante's arm. "What brings you here?"

"That's my line," said Eleanor. A tall barman approached, and she smiled up at him. "A bourbon, please, and — what would you like, Dante?" She relayed his order. "Sparkling water. In a bottle. Unopened. Thank you." Eleanor turned away from the barman and back to Avery. "Why are you back in my neck of the woods? I thought the case was closed, conviction reached, murderer behind bars, etc. No need to come back to tidy up loose ends. Or am I wrong?"

Avery accepted a whisky from the barman. "I'm here on holiday."

"I'll believe that when... when I believe a lot of other things. Like 'don't worry, you're just helping the police with their enquiries.'"

"Dante," said Avery. "Good evening."

"Yes," said Dante.

"Are you here undercover?" said Eleanor. "Because a key part of being undercover is that no one knows you're police. I'd say every primary school kid in Te Kohe could pick you out of a lineup by now."

Avery gave a deep sigh. "I am here on holiday. It was not my first choice of location. But the Orchid Symposium is here, and therefore so am I."

"You're an orchidist?" Eleanor's lips curved in amusement, and then she shook her head. "Not buying it."

"That's fine, since I'm not selling it."

"Excuse me," blared a voice behind them, "some of us are waiting to be served."

"Marjorie Everton," said Eleanor, "allow me to introduce Inspector Marcus Avery, who claims to be an orchidist."

Marjorie Everton, clad in a voluminous green silk dress, looked Avery up and down with two beady eyes set behind a beaky nose. "Hmph," she said. "One does not simply buy a Phalaenopsis from the supermarket and think one knows what one is doing."

"You're going to stand for that?" murmured Eleanor in Avery's ear. "Go on! Throw down!"

"Are you suggesting an orchid off?" murmured Avery.

"Absolutely. The honour of the New Zealand police force hangs in the balance."

"You give me no choice." He raised his voice. "Fine. I see your Phalaenopsis and raise you one Vanda coerulea."

"Aerangis articulata," snapped Marjorie.

"Oooh, burn!" smirked Eleanor.

"That's nice. However, I have a Dracula simia."

"Well." Marjorie huffed, drew herself up, and switched her attack to higher ground. "Strictly a foreign orchid man, are you? What's your best native, a Microtis unifolia?"

"I have one of those, but only to keep company with my Earina aestivalis."

By now, the small crowd around the bar had stopped talking to watch the repartee. They murmured approvingly with each orchid named. Eleanor wondered if everyone was keeping score and, if so, whether any of them would agree on what the score was.

"Huh," scoffed Majorie. "That's just what an orchid-of-the-month collector would say. I myself have a Caladenia alata."

"That's the best you've got? Pterostylis micromega beats Caladenia alata any day of the week."

"What about a European ghost orchid?" The new voice caused a sudden hush to fall. Marcel Lucier had joined the circle. "I mean, if we're comparing specimens." He spread his hands, a curl of his lips not quite making a smile.

The crowd muttered at this, a subdued chorus of recognition, and Eleanor smiled to herself. The orchid world looked to be more fun than she had anticipated.

"I think," said Avery, "a European ghost orchid beats them all. A trump card, if you will. And you are?"

"Marcel Lucier, at your service," said the man, shaking Avery's outstretched hand.

"A European ghost orchid," simpered Marjorie. "How amazing!" She all but curtsied, her green silks catching the light as she bobbed.

"Nice to see you again," said Marcel Lucier. "This is quite a turnout."

At this point, the crowd remembered their mission to get drinks, and the group broke apart, separating into knots of conversation and queues for the bar.

Eleanor took Dante's arm as he led her free of the crowd.

"You see? I am here for the Symposium," said Avery, who'd followed them out.

"You've done your homework," said Eleanor.

"Do you want to see my greenhouse?"

Eleanor fluttered her eyelashes. "I'm not sure I'm ready for that level of commitment."

"Here on holiday," growled Avery. "Which I need after last month."

"My sincere condolences," said Eleanor. "What happened? Oh, that's right, we solved a murder for you. Dante, I think Andrea's over there by the Greenhood orchid display stand. She looks lonely. Or possibly thirsty. I know she likes rosé."

With a silent movement, Dante vanished into the crowd, leaving Avery and Eleanor eyeing each other.

"I really am here on holiday," said Avery. "So I'd appreciate it if you don't trip over any more murders."

"I make no promises," said Eleanor.

5

In which Charlie misses a message.

Charlie Wilson slipped through the crowd, dodging both human and ghostly guests. The late members of the Te Kohe Botanical Society were out in force tonight, mingling with the living, clasping ghostly glasses of champagne in translucent fingers.

Charlie wondered if that was why alcohol was called 'spirits.' Any event where people consumed spirits seemed to draw ghostly company. Maybe the inventors of alcohol knew more about the other side than they let on.

A large screen in one corner was playing the hits — the top forty orchids around the world. Rain fell on a delicate orchid nestled in the trunk of a gigantic tree, its branches covered with rich moss and epiphytes. Then the Iguaçu Falls filled the screen, followed by the cloud forests of Venezuela.

"Takes me back, that does," came a voice at Charlie's shoulder.

Charlie didn't turn around. He knew the voice, and, more than that, knew the telltale brush of cold air and the sense that the sound you were hearing was mostly in your mind rather than your ears.

"You went to South America, Mrs Davison?"

"Oh, yes. With Mr Davison back in the sixties, when air travel was still glamorous. We went on a guided tour, although I'd say it was more of a misguided tour. Our guide eloped with the pastor. We had to make our own way back with no Spanish, and my husband delirious with dengue fever. For all that, I had a marvellous time."

"They don't make travel like they used to?" said Charlie.

"Cheek." She swatted playfully at Charlie's head, and the hairs on the back of his neck stood up with the chill.

"Ah, Charlie," came another voice behind him. This time, when Charlie turned, Professor Carroll had laid a heavy hand on his shoulder. "Just the man I was looking for."

"What's up, Professor?" asked Charlie.

"I'm feeling a bit off, lad. Do you think you could find me a place to sit down?"

"Of course." Charlie nodded goodbye to Mrs Davison as Carroll slung an arm over his shoulders. Even though the professor was a tall man, Charlie was struck by how thin he was under the tweed jacket and flannel shirt. He could feel Carroll's ribs rising and falling rapidly as he leaned on Charlie.

They made their way over to a series of couches, and Charlie helped the older man collapse gently into one of them. He sat next to Carroll and studied him with a worried gaze.

"You don't look so good, professor. Do you want me to call Dr Galway? He's probably here somewhere."

"Nonsense, young man. I just need five minutes' rest. I'm joining the panel soon. Will catch my breath, and then we can talk."

Carroll looked anything but alright. Tiny beads of sweat stood out on his forehead, and his breathing was rapid.

"Are you sure?"

"Quite sure. I wanted to tell you, Charlie, that I have a legacy." Carroll momentarily closed his eyes, as if gathering his thoughts. "I have a legacy to protect. And I'm running out of time." He swayed gently, like an old tree in the wind.

"I think I'll go find Dr Galway," said Charlie, rising to his feet.

In answer, the old man's arm shot out and caught hold of Charlie's wrist in a surprisingly firm grip. He drew the younger man down towards him.

"After the panel, we need to talk. There are some things," Carroll drew a shallow breath, "that you need to know."

"Of course, Professor."

"Just in case," said Carroll, his eyes squeezing shut as a tremor shook him, "it's in my house. My notebook. When you read it, you'll see." He leaned back, wheezing gently. "Going to do the panel soon."

"Please stay here, Professor," said Charlie. "I'll be back in five with the doctor."

Charlie took off at a half jog. This time, he plunged through several ghosts on the way to the reception desk. There were offended 'tsks' and 'watch where you're going,' but he ignored them. After all, living people walked into ghosts all the time. Ghosts only got offended when Charlie did it because they knew he could avoid them.

"Excuse me," he asked the young lady at the reception. "Is Dr Galway here tonight?"

"Is there something you need him for?"

"A friend of mine is really unwell. I think he might need urgent medical attention. I can call the doctor, but if he's already here, that's even better."

"Let me see." She ran a finger down the guest list. "Galway. Yes, he's here."

"Great!" Charlie pulled out his phone. From the coat rack behind the reception desk came a shrill 'brrrrr brrrrr.'

The young lady rolled her eyes. "Looks like he left his phone in his coat."

Charlie jogged back down the corridor. Dante would help him. With his skills, Dante could probably find the doctor in under a minute.

Charlie re-entered the hall to find the crowd gathered at one end of the space, all looking towards the raised dais where the four panel members sat at a white cloth-covered table.

Next to them, a speaker stood behind a podium, a cheery grin on his face.

"Hi, everyone! I'm Greg, president of Te Kohe Botanical Society, and I'm your MC for the night. You all know me, but you may not have met the fabulous members of our special opening night panel. Allow me to introduce you to..."

Charlie groaned. With everyone gathered here, it would be even harder to find the doctor. He wondered if he should storm onto the stage to grab Greg's microphone to make an announcement. The very thought of it made his heart pound with stage fright.

"...Dr Isabella Fiorelli, our keynote speaker and respected botanical historian. A big round of applause!" The crowd erupted as if Fiorelli were a rock star. "Next, Lord Martin Fairfax, of the Dorset Fairfax estate. Welcome, Lord Martin! He told us to call him Martin," said Greg in an aside to the crowd, "but it's not often we get a Lord here. So if anything, Lord Martin he is." The crowd laughed appreciatively. "Hailing from New Orleans, the famed Marcel Lucier. The Lucier orchid collection is second to none in the Bayou, and we're thrilled to have him here tonight. And, last but not least, our very own Professor August Carroll!" Greg drew the name out as if Carroll were a boxer at a high-profile match.

Enthusiastic applause filled the space as Carroll nodded in acknowledgement. The professor had a pallid cast to his cheeks that sent Charlie scurrying through the crowd again, searching desperately for the bald head and neat goatee of Dr Galway.

"Usually, we get each panel member to do a quick introduction, but since we're among friends, I thought we could kick off with some questions and get to the intros later. First question: in your opinion, what makes a real orchidist? Let's start with Dr Fiorelli and carry on from right to left."

"Grazie, thank you," said Dr Fiorelli, her lips parting in a stunning smile. With her raven black curls tumbling down her back, she looked more like a model than a botanist. "A true orchidist knows their forebears. They respect the history of our pursuit and honour the great botanists who came before them. New discoveries come because we are standing on the shoulders of giants."

Charlie darted through row after row of people, mumbling 'sorry' and 'excuse me!' as he navigated the tighter crowd near the front.

"Great answer," said Greg. "Lord Martin?"

"Please, just call me Martin," said Martin Fairfax, his voice low and beautifully modulated. His chiselled face broke into a smile that flashed white in his golden complexion. His perfect side part had a cowlick that broke the order in a carefully arranged curl. "I'd say a true orchidist chases the joy of discovery. Exploration and adventure make a genuine orchidophile."

"A wise answer for someone with your family history," said Greg, over the low murmur of appreciation. "Mr Lucier?"

Marcel Lucier steepled his hands in front of him, grey eyes looking into the distance. "I would say that the true orchidist is someone who is single-minded. The quest to build an extraordinary collection involves sacrifice, discipline, and a willingness to put everything aside in pursuit of your goal."

"That's where the phrase 'becoming an orchid widow' comes from," said Greg with a chuckle. "And our last panel member: Professor Carroll. What are your views?"

Charlie stared as Professor Carroll held up a hand. His mouth opened, but no sound came out.

"Professor Carroll?" said Greg uncertainly. "Are you ok?"

"He's not ok!" yelled Charlie, pushing through the crowd. "Please, Dr Galway, can you get over here right now?"

A small man, just a few feet from where Charlie had been standing, shot a hand up. "Right, folks, coming through, coming through."

Charlie reached Carroll as he pitched forward onto the table, his breathing harsh and laboured.

"Professor," cried Charlie. "Just... keep breathing!"

Other hands were there now, helping to lower Carroll to the ground. Dr Galway crouched by the professor's side.

Charlie found himself pushed back by the more officious members of the audience. Someone jogged his elbow, and he saw Marcel Lucier, his eyes unreadable as he gazed down at the fallen man. Then Lucier's jaw clenched, and he turned away.

Dr Galway yelled to Greg, "Call 111 now. He's having a heart attack."

The crowd noise grew louder at that, and Charlie shivered as the many ghosts pressed closer. A blue glow gathered around Carroll, visible to Charlie's eyes even through the backs of the gathered crowd. Carroll was dying.

"I'm doing CPR," said Galway into the phone Greg held to his ear as the doctor compressed Carroll's chest. "No, there's no pulse, patient is ninety-three years old, no previous heart condition. A few minutes away? I'll keep going until you arrive with the defib."

The blue glow coalesced into the form of Carroll floating five feet above his body, his face surprised. He looked down with interest at the scene.

"Why, that's me. Gosh, I look a bit buggered. How did I get so old?" His gaze swept to meet Charlie's agonised look. "Charlie! You can see me! I'm dying, aren't I?"

Too emotional to speak, Charlie nodded. The crowd noise grew even louder as Mrs Williams had hysterics, and various people tried to get other people to keep the noise down.

"It was probably about time," said the professor, drifting closer. "But look here, I still have this important thing to tell you. It's all at my house, Charlie. You need to go there and find—"

"Everybody stand back! Make a path for the ambulance officers!"

Charlie lost the thread of the professor's voice as Greg's voice blared over the loudspeaker.

"—and I want you to look after it, Charlie. It's vital. And keep it—"

"Clear the way, everybody!" called Greg again. "Ambulance officers coming through, make a path, people! Move!" It seemed Greg had wanted to be in a medical drama for years. Now that he had his chance, he was not about to stand aside and let more qualified people take over.

"—and that's it. All clear?" said Carroll.

"Professor, can you say that again—" began Charlie desperately, but the ghostly Carroll lifted his head in response to something Charlie couldn't see.

The professor's craggy face broke into a delighted smile. "Did you catch that scent, Charlie? It's Frangipani, the same as the garden when I was a boy. It smells wonderful. I think I'll go there now."

And with that, the ghost of Professor Carroll stepped from one reality to the next and vanished from Charlie's view.

A sigh went around the auditorium. It was a sigh uttered not by living throats but by the many Te Kohe ghosts who'd just witnessed a passing over.

"That was lovely," said Mrs Davison, just by Charlie's ear, and he resisted the urge to rub the side of his neck.

"Moving, people, moving!" called Greg again. Now, he was creating an exit path with broad, officious gestures.

Charlie glanced down at the figure of Carroll being strapped securely onto the stretcher. He had an oxygen mask over his face, but Charlie already knew it was pointless. Professor Carroll was gone.

6

On the disposition of law and breakfast.

The following morning (a Saturday), the Frog and Gumboot — Te Kohe's favoured cafe — was awash with speculation and rumour.

Eleanor sat at a table with her two best friends, Billy and Grace, ready to gossip and drink tea. Or, in Grace's case, black coffee.

"It's a shame, yes, but not a bad way to go," said Grace. "Perfect health until he's ninety-three, then bam! Gone in an instant. If you were to see some of the poor folk I look after at Saint Margaret's, you'd know how lucky August was."

"Does he have any relatives?" asked Billy.

"He's a local lad," said Grace, "but an only child. I don't know of any close relatives around here."

"I imagine the Botanical Society is already circling like vultures around his plant collection," said Billy.

Grace sniffed. "I bet Marjorie Everton is first in line."

"Wow," said Billy, eyes wide. "Looks like we have company."

Immaculately dressed in tan slacks, a blue button shirt and dark blazer, Lord Martin Fairfax had entered the cafe. With a bright and friendly air, he joined the queue leading up to the main counter.

There was a flurry of awkward gestures and embarrassed smiles, and Fairfax was quickly ushered to the front of the line, making half-hearted murmurs of denial the whole way.

"Ridiculous," said Grace. "It's not like he's royalty or anything."

"About sixty-ish in line from the throne, in fact," murmured Eleanor.

While Grace harrumphed, Billy watched with avid interest as Fairfax ordered a shot of espresso, a cup of tea, sourdough toast and one hard-boiled egg from the slightly flustered waitress.

As he turned to survey the crowded cafe, Billy waved a hand in the air, grinned maniacally, and indicated the empty chair next to her.

"I can't believe it," groaned Grace as Fairfax headed over. "It's like everyone reverts to being a peasant when an aristocrat waltzes in. I guarantee he goes to the loo just like you do."

"Shhhh!" hissed Billy. "He'll hear you."

"I don't care if he does," muttered Grace, but by then, Fairfax had arrived.

Eleanor noted the fine weave of his shirt, a luxury brand no ordinary person knew existed, bespoke from Jermyn Street, no doubt. The sunglasses casually tucked into Fairfax's shirt pocket probably cost as much as the coffee machine behind the cafe counter, and his wristwatch as much as her car.

"A good morning to you all," said Fairfax smoothly. "Is this seat taken?" He gestured the seat next to Billy.

"It is now," said Billy, with a winning smile.

Fairfax looked momentarily confused, so Eleanor stepped in.

"The seat is yours," she said. "We'd love you to join us."

"Splendid," said Fairfax, sitting down and positioning his order counter on the table. "Eleanor, good to see you again. And these lovely ladies are?"

"My friends Billy and Grace," said Eleanor. "We were just discussing the unfortunate events of last night."

"Such a shame!" said Fairfax. "Professor Carroll was a renowned scientist in the field of orchid hybridisation. I was looking forward to picking his brains about a couple of specimens we have back home."

"Is that the Fairfax estate?" asked Billy. "I've heard it's lovely." Her accent, normally a strong kiwi twang, was somehow turning British, with overtones of Downton Abbey. Eleanor sighed to herself. New Zealanders have a fine accent, she thought. Why change?

"Oh," Fairfax looked down, abashed. "I guess when you grow up with something, you can take it for granted. But I try never to do that. It is quite magnificent, but it was built on the back of colonisation."

"Exactly," said Grace, enunciating every syllable. She took a sharp swig of coffee.

"Grace," said Fairfax with a dashing smile. "Are you the Grace Henga who keeps St Margaret's Memorial Hospital running?"

Eleanor mentally applauded. Fairfax certainly knew how to hit the ground running in a small town like Te Kohe.

"Yes?" said Grace, a little gruffly.

"I've heard all about you," said Fairfax warmly. "I was planning to talk to the people back home about an exchange of medical trainees. We sponsor our local hospice in Dorset, and I've heard about the shortage of staff in rural New Zealand."

"That would be very... nice," said Grace. Eleanor could see her hackles, risen at the thought of an aristocrat trying to butter her up with a donation, slowly settling.

"I'll talk to the board about it when I get home," said Fairfax. "I had no idea Te Kohe was such a charming place. But I'm still truly distressed about Professor Carroll. I was so looking forward to talking with him. We'd been in correspondence, you see, and he was going to show me some of his research."

"I'm in charge of looking after Carroll's place until Leonard — that's his lawyer — gets in touch with his heirs," said Billy. "I could see if he had anything set aside for you." She shot Grace a defiant look. "I know Carroll wouldn't have wanted you to come halfway across the world for nothing."

"Oh, I wouldn't say that," said Fairfax with an easy smile. "But it would be marvellous if I could take a look at his correspondence. It might save you some time if I just went there with you — I can give you my number, if you like."

"Oh, yes." Billy's phone appeared like lightning in her hand.

"If you don't mind," said Fairfax. He reeled off a number — a New Zealand one, Eleanor noted, and Billy keyed it into her phone like someone receiving tomorrow's winning Lotto numbers.

Fairfax's breakfast arrived, and conversation settled into well-trodden lines: the weather, the best things to do in Te Kohe, what the Symposium organisers were likely to do now that Carroll was no longer with them.

"You could do a talk," said Billy, "about the Fairfax collection. I'm sure people would love to hear it."

"That's very kind of you to say," said Fairfax. "I'm happy to help, but I'd only do that if the organisers approached me. I'm certainly not up to Carroll's level and would never presume to replace him."

All nice sentiments, well put, thought Eleanor as she sipped her Assam tea. She noted that one cuff of Fairfax's shirt was just a tiny bit frayed. Was it a favourite shirt, perhaps?

"Well, this has been lovely," said Fairfax, rising to his feet. On his now empty plate, the knife and fork lay side by side, perfectly on the centre line, a clear signal that the meal was at an end. "I look forward to our next meeting."

"A pleasure," said Billy, a trifle breathlessly.

"Eleanor, Grace, Billy," Fairfax favoured each of them with a nod and a sunny smile. "Bye for now."

The three women sat in silence for a moment while Fairfax settled the bill at the counter and departed.

"He'll have paid our bill as well," said Eleanor serenely.

"I've always wanted to meet a lord," said Billy, leaning back in her chair.

"They're just like us, only posher," said Grace.

"I'd love to be posh for a day," said Billy. "Do you know, my cousin worked for a catering company in London. She once made morning tea for the queen in Windsor Castle Gardens. They had to make special little biscuits for her corgis."

"How wonderful," said Grace sarcastically. "You're awfully quiet, Eleanor. You're not starstruck, are you?"

Eleanor shook herself out of her reverie. "Not at all. I'm curious, though — are you going to message Fairfax when you go up to the Professor's house?"

"Of course," said Billy.

"Hmph," said Grace.

"When you're there, keep an eye on him, will you?" asked Eleanor. "I'd be interested to find out what he's looking for."

Billy huffed. "I hardly think he needs anything from that rundown cottage."

"You forget how noble families got their fortunes in the first place," said Grace.

"Possession is nine-tenths of the law," said Eleanor. "And when you're rich, you can possess a lot of law."

7

In which Charlie receives a visitor.

The morning after the opening gala, Charlie awoke from a strange dream. In it, something had gotten into his room and was trying to escape.

He awoke with the dawn to find out that his dream was true.

Something like a small bird was fluttering against his window. Rubbing sleep from his eyes, Charlie got up to investigate.

What he saw made him start and then switch on the light.

Trapped on the inside of his window was a moth, almost as large as his hand. It was a pūriri moth, its vibrant green wings perfectly matching the leaves of the pūriri tree.

Charlie reached for the moth, planning to capture it delicately in two caged hands. To his astonishment, the moth clambered onto his open palm, fanning its ornately patterned wings.

"Wow," breathed Charlie. Up close, the moth was gorgeous, its body covered with a fine green down almost like feathers. A name floated into Charlie's mind — the other name for a pūriri moth. "Ghost moth," he said out loud, and, as if in response, the moth's wings stilled.

Outside the window, the first rays of sun came over the hills behind Te Kohe. "It's too late to let you out now," murmured Charlie. Pūriri moths were nocturnal, and a moth attempting to fly during the day would be easy prey.

Another thought occurred to him. The life cycle of the pūriri moth meant that they spent five to six years as a bug, changing into a moth for only a handful of glorious days before they died. It always seemed unfair to Charlie. Why did nature give them such a short time to fly around and experience the world above?

"Your timing is off," Charlie told the creature resting in his palm. "Spring is your season to be a moth, not late summer. There won't be any other moths around for you to mate with. What are you doing here now?" He had the strongest sense that the moth had come to find him.

He held his hand up, and the moth walked delicately onto his shoulder, where it stayed as he wandered around the house, looking for a home for it during the day.

Eventually, Charlie settled on a large ice cream container with air holes punched in the lid. He furnished the inside with tītoki leaves and some sphagnum moss. Charlie carefully transferred the moth onto his palm.

From there, he planned to deposit it into the container, but it stubbornly refused to leave his palm. He cupped his other hand and tried to push it off, but it hunkered down, the tiny hooks on each foot catching on his skin in protest.

Charlie gave a deep sigh. "You really want to stay with me, don't you?"

The moth's wings fanned out, and Charlie didn't know if he was imagining a wave of relief emanating from it.

"I don't know what to do with you," said Charlie, at the same moment as he realised he did, in fact, know what to do. He lifted his hand, and the moth scrambled back onto his shoulder. "If I went for a walk with you, would you stay on my shoulder?"

I'm finally losing it, he thought — having a conversation with a moth. It wasn't that much weirder than talking with a ghost, he supposed. Except that ghosts usually talked back.

But taking this seriously seemed the right thing to do. A ghost moth had appeared in his room, quite out of season. He didn't know what it added up to, but he knew someone who might.

8

In which Dante takes an unprecedented risk.

Dante walked into the pet shop / veterinary clinic / hunting shop / post office situated on the main street of Te Kohe. He was hoping Andrea would be there. This would give him an opportunity to talk to her and maybe even ask her over for tea.

The tea invitation would depend on how the conversation went. Dante wasn't sure how to invite people. This was because he'd only done it once, fairly recently. Also, his therapist had told him that his questions came across as interrogative rather than inviting.

This was because, in the past when Dante had asked people questions, he was interrogating them. Not always at gunpoint, and not always when they were tied to a chair. But there was always the possibility of those things in the background, and it was hard to break old habits.

The bell jingled as he entered the store. To his disappointment (and secret relief) Andrea was not behind the counter. She was probably doing her vet rounds, visiting local farms to treat sick cows and pregnant sheep.

Behind the counter was a girl in her late teens with pierced ears, nose, tongue, and lip. Dante wanted to tell her how hazardous those kinds of piercings would be in a fight, but decided against it.

"Hi," she said in a bored singsong as Dante entered. "Can I help you?"

"I want cat food," said Dante, stepping up to the counter.

The teenager put down her phone and looked up at him. Her mouth fell open slightly. "Hi," she said in a quite different voice. "Erm, cat food is over there." She pointed with a tattooed hand.

"My cat," said Dante, "is getting fat."

The teenager sat straighter in her chair. "Um, have you been feeding it the same amount?"

"Yes."

"Did you get your cat from here?"

"No. It just showed up."

"Maybe someone else is feeding your cat. Her old owners? Someone else who thinks it's a stray?"

"I will talk to my neighbours." Something in Dante's tone made the teenager wince.

"You know cats can roam a long way during the night, right? Whoever's feeding her could be quite some distance from your place."

Dante considered this information. "I will put a tracker on my cat and find out."

"Ah, ok," said the teen. "Cool."

This not very promising line of conversation was cut short by the entry of Charlie Wilson. He wore a loose sweater and flannel shorts, a far cry from his usual button-down shirts.

"Hi, Maddy," he said to the teen. "Dante, what's up?"

"You're not wearing your normal clothes," said Dante.

Charlie made a face. "You wouldn't believe how hard it is to get dressed while holding a moth."

Dante checked the teen's face. Apparently, this statement mystified her, too. He was glad there was no moth-related aspect of country life he'd been unaware of until now.

"What the—" Maddy faltered. "Why do you have a moth on your shoulder?"

"Long story," said Charlie. "Hey, is Andrea in?"

"She'll be back," Maddy checked her phone, "pretty soon. Why don't you, ah, hang out with your moth and I'll help this guy get cat food."

"Ok," said Charlie. He seemed distracted, darting occasional glances at the large green moth perched on his shoulder as if afraid it would fly away.

Dante didn't know if this was normal moth behaviour. The only moths he'd ever tangled with were the ones that got into his surveillance equipment when he'd been posted in the Siberian Tundra.

Maddy pocketed her phone and slouched over to the cat food shelf. "Ok, so this one is supposed to be for lean cats — you know, lean and mean."

"My cat is not mean," said Dante with certainty.

"O-kay, but it might help it slim down. By the way, I keep saying 'it'—is your cat male or female?"

The question had not occurred to Dante. It was simply 'the cat.' He was saved from having to admit his ignorance by the arrival of Andrea.

She blew in through the door, her dark curls in disarray and several shopping bags hanging from each arm.

"Hi," she said a little breathlessly. Her gaze took in Charlie and Maddy, and then froze on Dante. "Hi," she said in a new tone. Dante tried to place it. It could have been surprised? A little put out? It was hard to be sure.

"Hi," he said in return.

They stared at each other for what seemed like a long time before Charlie cleared his throat.

"Can I help with your bags?"

"Uh, sure," said Andrea. "Thanks."

Dante hurried forward to help just as Charlie said, "I have to be careful taking them because of this moth on my shoulder—"

"Oh, it's a pūriri moth," exclaimed Andrea. "How beautiful. It's only going to be around for a couple of days, though. You know they don't last long."

"That's kind of what I wanted to talk to you about," said Charlie.

Distracted, Andrea let Dante take all six of the bags hanging from her arms. He then stood there, wondering where she wanted them to go.

"I don't know much about moths," said Andrea.

"I was hoping I could talk with your grandmother," said Charlie.

"Oh." Andrea's face cleared. "That sort of talk. She'll be at Mrs Haddock's."

"Thanks," said Charlie. He gave Dante and Andrea a distracted wave as he left. "See you later."

"Where do you want these bags?" asked Dante.

"Out the back, on the operating bench," said Andrea. Now, she sounded preoccupied. "Maddy, can you mind the counter for another ten minutes? I need to unpack this stuff."

Dante followed Andrea behind the counter and into the back rooms of the veterinary clinic. Here, the floor was blue vinyl, and the space smelled of antiseptic soap. It brought back memories of the many times he'd had wounds stitched, bullets removed, and bones set.

"Thanks, Dante." Andrea's voice sounded loud in the small space. She was busy opening cabinets and preparing to restock her veterinary supplies.

Dante placed the shopping bags on the vinyl-covered table. He drew in a breath. "I was wondering if you'd like to have dinner sometime. With me," Dante clarified as the silence dragged on.

"Oh," Andrea's eyes widened before she hurried on. "That would be lovely. How about the Pepper Tree Hotel restaurant? On Sunday evening at seven? It's a long weekend," she explained, as if that might mean something to Dante.

"Ok," said Dante, mentally noting it down. Location: Pepper Tree Hotel. Time: Sunday, 19:00 hours. Target: Andrea Kingi. Mission: dinner. "Should I bring anything?"

"Just yourself," she said with a smile. "I'll make a reservation."

Dante made another mental note to quiz Eleanor about potential hazards that might arise during dinner with Andrea. He was sure Eleanor would give good advice.

"Okay. See you then." Dante left the veterinary clinic, feeling that, all things considered, it had gone rather well. It was only on the walk home that he realised he had failed to secure the objective of his mission, namely, cat food that would stop his cat from getting fat.

This was unlike Dante, who always completed his mission. But some instinct told him it wasn't a good idea to go back to the pet shop right now. Timing was everything, and in this case, the important time to remember was seven on Sunday. Dinner. With Andrea.

9

In which Charlie receives confirmation of a sort.

Charlie climbed the steps to knock on the white front door, worried anticipation churning his gut. Entering the abode of Mrs Haddock brought to mind the many visits he'd accompanied his mother on when he was little.

When they thought he was too busy playing to listen, the talk always turned to him and whether he was acting normally. After his father died, the conversations got worse, and Charlie began hiding in the garden to avoid his mother taking him on visits.

The tidy cottage garden and the lingering scent of shortbread baking in the air brought it all back.

His first round of knocking brought no response. Charlie braced himself to try again when the 'clop, clop' of hard-soled shoes sounded from inside.

The door opened to reveal Mrs Haddock, her spry form clad in a dark green twinset set off with a dove grey shawl.

"Charlie Wilson, do come in." She looked neither surprised nor curious, which Charlie thought was deeply suspicious. Was there some secret network of octogenarians who passed information throughout the country? If there were, Mrs Haddock would be one of their kingpins.

The parlour was clad in faded floral wallpaper. Taking up the centre of the room was a round table covered with a thick brocade tablecloth. Around it sat what Charlie thought of as the Matrons of Te Kohe.

There was Mrs Ochinstan, a fierce lady from Myanmar who'd raised her seven sons alone after her husband died in a fishing accident. Next to her was Mrs Miller, a rose-cheeked lady whose Angora goats always won first prize at the jubilee and who hadn't missed a Sunday service in sixty-five years. Mrs Henga, Grace's mother, sat by the French doors. She had raised the money for the original St Margaret's Hospital in the sixties by ruthlessly running back-to-back lotteries, bake-offs, and collections until it was complete.

And there was Rawhiri Kingi. She was standing off to one side, a slim young woman in an old-fashioned dress. She turned as Charlie entered the room, and the bright morning sun glinted off her plait of thick black hair.

Her dark eyes traced from Charlie's face down to his shoulder, where the green ghost moth hunkered down, no doubt bewildered by the rapid change of scenery.

"Ladies, you all know Charlie," said Mrs Haddock, resuming her seat at what was presumably the head of the round table. Like an ageing King Arthur, she graciously indicated that Charlie should join them at the one remaining empty seat.

"Ah, thanks," said Charlie, sitting down.

"How are you doing, Charlie?" asked Mrs Ochinstan. "I heard you and your mother are well set up now."

"She is, thank you," said Charlie. "I mean, we are." He wondered how to broach the subject of wanting to talk with Mrs Kingi alone.

"Charlie," said Mrs Henga with a cheery smile, "would you like a biscuit?"

"Yes, please," said Charlie gratefully. A well-timed biscuit bite could forestall all sorts of awkward questions. Plus, Mrs Haddock's shortbread was legendary.

Like magic, a cup full of tea, a matching saucer, a milk jug, and an assortment of biscuits appeared in front of him. Charlie thought hard and took three: a shortbread, an Anzac biscuit, and an Afghan. If he was about to get the third degree, at least he wouldn't get it on an empty stomach.

The next few minutes were taken up by Charlie answering assorted questions (yes, the hotel was going fine, no, his mother hadn't met anyone, yes, the gardening business was going well, thank you) while he dipped biscuits in his tea and tried to catch Mrs Kingi's eye.

Finally, Mrs Haddock set her teacup down with a decisive clink. "Tell us why you're here, Charlie. You, and your moth."

Charlie finished his Afghan biscuit. "The moth turned up in my room this morning," he said, gaze veering off to the window where Mrs Kingi stood, silhouetted in the morning light. "It's February, so at least two months after the pūriri moth season. I wasn't sure what to do."

"You did the right thing, coming here," said Mrs Kingi. Her expression was sombre. "This is a serious matter."

"Perhaps you should contact the Department of Conservation," said Mrs Miller. "Is it a rare moth?"

Mrs Haddock looked between Charlie and Mrs Miller, her eyes shrewd. Then she stood. "Charlie, I've been meaning to ask you about my kumara patch. It hasn't been at its best since last season. If you'll excuse us for a moment, ladies?"

With that, she led Charlie out through the French doors and into the backyard, past neat rows of raised beds to the heaped furrows of kumara at the back. Mrs Kingi paced behind them, hands clasped together in an oddly formal posture.

"I'll leave you two to discuss whatever it is you need to," said Mrs Haddock. Her expression was sad.

"She's right beside you," said Charlie.

Mrs Kingi was beautiful in a classical way, the way that statues of Greek goddesses are beautiful, with a high forehead and an expression of grave serenity. She gazed at Mrs Haddock, and Charlie could see Mrs Haddock's garden through her transparent form.

"She still looks like we did at twenty?" " asked Mrs Haddock.

"The same," said Charlie.

"Very beautiful, then," said Mrs Haddock, a sad smile on her lips. "You probably already know this, Charlie, but when you lose someone young, they stay forever young while you gradually grow old."

"Tell Joyce that she's aged well," said Mrs Kingi. "Though not as well as I would."

Charlie relayed this message, and Mrs Haddock's smile deepened, though she still looked sad.

"We said we'd wait for each other, but I never thought..." said Mrs Haddock. "It was never meant to be for this long. I don't hold her to it."

"She knows," said Charlie.

Mrs Kingi inclined her head gravely.

"Alright," sighed Mrs Haddock. "Bye for now."

Charlie and Mrs Kingi watched her go.

"Now, Charlie, what have you brought me?" Mrs Kingi extended one slender finger to Charlie's shoulder. To his amazement, the ghost moth clung to her finger. It flapped its wings to get purchase, then climbed onto her hand.

"I didn't know moths could do that," he said.

"It's a ghost moth," said Mrs Kingi. "We call them that for a reason." She stroked its back gently with her thumb. "You've come a long way, little one."

"I was wondering if you know why it's here," said Charlie. "Seems unusual, turning up in my room months after they usually come out."

Mrs Kingi's dark eyebrows drew down. "This moth carries a message from the next world. It is a sacred trust, and it has come to you."

"Oh," said Charlie.

"A ghost moth comes when someone has died, and the spirit world is not at peace. It can carry many kinds of messages: a warning, an instruction, a prayer. But most often, it is a wish for justice to be served."

"I was hoping it wouldn't be that," said Charlie.

"If this call is unheeded, there will be much suffering, both in the spirit world and here." Mrs Kingi's dark eyes were intent. "Do you know someone who recently passed?"

Charlie nodded glumly. "Professor Carroll died just last night. It looked like a heart attack. I mean, he was ninety-three. But just before he died, he wanted to tell me something. We were at the gala, and then..." Charlie realised he was babbling, trying to drown out the sinking feeling in the pit of his stomach. He took a deep breath and asked the question he didn't want to hear the answer to. "Are you saying the moth is here because the professor was murdered?"

"What do you think, Charlie?" asked Mrs Kingi.

He shrugged unhappily. "I don't know. I don't want it to be true. I mean, he was such a nice gentleman. And he's moved on, so he's at peace now. But..."

"Charlie," said Mrs Kingi gently, "you're avoiding the question."

"I'm going to have to find out, aren't I?" said Charlie.

Mrs Kingi held out one ghostly hand, and the moth fluttered into the air to rest a moment later on Charlie's shoulder.

"It came to you, Charlie."

It appeared that was all the answer he was going to get.

10

In which Dante is given advice of a questionable nature.

"I'm going on a date," said Dante.

The four members of his Assassins Anonymous group stared at him, expressions ranging from calm, to bored, to concerned, to encouraging.

"That's a positive step, Dante," said John. "How do you feel about it?"

"I feel like just before I took out a machine-gun nest camped out in the middle of a minefield," said Dante.

"Worried? Trigger happy? Terrified?" guessed Aubrey.

"Focused," said Dante.

Frankie snorted a laugh. "Man, you're more on edge than a snitch at a mob wedding." He froze under Dante's stare. "Just sayin', man."

"I think it's lovely you're starting a relationship," said Jasmine. "Are you going to give her flowers? I used to love getting flowers from my targets."

"I haven't thought of what to give her," said Dante.

"Just don't let her stay over," said Aubrey. "Or she might ping the tripwire on your weapons stash, and you'll have to run for it before the basement blows." He scowled. "Lousy landlords and their tenant bonds."

"I think what you need to remember, Dante," said John, "is that a date is just a first meeting."

"Like an initial reconnaissance," said Dante.

"Exactly," said John. "You're not giving any commitment beyond meeting for a meal."

"I think," said Dante slowly, "that she's a good person. So it probably won't work."

"Just take one day at a time, Dante," said John. "What do we say?"

"The past is dead, the future unknown, the present is where we can live," chorused the group.

Dante felt that he had not, perhaps, properly expressed the sense of impending doom his upcoming date evoked. If he were to do so, it might come out something like: 'What if she likes me?' That was by far the worst outcome he could imagine. A normal, non-lethal person liking Dante meant they were probably going to end up dead, one way or another.

"Dante," said John, and Dante realised he'd been silent a long time. "Here's what I want you to think about. What's the worst that can happen with your date?"

"She ends up dead," said Jasmine.

"You end up dead," said Aubrey.

"Everyone ends up dead," said Frankie. "Double tapped with a 9mm bullet to the back of the head and buried under eight feet of concrete."

"That's always a possibility," said John. "But it seldom happens."

"It does around here," said Frankie darkly.

"To put things in perspective," said John, "the universe is 93 billion light-years across. Our Earth is so tiny in comparison, we can't even comprehend its vastness. In the larger scheme of things, nothing we do really matters."

A silence greeted this statement. Even Frankie appeared to be thinking.

John fixed Dante with his dark eyes. "Dante. Sometimes a date is simply a date. You're going to be all right."

11

In which Charlie recruits allies.

Dante stood outside the back entrance of the Bughouse, sipping a bottle of sparkling water. The first Symposium lecture was due to start soon, but Dante had felt the need for some fresh air before he met up with Charlie and Eleanor.

The wide rectangle of lawn outside gave way to a formal garden, then a hedge, then an ordinary wire fence. Across it lay the rolling green fairways of the Te Kohe golf course, with rows of evergreen trees and the occasional sheep busily cropping the grass.

He sensed someone approaching and turned to see Charlie with an orange juice in his hand, a moth on his shoulder, and a worried expression on his face.

"Dante," said Charlie, "can you help me?"

"Yes," said Dante.

A month ago, Charlie had banished Dante's ghosts. This meant that in his book, Charlie could ask him for help with anything up to murder. Dante wouldn't even draw the line at helping Charlie dispose of a body. He was good at that and preferred that if such things were done, they were done properly. His AA commitments meant that the creation of fresh corpses was his only sticking point.

“I think Professor Carroll was murdered,” said Charlie.

“Did his ghost tell you?” asked Dante.

“No,” said Charlie. He looked a bit flushed, but Charlie changed colour from almost anything.

“Did you see him being murdered?” asked Dante.

“A moth told me,” said Charlie, then snapped his mouth shut and hunched his shoulders. The moth on his shoulder waved its antennae as if in silent agreement.

“Ok,” said Dante. “What do you want help with?”

“Uh, did you hear the part about the moth?” asked Charlie. “I can explain.”

“It’s ok,” said Dante.

“Oh. Alright then.” Charlie took a moment to regroup. “So, I want to find out who murdered him.”

“Why?” asked Dante.

“Er, because murder is wrong,” said Charlie. “And I can’t go to the police because I don’t have any evidence they’d believe — yet. And the moth is here because if Carroll doesn’t get justice, bad things will happen in the spirit world, and this world.”

“When you find out who did it, what are you going to do?” asked Dante.

“I’ll go to the police,” said Charlie.

“Because I don’t kill people anymore,” said Dante. “Even murderers.”

“I would never—!” Charlie looked shocked. “I just could really use some help in figuring out who did it. And since we’ve done this kind of thing before, I thought maybe you’d be ok with doing it again.”

Dante recalled their last investigation. It had been interesting. Several parts, like the one with the cliff and the ghosts, had been nearly fatally interesting. He wondered if this time would be similar.

"I will help you," said Dante, "because you'll likely end up dead otherwise."

"Oh." Charlie's eyes widened. "I suppose that's... possible."

"It's probable."

They sat in silence for a minute, watching the distant sheep graze the golf course fairways.

"What are we going to do first?" asked Dante.

"Erm," said Charlie. "I'm going to find Eleanor and see if she can come up with a good plan."

"That is a good first step," said Dante.

Further silence followed, punctuated by sheep baa-ing.

"But Dante," said Charlie, "doesn't it worry you? To go looking for a murderer?"

Dante shrugged. All he had to do to find a murderer was look in the mirror, and he did that every morning when he shaved.

"It looked to me like Carroll died of a heart attack. But you say it's murder," said Dante. "That means poison. Poisoners are cowards and not to be trusted."

Charlie swallowed. "I guess you're right." On his shoulder, the moth gently fanned its green wings.

The afternoon sea breeze moved the trees and pushed the puffy white clouds across the sky. Charlie appeared to be thinking again, his forehead furrowed in worry.

"Do you think justice is important?" said Charlie.

Dante considered.

It wasn't a simple answer because Dante had realised long ago that justice came in various weights. For instance, killing a human trafficker, while it offered a measure of justice, didn't shift the scales all the way to absolute good. The trafficker might have children who loved him or an aged mother who relied on him. Removing the trafficker would benefit those he preyed on, but harm others.

"Justice is important," he said at last. "But perfect justice is not possible."

"Sometimes I don't believe in justice," said Charlie. His eyebrows drew together in an uncharacteristic scowl as he gazed out over the rolling fairways. "So many good people die young. They'll never get the chance to be alive again. But when ghosts move on...it's beautiful. Maybe I don't see the justice of it because I'm looking at the problem up close. Maybe if I looked at things from far away and saw the bigger picture, then it'd all make sense. What do you think?"

Dante shrugged. Death was a fact. No amount of thinking would change that. But Charlie was waiting for an answer.

"Sooner or later," said Dante, "everyone ends up dead."

Charlie's frown deepened, then cleared. Now, he looked unexpectedly cheerful. "I suppose death is the great leveller."

Dante agreed. In his experience, death was remarkably impartial. It never discriminated, never hesitated, never deviated from its purpose. Death could be relied upon.

"Let's go find a murderer," said Dante.

12

Which contains certain disruptive elements.

Eleanor relaxed into a mid-row seat near the back of the hall. The first lecture of the Symposium was by Marcel Lucier, and she admitted she was intrigued. Eleanor was good at assessing people, and the man she'd met yesterday radiated both secrets and danger. It was a combination she found irresistible.

The lights were dimming in preparation for the talk when someone sat next to her.

"Coming to level up your orchid game?" asked Avery.

"I thought you were avoiding me for a complication-free holiday," she said with a sweet smile.

"It's a policeman's instinct," he said. "If any trouble occurs during my stay, it's bound to be centred around you."

Eleanor fanned herself with the program. "Such accusations wound me deeply. Just admit what you're really up to, and we'll call it quits."

Whatever Avery was going to say was drowned out in the applause as Greg walked onto the stage, followed by the elegant figure of Marcel

Lucier. Today, he wore a light blue silk suit with a white folded handkerchief in the breast pocket.

"Not many people can bring off a blue suit that isn't navy," murmured Eleanor as the applause died away.

"And he does?" asked Avery.

"With style to spare." Eleanor caught the slight frown on Avery's face and smiled to herself.

"I'd like to introduce Marcel Lucier, scholar and collector, patron of the arts, and the pre-eminent authority on the ghost orchids of the Southern States. Please join me in welcoming him," said Greg.

As the applause died down, Lucier stepped up to the podium. With one hand, he pressed the small controller, and an aerial photo filled the screen behind him: lush green wetlands stretching as far as the eye could see.

"This," said Lucier, "is the Florida Everglades. It is the home of the ghost orchid and the place where my brother and I spent years exploring and discovering rare plants."

There was a collective hush as the audience waited for him to go on. The pause stretched, and Eleanor watched with fascination as Lucier remained, head bowed. His hands clenched around the podium. When he looked up, his gaze was sombre.

"I am sorry. This is the first lecture I have given since my brother passed. Between us, he was the true scholar. He planned, I put his plans into action. The credit for our extraordinary collection must go primarily to him, so it is hard to be here, talking about it and knowing that he is not with us."

The silence grew heavier as people realised that the correct thing to do in this situation was for someone to say, 'I'm sorry for your loss.' However, the problem with a crowd is that responsibility rests on everyone, and therefore no one.

The silence stretched on. Greg looked like he was about to get up from his chair in the front row and say something when Lucier sighed and then spoke.

"And so it falls to me, and I must carry on. I can almost hear him now, scolding me for the delay in getting to the orchids."

The laughter that scattered through the auditorium was relieved and sympathetic. Lucier knew how to get a crowd on his side.

"Many mysteries surround the ghost orchid, and the first is how it is pollinated..."

Lucier dove into the theories on how the ghost orchid plant spread its pollen, and Eleanor became more and more intrigued.

This was a world with as much detail, history, and obsession as the high art market. She wondered how much a ghost orchid would fetch on the black market, and the logistics of how said black market worked.

Plants would be trickier to transport than fine art. They needed food, light, and water. You couldn't just leave them in an airtight container in your attic for years, waiting for the right buyer to wander into your network.

Her growing interest in Lucier's talk was interrupted by the back doors of the auditorium cracking open and then quietly closing as a figure slipped inside. Eleanor raised her eyebrows when she saw the latecomer was Charlie.

Charlie spotted her at the same instant and hurried over, ducking low to avoid blocking people's view.

With murmured apologies, Charlie made his way through the row of seated people to take the empty seat next to Avery. The next moment, he leaned across Avery to whisper. "Eleanor, can we talk for a moment?"

Eleanor nodded distractedly. Right now, Lucier was explaining the difficulty of propagating wild orchid seeds.

"The thing I want to talk about... it's a bit urgent," said Charlie.

Avery made an annoyed noise in the back of his throat.

Eleanor's gaze flicked over to Charlie, then back to Lucier. "Right now urgent?"

"Well... yes," admitted Charlie.

"Surely it can wait," growled Avery.

"Not really," said Charlie.

Reluctantly, Eleanor looked away from the lecture.

"What's the problem, Charlie?"

"Erm..." said Charlie.

"Wait until the talk's over," hissed Avery.

"I'm sorry," whispered Charlie. "But this is important."

Lucier switched to a photo of smuggled ghost orchids being seized by customs, and Eleanor's attention returned to the lecture.

"Just a minute," she said.

"I think something bad has happened." Charlie continued to lean across Avery.

This was very un-Charlie-like behaviour, and Eleanor gradually disengaged from Lucier's talk to study him. His face was creased in earnest worry, and there was something on his shoulder.

She did a double-take. "Why do you have a moth on your shoulder?"

The large green moth seemed to fix her with its multifaceted black eyes as it waved its antennae.

Charlie's eyes rolled upwards to Avery. "Can we swap seats?"

"No," said Avery.

Eleanor leaned over to get closer to Charlie. "Charlie, what's going on?"

Avery made an annoyed noise and folded his arms across his chest.

"I think that Professor Carroll's death may not have been accidental." Charlie's whisper buzzed in her ear.

Eleanor's eyes widened, and then she fought to stop a slow smile from spreading across her face. "Why do you think that?" she whispered back.

Charlie glanced up at the glowering inspector. "Evidence received."

"Ah." That meant ghosts. Not something Charlie would want to discuss in front of the inspector. "Do you have anything more than that?"

"He didn't have any history of heart trouble," whispered Charlie.

"He was ninety-three," murmured Eleanor. "You'll need a bit more than that."

"Stop playing detectives, and let me listen to the lecture in peace," growled Avery.

To Eleanor's delight, a rich voice erupted behind them.

"Will you three keep it down there? Some of us are trying to listen." Marjorie Everton glared as Avery turned to see who was telling them off.

"Sorry," he mouthed.

She gave an outraged huff and smoothed her immaculately coiffured hair into place. "Aucklanders."

Eleanor's shoulders shook as she laughed silently.

"Shut up," Avery whispered.

Eleanor leaned towards Charlie again. "Are we getting the band back together?"

"Yes, please," whispered Charlie.

Marjorie jabbed Avery between the shoulders. "You are disturbing the lecture!"

"I'm not saying anything," snapped Avery. "Get your facts straight before you make accusations."

"That's the pot calling the kettle black," murmured Eleanor, and Charlie gave a startled snort of laughter.

"I'll have you know—" Marjorie's voice volume rose to a trumpeting blare as she lost control of her temper.

A loud chorus of shhh's came from the people sitting all around them, and Marjorie subsided in impotent fury.

On the podium, Lucier paused in his presentation, a bemused look on his face. "Is something the matter?" he asked. Audience members in the front rows craned their heads around to see who was responsible for the disturbance.

Charlie froze, looking panicked, and Eleanor decided to redirect the crowd's ire. Charlie was obviously having a tough day. She sat up straight and raised her hand skyward.

"Yes?" asked Lucier. His grey eyes fixed on Eleanor with laser beam focus.

"My good friend, Marjorie, has a question," said Eleanor. "You're a major player in the orchid collecting market. Won't Dr Fiorelli's work on cloning rare and extinct orchids put you out of a job?"

"Bloody unbelievable," muttered Avery.

Lucier's eyes narrowed, and one hand gripped the podium.

Behind them, Marjorie uttered a sort of breathless squeak, like a mouse surprised by the sudden appearance of a rattlesnake.

Carefully, Lucier relaxed his stance and let out a breath, nostrils flaring. "I have the deepest regard for all scientific research, Dr Fiorelli's included. Now, if you would let us continue, we were talking of the giant sphinx moth and its possible role in the pollination of the Florida ghost orchid..."

The crowd settled back into place.

"I can't *believe* you said that," whispered Marjorie, her voice hoarse. "I shall never live this down."

"I'm sure you will, though," murmured Eleanor. Her thoughts were far away as she turned over the possibility of Carroll's murder in her mind. She had liked the elderly gentleman. If someone here had cut short his life, uncovering the truth was a worthy cause. And if she upset the gathered orchidists while doing it, well, that could be an unforeseen bonus.

13

In which the investigation becomes official.

Dante, Charlie and Eleanor met during the morning tea break in a small alcove that opened off one of the many long corridors of the Bughouse. Every so often, serving staff hurried by, bearing trays of drinks or pushing trolleys laden with coffee and biscuits.

Dante didn't think much of it as a meeting place. He would have preferred a soundproof room with scramblers installed to block electronic surveillance.

"It'll be fine," said Eleanor when he brought this up. "We're just going to compare notes and decide on the next actions."

"Right." Charlie pulled a small notepad out of his pocket. The ghost moth tucked close to his neck, as if seeking shelter.

The back of Dante's neck prickled, and he stepped out of the alcove to look up and down the corridor. There was a slight scent of coconut sunblock in the air. He frowned. "You're going to burn that notebook after this meeting."

Charlie's smile faded when he saw Dante was serious. "Er, I wasn't planning to. Otherwise, how would I refer to it later?"

"Perhaps," said Eleanor, "you could write in it now, and then we can all agree to remember whatever was most important. Then you can burn it."

"I'd rather compost it," said Charlie. He pulled a hotel pen out of his other pocket and held it up. "Where do we start?"

"You two were at Carroll's house yesterday morning," said Eleanor. "If someone poisoned him, they must have come to his house after you. Or he was poisoned at the Symposium."

"I don't like poisoners," said Dante. When his time came, he wanted to go down fighting a dozen well-armed combatants. Poison seemed an anticlimactic way to go.

"We need to establish a timeline of events," said Eleanor. "I can think of a few common poisons that would look like a heart attack. Some of them act quickly, others slower. If we knew what the poison was, it would give us a time window for the murder. I suggest we start by examining events within four hours of Carroll's death."

"You said we'd need evidence of murder to get a postmortem," said Charlie.

"It's a catch-22," said Eleanor. "And you're right — our first action item should be to find evidence sufficient to request a postmortem."

"If we were in Britain," said Dante, "I could get it done today."

"That's a good point," said Eleanor. "Maybe we could get the inspector onside with this one. He could smooth the way to a speedy postmortem."

"I don't want him involved," said Dante.

"Because he tried to arrest you?" asked Eleanor.

"I don't really want him involved either," said Charlie.

"Why?" asked Eleanor. "Much as I respect Sergeant Hemi, Avery's got more clout."

"It's like this..." Charlie chewed the inside of his lip as he thought. "There's a certain amount of disbelief I can take in any given week. You've both been great on that front. But if we bring Avery into this, there'll be so much that we can't explain. Starting with why I'm sure it's murder."

On Charlie's shoulder, the moth hunkered down, looking as defensive as its bearer.

"What happens if you go over your disbelief quota?" asked Eleanor.

"It brings up a bunch of stuff from when I was a kid," said Charlie, "and it's exhausting. I haven't used up my disbelief quota yet, but I have the feeling we're headed for some tricky conversations."

"I don't want him involved because he's a police officer," said Dante.

"And why is that a problem?" asked Eleanor.

Dante considered how to explain his objection to police officers. In general, he approved of them. They kept things orderly and stopped many domestic crimes from occurring. But in his professional capacity, they always got in the way. Moreover, they tended to insist their rules applied to him, too. Dante had a successful career that proved this was not the case.

"Police officers are too... rules-y," he said at last.

"We don't have to bring him in on everything we plan to do," said Eleanor. "Just enough to get a postmortem approved. I'll manage Avery. Will that work for you?"

"Ok," said Dante.

Charlie wrote: 'Eleanor to manage Avery on postmortem.' The ghost moth leaned out from his shoulder as if reading his notebook.

"Are there any ghosts in Carroll's house?" asked Dante.

Charlie shook his head. "I think it's all the potions he made. At least one of them keeps ghosts away. I wish I knew which one."

"What about ghosts who might have seen people walking up to his house?" asked Eleanor.

"Good idea." Charlie added 'talk to ghosts about Carroll's visitors' to his list.

"You said Fairfax was keen to visit Carroll's house," said Dante. "Put him on the suspect list."

"Our first contender." Eleanor rubbed her hands together. "This is going to be fun."

"It's not meant to be fun," said Charlie, giving Eleanor a reproachful look.

"Oh, I know," Eleanor waved away his comment. "But we can't change what's already happened. While some might view a scarf as an appropriate gift for someone my age, a murder to solve is so much better. If I ever end up suspiciously dead, I hope you enjoy solving my murder as much as I intend to enjoy solving this one."

Charlie shook his head. "Not helping," he murmured.

"What's the motive?" said Dante.

"Let's see," said Eleanor. "The timing is suggestive of motive. An International Orchid Symposium begins. Carroll was a famous orchid scholar. Maybe he'd made a scientific breakthrough that a rival wanted to steal. Or perhaps he had an uber valuable orchid that someone with orchidelirium just had to own."

"The professor said something to me just before he died," said Charlie. "He said he had a legacy and a book I should study to understand it. I haven't had time to look for it since the moth showed up."

"We'll do that next," said Eleanor. "If the murder is connected with the Symposium, we have three days to solve this before the guests fly away." She smiled, bright and sharp. "It's nice to have a deadline. Oh, don't look at me like that, Charlie. I know it's sad about Carroll, but we're trying to find his killer, after all."

"He knew it was important," said Charlie slowly. "And there's the moth. Mrs Kingi said they show up when an injustice has occurred."

"I never thought I'd be a pursuer of justice," said Eleanor. "Which goes to show you never know how life will go."

Dante privately agreed. He hadn't expected to live past thirty, and yet here he was, almost thirty-eight, and about to embark on a mission to bring balance to the spirit world, based on the evidence of a green ghost moth.

His therapist had told him to take one day at a time and let life happen. It wasn't good advice for people who were regularly shot at. But perhaps it applied to life in Te Kohe. Time would tell.

Dante checked the corridor once more for spies, surveillance, or micro-drones. It was empty of everything except a loud red and blue eighties carpet and a dark pink dado that clashed to an impressively awful degree. It was time to search Professor Carroll's house.

14

In which a search uncovers more questions.

Half an hour later, Dante, Eleanor and Charlie crested the top of the hill. Dante paused on the forest track to check for watchers in the treeline, but found nothing. Something was bugging him though — his sixth sense was sending him an error signal. This was the kind of message that he never, ever ignored.

"The way I see it," said Eleanor, "we have two tasks. Firstly, we want to look for any evidence that Professor Carroll was poisoned, and secondly, we need to find this notebook. Did Carroll look unwell when you and Dante went to see him?"

"He looked fine," said Charlie. "Although there was one thing — the professor asked who was coming. When I said Marcel Lucier, he looked worried."

They rounded a corner, and Carroll's cottage came into view, nestled back into the New Zealand bush.

"That's interesting," said Eleanor slowly. "Most of the guests arrived on the day of the Symposium. It only started in the evening, so any of them could have visited Carroll that day and given him a slow-acting poison.

We also need to find out if Carroll ate or drank anything at the Symposium. Speaking of suspicions, Lord Martin Fairfax's story about letters from Carroll could be true, or it could be total bunkum."

"There're probably quite a few suspects," said Charlie. "Can we make one of those walls? You know, the ones in thrillers with the photos and red string?"

"I've always wanted to do one of those," said Eleanor as they climbed the steps to Carroll's front porch.

"I've been featured on a few," said Dante. "Only as a blurred image, though."

They digested this information in silence as they contemplated the closed front door.

"Do you want me to pick it?" said Dante. "Old locks are easy."

"I doubt you'll need to," said Charlie. "Most people around here don't bother locking up if they're only going out for a short time." He proved this by turning the handle and opening the door.

Dante took in the scene, then swung around to check the treeline behind them again.

"It looks like we're late to the party," said Eleanor, breaking the silence.

The entry hallway was a mess. Books lay scattered on the floor, and loose pieces of paper blew away from them as a sudden gust of wind whistled through the open door.

"This is awful," said Charlie. "Should we call the police?"

"We definitely should," said Eleanor. "But first we need to do a quick search and see if whoever ransacked this place missed what they were looking for."

"I'll go check the greenhouse," said Charlie. "There's a lot of valuable orchids there, and I'll know if anything's been taken." He vanished around the side of the house.

"Dante," said Eleanor, "if you were an old professor who never locked his doors, where would you hide something valuable enough to be murdered for?"

Dante thought about this. "Under the floorboards or in the attic. The walls are another good place. There might be movable panels or bookcases."

"I'd love to find a secret room behind a bookcase," said Eleanor. "I've gone so long not finding one, I might have to build one myself."

Eleanor drew a pair of cotton gardening gloves from her handbag and put them on. "Let's start the search. We'll give it forty minutes, and then I'd better call Sergeant Hemi."

Dante pulled his own gloves from his pocket and stood in the doorway, scowling out at the forest. He didn't like murders when he didn't know who was responsible. In his previous line of work, he'd always known who the killer was — himself. But in this town, it could be anyone.

Charlie ducked back around the house, his hair sparkling with water droplets. "I've checked the greenhouse. As far as I can tell, nothing's missing." He looked rueful. "The automatic sprinkler system still works."

"Charlie, could you be a dear and stand guard out front?" called Eleanor from inside. "Let us know if anyone's coming. Dante, can you help me search? We'll divide up the rooms and see what we can find."

Dante reentered the house and sniffed the air. It was redolent with many scents: old books, beeswax, rubbing alcohol, herbs, and flowers. There was something else — a fragrance that he did not think belonged to the house. It was very faint, a perfume that reminded him of a delicate white and yellow flower. Frangipani, that was it. One of Charlie's favourites.

Sampling the air every few feet, he tracked his way into the living room. Eleanor was there, tapping at the tiles around the fireplace.

Here, the mess was, if anything, worse, but Dante ignored it, focusing instead on that elusive scent. He followed it into the kitchen, where the long bench was scarred with years of chopping herbs. A black potbelly stove squatted in the corner, the wall behind it lined with red ceramic tiles to reflect the heat.

Dante sniffed. The scent was fainter here. He backtracked and arrived at Carroll's study.

The room was small, with a single window that looked out on flowering honeysuckle and a green lawn studded with clover and tiny white daisies. One wall was occupied by an immense mahogany desk. A curve-backed chair sat in front of the desk, its red leather seat worn nearly bare.

Here, the scent intensified. It was time to begin a thorough search.

With a grunt, Dante shifted the desk away from the wall. There was nothing hidden between the wall and the desk, but he could evaluate the depth of the desk. Next, he opened each drawer, checking them against the width of the desk to see if any had false backs.

After that, he took each drawer out and tapped the bottom. A false bottom was relatively easy to install, but all the drawers were quite normal.

"Hey, guys," Charlie called from the front porch. "I think someone's coming. I saw them through the trees — they're about two minutes away. What should I do?"

Eleanor gave a muffled curse, then called back. "Call the police and report the break-in."

"What should I tell them about why I'm here?"

"Say you came to check on Carroll's orchids," said Eleanor. "You've been looking after them, so that's believable. Stay and find out who's coming. Dante and I will leave through the back door."

Dante tapped the sides of the desk. It all sounded perfectly solid. He sat in the seat, which swivelled gently. He swivelled ninety degrees one way, then ninety degrees the other.

The study had a peaceful feeling, and for the first time in his life, Dante wondered what it would be like to be a man who sat on a swivelling seat in front of a big desk with a window that looked out on a garden and thought things. He wondered if that kind of life could be his one day.

Eleanor popped her head through the study doorway. "Dante, I think we'd better be going— oh, that's a lovely desk. It's a Chapman-Taylor, I think. Have you found anything?"

"I think there might be something here," said Dante.

"It'd be easy to hide a secret compartment in this desk," said Eleanor, "but I'm afraid we've run out of time."

From the porch, they could hear Charlie relaying news of the break-in to the ever-vigilant police force of Te Kohe.

Dante swivelled the seat again. He was enjoying the feeling. What was it Carroll had said? 'I do my best thinking when I'm off my feet.' A thought struck him, and he put a hand under the seat and knocked. It sounded hollow.

In an instant, he was off the chair and turning it upside down.

"Very good," said Eleanor approvingly. "We could have spent an hour checking that desk."

On the underside of the chair was a hinged panel secured with a simple latch. Dante released it and lifted the flap.

Inside was a small leather-bound notebook. It was tied shut with a silk ribbon and looked old.

"Hi, Billy, Grace. Lord Fairfax? Pleased to meet you," came Charlie's voice from the front door. "I'm afraid there's been a burglary. I came up to check on Professor Carroll's orchids and found this. Yes, the police are on their way."

"Time's up," murmured Eleanor, accepting the book from Dante and tucking it into her handbag.

Silently, Dante closed the hidden panel and returned the chair to its upright position. They crept out of the study and into the backyard. Dante resisted the urge to pick Eleanor up and hurry her out of sight. He didn't relax until they'd ducked behind the greenhouse.

"We can't stay here," said Eleanor. "Fairfax is bound to snoop through the garden. I want to be somewhere we can spy on him and see what he's up to."

Dante looked around. The forest pressed in close at the back of the garden. Voices coming from the kitchen made him put one hand under Eleanor's elbow and direct her into the woods.

They made their way swiftly uphill. Dante was careful to avoid the slippery mud and wet leaves from the recent rainfall. He kept one hand on Eleanor's arm and caught her twice as she slipped.

"Thank you," murmured Eleanor as he drew her behind a broad totara trunk, one side of it still wet with rain.

From here, they had a view of Carroll's back garden and greenhouse.

A few minutes ticked by.

"He's probably searching the bookshelves and the study," said Eleanor. "He may have been the burglar, coming back for a second try. Or it may have been someone else. Hard to say at this stage. Ah, here we go."

The back door opened, and Fairfax strode out of the door. Gone was his charming smile. Instead, his face was set in a thunderous frown, mouth turned down, fair eyebrows drawn together.

"Someone's not happy," said Eleanor.

Fairfax glanced behind him, then opened the greenhouse door and stepped inside.

"It's a pity the greenhouse glass is fogged up with condensation. I'd like to see what he's doing," said Eleanor.

A minute later, Fairfax exited the greenhouse and stalked to the centre of the lawn. He stood, hands in pockets, and slowly rotated in place, looking at the treeline.

"That was quick," said Eleanor. "I wonder if what he's after is missing — or still there."

Dante felt Fairfax's eyes rake past their hiding place. He knew they couldn't be seen through the trees, but he still tensed minutely as the lord's eyes traced over where they were crouched.

"He knows someone's watching," muttered Eleanor. "I suppose we left footprints on the muddy lawn. Lords and their hunting hobbies. Do you think he could track us?"

"Yes," said Dante. With the ground this wet, it would not be difficult. "I could stop him."

"I think it would be better if we simply retreated," said Eleanor drily. "Can you lead us back around to the track?"

Dante checked his mental compass. "Yes."

"Very well then." Eleanor smoothed her skirts and looked around the sodden forest with a wry smile. "Let's go."

"Once the police have finished, we need to return everything to where we think it might have been," said Grace. She stood in the middle of Carroll's living room, hands on hips, glaring at the wreckage.

"Shall I start tidying now?" said Charlie. He was glad he'd dropped the moth at home before taking the trip up to the cottage. Grace would have been very curious.

"Hemi?" called Grace. "Can we start tidying?"

Sergeant Hemi was the chief police officer in Te Kohe and Grace's nephew. That meant she got to shout questions at him from the next room.

Hemi put his head around the door. He was a big man with a large, expressive face. Charlie remembered him having a thick Burt Reynolds moustache in the early 2000s, and he missed its presence. He wondered if he could ask Grace to recommend that Hemi grow it back.

"Yeah, you can start tidying up. I reckon it was kids who found out this place was empty and decided to trash it." Hemi shook his head in a silent indictment of people in general and kids in particular. "I'll ask around, find out if anyone knows anything."

"Right." Grace flexed her fingers. "Charlie, you start in the kitchen, and I'll do the living room. As soon as Billy gets back from mooning over his royal highness, I'll put them to work on the other rooms."

"Yes, ma'am," said Charlie.

Grace gave him a wry smile. "Go on - get to it."

Charlie entered the kitchen, where bottles had been pulled off the shelves and lay, some broken, all over the kitchen floor. He got the impression of someone searching in increasing frustration and then rage.

The kitchen bench was empty except for an old-fashioned dish drainer with a kettle and two cups and saucers left on it to dry. Charlie shifted the drainer onto the table and began picking up the bottles that were whole and stacking them on the bench, ready to wipe down and return to their shelves.

He was halfway through this task when a small brown bottle caught his attention. It was stoppered with a rubber cork and filled with a clear liquid. Charlie studied the label.

'Digitalis purpurea (Foxglove) Extract 2% Solution – For Cardiovascular Support. Take 2 drops, morning and night. Do not exceed recommended dose.'

"Foxglove," murmured Charlie. "For cardiovascular support." He picked the bottle up by the cork and read the label again. It appeared to be the professor's neat handwriting.

Charlie picked a similarly sized bottle up by the cork and looked at the two labels side by side. Digitalis came from foxglove leaves, and could be poisonous. A quick search of the kitchen drawers revealed an empty Ziploc bag. Charlie carefully put both bottles in the bag, sealed it, and wrapped it in his jacket.

He felt guilty about this. He should be showing the bottles to Hemi, but what would he say? That he thought Carroll's death was suspicious because of a moth? Better to gather evidence with Eleanor and Dante and then present it all at once.

At last, the kitchen looked presentable. Charlie swept up the broken glass and went looking for a mop in the laundry. He'd found one when a thought popped into his mind.

He stepped out into Carroll's garden and studied the plants growing there. The last foxgloves should still be in bloom, but he couldn't see any stems bearing the distinctive purple blossoms.

"No foxgloves in the garden," he murmured to himself. He walked out onto the lawn to check behind the greenhouse. Turning the corner, he happened on Fairfax, studying some impressions on the lawn.

"Hello there," said Fairfax, giving Charlie a breezy smile. "Just wondering, was anyone here before you?"

"Not that I know of," said Charlie truthfully. "Except for whoever trashed the professor's place."

"Yes, such a shame, that," said Fairfax. "Charlie, you seem a decent chap. Have you any idea who would do something like this? The professor was going to give me an important document, and it looks like it's gone."

"Sergeant Hemi thinks it was just some kids being destructive," said Charlie.

"Was there anything on the desk when you went in there?"

Charlie didn't see any point in denying he'd been in every room. "I didn't see any letters. Is that what you were looking for?"

"No," said Fairfax slowly. "It would be a small parcel, about this big," he held up his hands to indicate something roughly book-sized.

"And it's for you?" asked Charlie.

Fairfax nodded emphatically. "We've been writing letters for quite some time. He wanted to share something important with me."

"Maybe it's already en route?" said Charlie. "It could be waiting for you when you get home."

Fairfax pushed his hand distractedly through his hair. "I'll have my people check, but the chances are slim. He knew I was coming here."

"I better get back to tidying," said Charlie. "I'll look out for it for you."

"Thanks, old chap," said Fairfax.

Charlie felt Fairfax's gaze between his shoulder blades as he retreated into the house.

15

In which Dante evaluates the merits of small talk.

"That was interesting," mused Eleanor. She and Dante had traversed the track down from Carroll's house to arrive on the outskirts of Te Kohe. "It certainly lends credence to Charlie's theory that Carroll was murdered. I believe Charlie — his heart's always in the right place. But it's nice to have supporting evidence."

"The murderer wanted something in his house?" Dante could think of a dozen ways to safely search Carroll's house that didn't involve murder.

"It's likely," said Eleanor. "And yes, murder is a bit of an extreme way to get access, so there must be something more going on."

"And Fairfax is the prime suspect?"

"He's certainly on the list," said Eleanor. "He was looking for something, and we found something. We need to find out who else had the means, motive, and opportunity to poison Carroll yesterday."

Dante reflected on how much easier it was to solve murders when you were the one doing the killing. Of course, he would never have terminated a professor of botany whose chief desire was to be left in peace to tend his garden.

His targets had all been drawn from the darker side of life – drug smugglers, human traffickers, arms runners, despots, and killers. Although calling it the darker side of life was an understatement. His targets had been drenched in blood and hues of blackest midnight. Their deaths had made the world a brighter place.

Dante returned from his reverie as Eleanor spoke.

"How about you and Andrea? Have you caught up lately?"

"We're going on a date," said Dante.

"Wonderful. How do you feel about that?"

"I'm not sure."

"What's worrying you?"

Dante thought about this. "The point of a date is to get to know someone, right? By talking to them?"

"Yes, Dante. Talking is the conventional method. You could do an interpretive dance, but I can't really see that happening." Eleanor put a hand on his shoulder to steady herself as they stepped down onto the pavement of Te Kohe's main street.

"I'm not good at talking," said Dante. "Also, Andrea getting to know me would not be a good thing."

"Maybe," said Eleanor. "I assume you have a cover story and false history supplied by your previous employers?"

"Yes," said Dante. "But that wouldn't be Andrea getting to know me either."

"You are more than your previous job," said Eleanor. "You are more than your history. One way to look at this is that Andrea wants to know who you are now. She wants to find out if you and she might have a future together."

"I don't like to think of the future," said Dante.

"I have a feeling that Andrea might think of the future quite a bit," said

Eleanor. "It's a common pastime for women in small towns in their mid-thirties."

Dante filed this piece of information away for later consideration.

"So what do I talk about if I can't talk about the past, and I don't want to talk about the future?" he asked.

"Let's see you smile," said Eleanor. She stopped walking and studied his face while Dante dutifully turned the corners of his mouth upward.

Eleanor made a 'hmmm' noise. "I'm not sure smiling is your thing — yet. Let's see your interested listening face."

Dante used the focused stare he employed while sighting through the scope of an L115A3 sniper rifle.

"I'm not sure that's going to help you either," said Eleanor. She snapped her fingers. "I know — what about when you're gardening? Channel that."

Dante felt his muscles relax. Eleanor's face broke into a delighted smile. "That will work. I'm now going to share with you the secret to good conversation. Have you watched a tennis match?"

"I once tailed an operative to the Spartak Tennis Club in Moscow."

"Perfect. Good conversation is like a tennis rally. Whenever Andrea asks you a question about yourself, give her just enough of an answer to satisfy her, and then turn it back into a question about herself."

Dante stopped walking and crossed his arms. "Give me an example."

Eleanor tapped her lip, thinking. "Imagine I'm Andrea."

"Ok."

"And I say: 'Dante, what did you want to be when you grew up?'"

"When I was a kid, I wanted to be a stormtrooper," said Dante. "But one that could shoot and hit the target. After that, I wanted to be the Terminator."

"Was that until you became an agent?" asked Eleanor.

Dante shifted his feet.

"Dante, do you still want to be the Terminator?"

"Maybe."

Eleanor stifled a smile. "Maybe don't share that piece of information. Next step — you turn Andrea's question for you back into a question about her."

"Ok," said Dante. He drew a deep breath. "What did you want to be when you grew up?"

"You don't have to phrase the question back exactly," said Eleanor. "You could just say, 'How about you?' Or, 'Did you always want to be a vet?'"

Dante wondered briefly if he could get his hands on a remote earbud system in time for his dinner with Andrea. That way, Eleanor could feed him the right questions and answers in real time.

Their walk had carried them into the town centre. The Pepper Tree Hotel came into view, filling the street corner with Victorian charm.

A thought occurred to Dante. "What if I told Andrea the truth about me?"

"I can't advise you on that," said Eleanor, "but I can tell you a story."

"Ok," said Dante.

"I once fell in love. It was the eighties, and I was in Paris, lying low after a big job stateside. I had time to spare, money to blow, and there was this gorgeous man. I felt like we were meant for each other."

Dante tried to look as if he knew what Eleanor was talking about.

"I thought he felt the same way. And perhaps he did. Right until the point when, in a fit of moonstruck madness, I told him exactly how I made a living." A look of wry amusement flitted across Eleanor's face. "I left my apartment early that morning via the fire escape, just ahead of the gendarmes my beau had called. I didn't stick around to find out whether he was an undercover cop or just a dutiful citizen." She turned to face Dante, her eyes serious. "Would you like to know the moral of the story?"

"Yes," said Dante. It was always good to avoid ambiguity.

"Never stay the night in a room with only one exit."

Dante nodded. This was good advice, and a rule that had saved his life before.

"And remember that trust must be earned, not given." Eleanor looked speculatively at the hotel, drawing nearer with every step. "I have an idea. I'd like to study the notebook we found, but right now, all the hotel guests will be at the Symposium. Let's do a bit of light breaking and entering to find out more about Fairfax. Then, we'll have lunch, and we can carry on practising the art of conversation. How does that sound?"

"Ok," said Dante. A bit of B&E would provide light relief from this difficult topic.

With that, they turned and climbed the steps into the Pepper Tree Hotel.

16

In which the circle of suspicion widens.

Inside the hotel was quiet. Eleanor and Dante walked nonchalantly down the thickly carpeted foyer, then up the stairs to the top of the building.

“I imagine Lord Fairfax will have the executive suite,” Eleanor nodded at a heavy rimu timber door to her left. “I’ll keep watch, you pick the lock.”

Dante knelt by the door, and in an impressively short time, he swung it open.

“Hello,” called Eleanor softly. It would never do to search an occupied room, and she had several entertaining stories to explain their presence if someone did emerge. After a few seconds had passed, and no one replied, she walked in briskly, as if on a thoroughly above-board mission.

The bedroom was empty, as was the bathroom and a large adjoining room she supposed you could call a sitting room, if you were feeling especially formal.

“Good,” she said. “Dante, could you relock the door? If anyone comes in, we can leave by the fire escape. Quite handy having these outside every window.”

"I don't like it," said Dante. "If we leave that way, we could easily be seen from the street."

"I know," said Eleanor, "but I can come up with some pretty good explanations if anyone objects. Let's search this place."

Eleanor started with the walk-in wardrobe. "Gucci suitcases," she said. "I'd expect Burberry for Fairfax, or a custom English craftsman. Ah." She popped open the first suitcase to display some genuinely gorgeous lingerie. "Unless Fairfax has an unexpected side to his character, I think we might be in Fiorelli's room. Yes, there's one airline tag still attached to this bag. Dr Isabella Fiorelli, via Milan. And some handmade leather walking shoes with," she leaned down to examine them closely, "a touch of distinctive pink clay on them. The same clay as the path up to Carroll's house."

"What about this?" Dante drifted over to the desk, where various papers were laid out. He picked up a small locked leather case, small enough to fit in a satchel.

"I like the look of that," said Eleanor. "Can you open it?"

Thirty seconds later, the case clicked open. Eleanor leaned over Dante's shoulder to get a better look.

"I love a good mystery," she murmured.

The case contained papers written in flowing copperplate cursive. Eleanor, whose career meant she knew quite a bit about old documents, judged them to be at least a hundred years old. Each paper was encased in a plastic sheath to preserve it. Eleanor carefully leafed through the collection.

"This looks like a ship's manifest," she said. "A list of cargo carried by the *Whitby*. Does that name ring any bells for you?"

"No," said Dante. He retreated to the door and listened.

Eleanor spread the papers out on the table and photographed them, working quickly. Her instinct told her this was something important, though she didn't yet know why. Dante's frown also told her they were running out of time.

She shoved the papers back into the case and clicked the lock closed.

They both froze at a small, metallic sound from the room door. Someone was about to enter.

“Time to go,” whispered Dante.

He crossed the room so fast that Eleanor gasped.

The next moment, he’d opened the timber sash window and lifted her outside onto the fire escape walkway. He closed it silently behind them before herding her around the corner of the building.

“Wait,” whispered Eleanor. “Is someone else breaking into Fiorelli’s apartment?”

Dante nodded, his eyes fixed on the walkway they’d just traversed. Their position overlooked the quiet hotel courtyard. Behind them, the timber walkway wrapped around the building, with ladders and stairs going down at intervals. It was 1900s fire safety, and Eleanor approved. Also, as per usual, no one going about their business in a busy hotel was looking up.

“Can you see who’s in there?” she whispered.

Dante moved soundlessly back around the corner, where a small side window gave him a view inside Fiorelli’s room. “It’s the man from New Orleans. The one with the ghost orchid.”

“Marcel Lucier,” breathed Eleanor. A satisfied smile crossed her face. This *was* going to be fun. “What’s he doing?”

“He’s lock-picking the case we just broke into,” reported Dante. “Now he’s looking at the papers.”

“What does his face look like? Any emotion there?”

There was a long silence. “He looks…” Dante was saved from answering this question by Lucier moving to the window.

Eleanor found herself whisked further along the walkway so quietly and swiftly it was like magic. There was a quiet sound as the sash window slid up.

Dante tensed, then slowly relaxed. There was a quiet 'thunk' as the window closed again.

They waited, frozen in place, for a full minute, then made their way down the next staircase to the ground.

"I think," said Eleanor, as they reached the pavement, "that it might be time for lunch." All things considered, they had probably pushed their luck enough for one day.

17

In which Dante is disquieted.

Dante scanned the diners at the Pepper Tree Hotel restaurant. Even though it was Saturday, there were only a handful, possibly because most of the guests were still at the Symposium. He and Eleanor were sitting in a quiet corner near the low window that overlooked the sun-filled courtyard.

"So that's how I came to Te Kohe," said Dante. "How did you come to Te Kohe?"

Eleanor shook her head slightly. "As far as I know, Andrea was born in Te Kohe. A better question would be: Did you grow up here in Te Kohe? What was it like?"

Dante fought the urge to stab his fork into the white dinner plate in front of him. He knew he could do it with enough force to crack the plate and drive the fork tines into the wooden table beneath. He was fairly sure the hotel staff would not appreciate this, so he carefully placed the fork down on the plate instead.

"So, Andrea, what was it like growing up in Te Kohe?"

"Good," said Eleanor, "but try not to look so murderous."

"This is how I usually look."

"Let's take a break from practising the art of conversation," suggested Eleanor. "Do you like dessert?"

"I like tiramisu." Dante had once been present at the unfortunate demise of a Sicilian crime boss. Since the man had died before having the chance to sample his dessert, Dante had eaten it for him, on the pretext that it was wrong to let good food go to waste. The dessert had been tiramisu, and Dante had found it delicious.

Eleanor scanned the menu. "They do tiramisu, but I have to say it's not their best dish. If you're willing to try something new, I'd recommend the butterscotch pudding with Kapiti Island vanilla ice cream. It's a classic."

"I second that." The voice came from behind Dante's shoulder, and he resisted the surge of adrenaline and the urge to attack immediately. No one should be able to sneak up on him like that.

A red-haired woman stepped into view. She was in her early twenties, with a pretty, heart-shaped face and bright green eyes. She wore a tight-fitting green dress that ended at the knee, revealing tanned calves and dainty leather sandals. Dante sniffed the air. Coconut sunblock. He'd smelt that same scent recently, and he set his mind to remembering where.

Eleanor took off her reading glasses, put the menu down, and faced the new arrival. "Hello, there. I take it you're a dessert aficionado?"

The newcomer's cheeks dimpled. "I am! So loving the after-dinner treats here."

Eleanor's quick gaze took in Dante's carefully neutral pose, as well as their visitor's posture — leaning in, one hand on her handbag strap. "Would you like to join us?"

"That'd be fabulous." The redhead favoured her with a brilliant smile and slipped into the seat across from Dante.

"So, you're new in town?" asked Eleanor.

"I'm here on holiday." The red-haired woman tucked a stray lock of hair behind her ear. “I’m Stephanie Church.” She stuck out a hand and shook Eleanor’s, then turned to Dante. “Are you visiting too?”

“I live here,” said Dante. The hairs on the back of his neck had not subsided. He did not like being surprised, and he discovered he did not like Stephanie Church either.

“We both live here,” said Eleanor, “though Dante is a more recent resident. I’m Eleanor, and this is Dante. You’re from Australia?”

“Guilty as charged.” Stephanie’s eyes tilted upwards as she smiled. “I’m touring New Zealand for a few months, and this sounded like such a charming town.”

Dante turned his focus inward as Eleanor and Stephanie did small talk. Something was bugging him about their guest, and he wanted to work out what it was. He took the menu lying next to his plate and felt the stiff cardboard in his hand. It would do.

Sliding it carefully over his plate, he positioned the edge of it next to the salt cellar between him and Stephanie. Next, he leaned one elbow on it and gently nudged the menu sideways.

The salt cellar, rocked off balance, teetered on the edge of the table for a moment. Then it fell. In almost the same instant, Stephanie’s hand shot out to catch it.

To a casual observer, it would look like she’d fumbled. But Dante was never a casual observer. He saw her grip the cellar and then abruptly let it go. The cellar hit the carpeted floor, spilling salt in a plume of white.

Eleanor leaned over to eye the fallen vessel. “Apparently, you’re supposed to throw some salt over your shoulder now. To avoid being visited by ghosts.”

Stephanie laughed, her even white teeth showing. “How superstitious. Is that an American thing or a you thing?” She bent down to pick up the offending salt cellar.

“It’s a me thing,” agreed Eleanor. “Dante, what do you think about ghosts?” She raised a hand to attract the waiter's attention.

"I don't like them," said Dante. His fingers extended, feeling the pull of the handgun in his underarm holster. There were only a few reasons someone would have reflexes that good. And even fewer why they might want to hide it. "Do you do sports?"

"Beach volleyball," said Stephanie. "It's kind of a given when you grow up on the Goldie."

Eleanor's eyes flicked between Stephanie and Dante. "Are you a professional?"

"Oh, no," Stephanie smiled. "Just fun with friends. I work in advertising."

"I'm afraid we've spilt some salt," said Eleanor to the waiter who'd appeared at her shoulder. "I'm so sorry - would you be able to clean it up?"

"Certainly." The waiter bustled off to get cleaning gear.

Dante pondered what his next question should be. This was not his area of expertise. Normally, the question of who was dangerous became abundantly clear once bullets began to fly. Talking didn't figure into the equation.

As questions went, 'Are you a hit woman?' seemed a trifle obvious and unlikely to get a truthful answer. 'Do you shoot a lot or fight with edged weapons?' had the same drawbacks. He'd settled on, 'If you had to shoot someone from the fifth storey of an apartment at a distance of 1500m, what firearm would you use?' and was about to ask it when Eleanor spoke again.

"I'm detecting a hint of Yorkshire in your accent."

Stephanie's smile hitched just a fraction. "You have a good ear. I grew up in Australia, but my parents are English. We moved back when I was a teenager."

As the small talk resumed, Dante's hindbrain passed a message up to his frontal cortex. There was something very off about Stephanie. It was there in her movements and how she held herself. The question was: what kind of threat was she? And what was she doing in his town?

"Well, it has been lovely meeting you," said Eleanor. "And I'm sure we'll see you around soon. Unfortunately, I have another appointment. Dante, are you staying?"

"No," said Dante. If he left now, he wouldn't be tempted to follow her back to her room, ambush her, and find out why she was here. Down that road lay breaking the code. One hundred and thirty-eight days, no bodies, he chanted to himself like a mantra.

But on the other hand, if he ignored her and ended up dead, the code wouldn't matter. It was a difficult decision, one he wished he could have made over tiramisu.

"Can we have the bill, please?" asked Eleanor as the waiter reappeared to sweep up the salt.

"It's been taken care of," said the waiter.

"Really?" Eleanor raised her eyebrows. Then she followed his gaze to a figure leaning nonchalantly on the bar. "I see. Lovely meeting you, Stephanie. I'm sure we'll see you around."

With that, Eleanor sashayed over to the bar, where Avery waited.

Dante sat for a few heartbeats longer. Every cell in his body inclined towards violence, but he deliberately relaxed and offered Stephanie one of the smiles he'd been practising. "Nice to meet you, Stephanie Church."

She smiled back a little uncertainly. "You too."

Maybe Stephanie was here on holiday, he thought. But Dante's shoulder blades itched as he made his way over to the bar.

He didn't think Stephanie was here on holiday. And he was going to ensure (forcibly if necessary) that she did nothing to disrupt his new home.

18

In which Avery resists temptation, and Eleanor doesn't.

"A funny thing happened just now," said Avery. "I was taking a walk along the waterfront when I saw two people climbing out of the window of one of the hotel rooms. Top floor, I think it was."

"How extraordinary." No good deed goes unpunished, thought Eleanor. "Two hotel guests getting some fresh air, no doubt."

"No doubt," agreed Avery.

"And at that distance, I doubt you could identify them," said Eleanor. "Unless you routinely carry binoculars."

"It might be time to start." Avery scowled at the bottles of spirits lining the back wall of the bar. "Do you realise how impossible it is to enjoy my holiday with you running around doing who knows what with your hulking shadow?" he inclined his head toward Dante, who was studying the redhead still sitting at their recently vacated table with a worrying blank expression.

"I suggest you try," said Eleanor. "I hear yoga is good for relaxation. Possibly Kama Sutra yoga? Or is it Kundalini?"

Avery buried his face in his hands. "I can't believe I'm having this conversation. God give me patience."

"Do you want to know what your problem is?" asked Eleanor.

"No," said Avery.

"Secretly, you're dying to know what we're up to."

"I want you to stop whatever it is you're up to."

"You are the proverbial cat, filled to the brim with curiosity, unable to let a mystery go until you've unravelled it like a ball of yarn."

"Please," Avery raised his head from his hands, "indulge my catlike sensibilities."

"No," said Eleanor. Then she smiled like the cat who'd drunk all the cream. "But I know you'll like it."

"Why is that?"

Eleanor thought over the ship's papers she'd seen and Carroll's notebook, nestled in an inner pocket of her handbag. "It involves your alleged favourite hobby."

"Alleged." Avery narrowed his eyes. "I can ask Hemi and Rosie to do their legal best to obstruct whatever rule-breaking you're up to."

Eleanor shrugged. "Much as I like and respect our constabulary, I doubt they'd be up to the task."

"If you continue to hold out on me," said Avery. "I'll be forced to—"

"Yes?" asked Eleanor.

"—ask nicely," finished Avery.

"Alright then," said Eleanor. "Let's hear it."

"Eleanor, alleged surname Graham," began Avery, and Eleanor gave a slight smile. "Will you please tell me what mad and possibly illegal scheme you are perpetrating at this respectable Orchid Symposium where I am trying to have a relaxing, crime-free holiday?"

"Not bad," said Eleanor. "Though you could drop a few modifiers. In fact," her eyes narrowed as she studied the inspector, "you might even be quite useful—"

"I shudder to think how," said Avery.

"—and I might let you in on this, with a few conditions," finished Eleanor.

"No," said Avery, turning away. "I know this is a bad idea, and just this once, I'm going to listen to my better instincts."

"Pity," said Eleanor. "It's turning out to be quite the floral mystery."

"Excuse me." Avery signalled the barman. "A ginger beer, please."

"Ginger beer." Eleanor sighed. "Better instincts?"

"Exactly." Avery leaned on the bar and swigged his beverage. Now, he looked satisfied. "I'm on holiday, and I'm going to stay on holiday, thank you very much."

"Good luck on that front," said Eleanor.

Avery checked his watch. "The next lecture is in forty-five minutes. Care to join me?"

Eleanor shook her head. "Thank you, but no. Dante, shall we go?"

But Dante had vanished.

Avery huffed a laugh. "When you and the whole Scooby Gang end up getting arrested, I will absolutely remind you that I told you so."

Eleanor thought of Charlie's ghosts, and the corners of her mouth turned up. "Scooby-Doo? You have no idea."

"Excuse me," came a voice with a southern American accent. "I'm sorry to intrude, but may I buy you a drink?"

Eleanor turned to see Marcel Lucier leaning against the bar, the elegant line of his shoulders accentuated by the well-tailored cut of his jacket.

"I appreciate the offer," she said. "But I haven't decided whether to return home now or not."

"We met at Marjorie's tea party," said Lucier. "I'm sorry — could you remind me of your name?"

"Certainly," said Eleanor. "I'm Eleanor Graham."

"Enchanté," said Lucier. "Marcel Lucier."

"You remember my friend Marcus Avery?" Eleanor nodded towards Avery.

"Afternoon," said Avery.

Lucier gave a small gesture of acknowledgement, his eyes never leaving Eleanor's. "If you're ready to leave, perhaps we could walk and talk. I hear the waterfront is quite charming."

"That would be lovely," said Eleanor. "Thank you." She was aware of Avery's eyes boring into the back of her neck as she retrieved her handbag from the hook under the bar.

"*Allons-y*," said Lucier and offered his arm to Eleanor. She took it, and they walked down the hotel steps into brilliant sunshine.

19

In which Dante seeks counsel.

Dante walked along the waterfront, the sea breeze cooling him and the pohutakawa branches casting patterns of shade on the path.

His gaze fell on the wristband around his left wrist. One hundred and thirty-eight days, no fatalities. This was a new life, and it came with a cost.

Out of habit, he checked the path behind him, then ducked out of sight behind a broad tree trunk and waited for two minutes.

A jogger with a boxer dog passed by, followed by a couple of teenagers dressed in loose black Goth clothes. No Stephanie Church.

Dante considered. It was time to do something he hadn't done since he'd moved to Te Kohe. It was time to make a call.

Back in his house, Dante waited. After a few seconds, the connection fired, and John's name appeared on the screen. Just 'John,' white letters on a black background. No surname. And also, no video feed.

"Dante?" John's voice was quiet.

"Hi, John," said Dante. "Is this a good time?"

In the background, a gong sounded, and a low hum of voices rose in Dorian harmony.

It reminded Dante of a temple he'd once visited deep in the Golden Triangle jungle. The man he'd been hunting had gone to ground there, and the abbot of the monastery had counselled peace and forgiveness. Dante assured the abbot held no grudges against his target. He simply intended to kill him for his crimes. And he had, as soon as the man broke cover.

"I have a few minutes to spare," said John. "Tell me what's going on."

"Someone's appeared in my town," said Dante. "She could be from my old life."

"I see," said John. The chanting faded slightly as John walked away from its source. "You are wondering if she's a threat to be neutralised."

"Yes," said Dante, "but doing that would go against the code."

The reverberating tone of a gong sounded loud enough to max out the small speakers on Dante's laptop. It took a long time to fade.

There was a drawn-out silence. Perhaps John was meditating.

"The way I see it," said John, "you have two options."

This was good news. Dante felt he could deal with a simple choice of A or B.

"Option one is to retreat," said John. "There's no shame in a tactical withdrawal until you know the lay of the land and have a plan to deal with any attacks."

"Ok," said Dante.

"Option two is more difficult," said John. "You face your adversary without the possibility of lethal violence if things go badly."

Dante was silent while he thought this over. The gong sounded again, low and sonorous.

"Have you ever done that?" asked Dante.

"Once," said John.

"And your adversary is still alive?"

"Yes."

"Your adversary is healthy, with all their limbs attached?" Dante probed this scenario, looking for an angle.

"We talked," said John, "and reached an understanding."

Dante's shoulders slumped. Talking was not his forte.

"I have confidence that if you truly desire it, you too can find the harmony hidden within conflict," said John.

Dante had difficulty finding the harmony within harmony, so this seemed an unreasonably optimistic point of view. Still...

"Thank you for your advice, John."

"Sure, Dante."

The connection broke midway through a third ringing gong note.

Dante noticed John had not wished him good luck. The reality was, people died. People in his profession died a lot, even when they were trying to kick the habit. And good intentions were no guarantee of success.

The doorbell rang. Dante checked his watch to see who was on the front porch camera. It was Charlie, looking excited. Dante stowed his laptop in the desk drawer and stalked into the front hallway.

"Hi Dante," Charlie said as soon as Dante opened the door. "Eleanor messaged me about the papers you found. The ship was called the *Whitby*, right? I've heard of it. It's part of Te Kohe's history. We could go check the library and find out more."

"The library." Dante shifted on his feet. A memory surfaced of a pursuit through the Vatican Library with its huge vaulted ceilings and tall shelves loaded with books. He scowled. It was not a good memory. "Fine. Let's go see some books."

20

In which Eleanor discovers more about orchids and their collectors.

The Te Kohe waterfront was charming. The promenade wound around an aquamarine harbour, and across the road, little villas and bungalows with immaculately kept gardens basked in the sun.

Once they reached the walkway, Lucier released Eleanor's arm, and they walked in silence, a couple seemingly out to enjoy the fresh air. Lucier waited until the hotel was out of sight behind the first curve in the road before he spoke.

"I want to know why you are interested in Doctor Isabella Fiorelli."

Eleanor had expected something along these lines, but still, she paused. A direct approach seemed Lucier's style, although she was sure the man could be subtlety itself when required. He was confident in a way that spoke of intelligence but also experience. Such confidence was seldom misplaced.

She also wondered how much he'd seen of their recent entry into Fiorelli's room. Eleanor decided to proceed with caution.

"What makes you think I'm interested in Fiorelli? Aside from her amazing achievements in the orchid world, of course."

"She has accomplished some truly groundbreaking research," said Lucier, "and doesn't usually venture outside Europe. This is a rare occurrence."

"You must know her quite well from your many trips abroad to collect orchids," said Eleanor.

"Not so well," said Lucier. "My brother had more contact with her."

"Your brother was an accomplished researcher?" asked Eleanor.

"He was." Lucier gazed off into the distance, and Eleanor noted the slight hollowness around the eyes, the sunken cheeks below high cheekbones. It was hard to say without having known Lucier longer, but to her, he looked like a man consumed by some powerful emotion. Grieving a lost brother, perhaps? Obsessively searching for something?

She decided to fish a little. "Do you have a professional interest in Fiorelli? Or a personal interest?"

Lucier turned to face her, and she caught the flicker in his expression. It was a personal interest, she guessed.

"I saw you and your ominous friend outside her room earlier today. It seemed a strange place for two non-hotel guests to be."

Eleanor knew no one had seen Dante picking the lock — she'd been checking the corridor. When had Lucier seen them, then? Perhaps he'd passed by on the stairs just as they were preparing to break in.

"Oh, I'm a good friend of Delia, the hotel owner," said Eleanor airily. "Her office is just down the hall from the executive suite."

"I see," said Lucier.

"I was a friend of Professor Carroll, too," said Eleanor. "I was wondering - did you visit the professor on the day of the opening gala?"

"The day he died." Lucier's cool grey eyes betrayed no emotion as he met hers. "I did, as a matter of fact. The late professor had been in contact with my brother, and I had some private questions to ask him."

"Did the professor seem well at the time of your visit?"

"He did. Our conversation was... opaque. Rather like the talk we are having now." Lucier's eyes showed a glint of humour. "He was hinting at something, but I was unable to pick up on his cues. Perhaps my brother would have." The humour vanished, to be replaced by bleakness.

"Did you see anyone else on your way up to the house?" asked Eleanor.

"Only Fiorelli," said Lucier. "She was coming back down the path, I assume having already visited Carroll. She did not see me, though."

So now they had three suspects, thought Eleanor. Assuming Lucier was telling the truth, which was far from certain. But they had no motive for murder beyond wild guesses. Her mind went back to the documents she'd found in Fiorelli's locked case. A cargo list from an 1850s ship. Was this a treasure hunt? Had Lucier's brother been involved? Had Carroll?

"No doubt those two academics had much to talk about," she said, keeping her tone neutral.

"No doubt," said Lucier drily.

"Did your brother have an interest in the history of orchid collecting?" she asked innocently.

Eleanor was paying close attention, or she would have missed the tiny hitch in Lucier's stride.

"He was interested in everything," said Lucier. "Modern-day orchid propagation, the mysterious symbiosis between orchids and fungi, and yes, the history of orchid hunting. Mainly, he was interested in that most elusive of flowers: the ghost orchid."

Eleanor wondered briefly whether orchids could become ghosts and resolved to ask Charlie. She quite liked the idea of a ghostly garden populated by the departed flowers of seasons past. It put her in mind of the Persephone mythos.

"Such a strange name for a flower," she said. "Quite lyrical. It seems orchidists get carried away by their obsessions. Is that why you are interested in Fiorelli?"

"Would you believe me when I say it is none of your business?" Lucier's tone was light, but she didn't miss the coldness in his eyes.

"You're the one who asked me to join you on a walk," said Eleanor, "so you could ask me about Fiorelli. I rather think it is my business. Are you similarly interested in Fairfax?"

This time, Lucier betrayed no reaction. Either she'd missed the mark, or he'd regained enough composure to hide any tells. "My interest in Fiorelli is strictly professional," he said at last. "However, I would advise you to stay away from both her and the English lord."

"And you?" asked Eleanor. "Am I also meant to avoid any further contact with you?"

Lucier smiled faintly. "I have asked you out for a harbour promenade on this lovely day. It would be impolite to make threats or warnings now, would it not?"

"And yet, here we are," said Eleanor. "You should know that warning me to stay away from someone is the surest way to make me curious."

"I had suspected that," said Lucier gravely.

"Perhaps if you gave me a reason to take your warning seriously?" prompted Eleanor.

"It was an interesting question you asked the other day," said Lucier. For a moment, Eleanor wondered if this was about her impertinent question during his lecture. "At Marjorie's tea party — you wanted to know the lengths people will go to satisfy their orchid obsession," Lucier clarified.

"I've met many collectors — not of orchids, but in the art world," said Eleanor. "The pursuit of something beautiful can reveal the uglier side of human nature."

"My fascination with orchids is tied to the qualities of the orchid itself," said Lucier. "They are the masters of camouflage — did you know that?"

"I did not."

"The orchid produces no nectar of its own," said Lucier. "There is no sweetness to draw in the honeybee or the butterfly. But it needs their help to reproduce. So, it disguises itself. Its ruses are many. Some orchids imitate the female insect of their pollinators. Others have evolved to look similar to other nectar-rich flowers. Still others — like the ghost orchids — have no leaves, but live in symbiosis with specific fungi."

"So orchids are the con artists of the floral kingdom," said Eleanor. "I rather like that."

Lucier inclined his head in acknowledgement. "Orchids have captured the imagination of plant collectors for more than a hundred years. Scientists like Fiorelli want to change all that. She has attracted much attention with her method of bringing extinct orchids back to life. She has some very wealthy backers. And yes, I am an orchid collector, and this puts my business at risk. But I am not someone who knows the price of everything and the value of nothing. There have been times when I have found a rare orchid in a remote place, and I have left it untouched. There is a certain magic to knowing something is there, pure, pristine, where no one else will ever find it."

Lucier paused in his oration to stare out over the harbour.

"You think scientific advances will ruin the magic of orchid hunting?" asked Eleanor.

Lucier shook his head. "I am a realist. The orchid world is always changing — this is just one of many upheavals since the beginning of the craze back in the 1800s. I'm saying that some secrets are dangerous, both to keep and to seek."

"Thank you for the warning." In her mind, Eleanor moved Marcel Lucier up her suspect list to just below Fairfax. "Perhaps you can answer a question that's been on my mind?"

"Yes?"

"Carroll's death — it seems more than coincidental, don't you think? Three orchid experts arrive in a small town, and that very night, the local orchid scholar dies."

"The old man's passing had nothing to do with me," said Lucier coolly.

"You left his house unsatisfied — with more questions?"

"I did," said Lucier. "I wanted to talk with him again."

It was hardly an alibi, but Eleanor nodded as if this satisfied her. "Perhaps you can tell me more about New Zealand native orchids," she said. "I've lived here for years and had no idea they existed before this week."

"Of course," said Lucier, and they walked on as if murders, deception, and intrigue never came within a mile of Te Kohe.

21

In which Charlie invokes the librarian's code of secrecy.

Charlie always felt sad walking past the monument outside the Te Kohe Library. A set of names from the Great War was carved on the front face. But another, longer list had been carved on the Western face. These were the young men who had gone overseas to fight in World War II and never come back.

To Charlie, the names held a gravitas that reached over a hundred years. And it was lent weight by the occasional foot soldier who had made his way home and still hung around, in ghostly uniform, at the Returned and Services' Association.

"How do we get into the records?" asked Dante.

"That's easy. We'll ask Mrs McGwiggan," said Charlie. "She's the librarian and the record keeper. There's bound to be information about the *Whitby*. It was a big event back in the day."

Charlie strolled through the double doors of the library, Dante in his wake.

The library consisted of a tiny children's corner, with brightly coloured kids' books and a pile of beanbags; the adults' section, with ten aisles packed with books; and a large hunting and fishing section, filled with almanacks, magazines, and a large coffee table stacked with books full of photos of dead fish.

This last section had been made by the previous librarian, who was a keen fisherman. Over the last five years, Mrs McGwiggan, the current librarian, had whittled it down to make room for other books. She'd had to do this at a glacial pace, so no one in town would notice. Thus far, she'd succeeded in adding an entire row of bookshelves filled with literary classics like *'A Christmas Carol,' '20,000 Leagues Under the Sea,'* and *'Pride and Prejudice.'*

Charlie approached the reception desk. Behind it, a large window to the office allowed the librarian to spot any miscreants making away with books they hadn't checked out.

"Hello?" called Charlie. "Mrs McGwiggan?"

"Over here," called a voice from the literary end of the library. A hand waved above the bookshelves, and Charlie hurried over to the 800s section.

Mrs McGwiggan was a small lady with round glasses that sometimes sat on her nose and sometimes hung on her chest, suspended by a beaded string. She was wearing a knee-length brown wool skirt, a soft blue blouse, and a bright red cardigan.

"Charlie!" Her face lit up as he came into view. "And this is?"

"Dante, Mrs McGwiggan." Charlie introduced them. "Mrs McGwiggan's in charge of all the books in Te Kohe."

"Well, not quite all," said Mrs McGwiggan. "Just the ones here. And those currently being lent out. Pleased to meet you, young man." She held out a gnarled hand, which Dante shook carefully.

"We'd like to look over the records if that's ok," said Charlie. "We're doing a research project. Something for the Professor."

"I heard about poor August Carroll," said Mrs McGwiggan, her mouth pursing in sympathy. "So sad."

Charlie nodded and scrubbed a hand through his hair. He knew he should feel sad about the professor, but he'd seen how happy the old man had been when he'd left. The moth was his chief concern. It was resting at home on his coffee plant, looking more tired and ragged each time he saw it. It was a messenger that had come for a serious purpose, and it didn't have long to live.

The librarian led them to the back of the library, where old and dusty double doors guarded another room. She took an old key from the keyring at her belt, turned it with a click, and pushed the door open.

"The records room," said Charlie in a reverent tone. Beside him, Dante's face was expressionless, but in such a way that conveyed he did not hold the same regard for a room full of old paper and dust.

Like the library, the records room had been built in the 1920s, but on a much smaller budget. A skylight illuminated rows of steel shelves packed with boxes and crates. Steel file drawers and the occasional old-fashioned pigeonhole cabinet lined the walls.

"What time period do you want?" asked Mrs McGwiggan.

Charlie stuck his tongue in his cheek, wondering if he could ask her to swear a librarian's oath of secrecy and whether such a thing existed. "Mid 1800s."

"Ah," her eyes lit up. "You're researching the wreck of the *Whitby*."

"Did Carroll ever come here looking for information?" asked Charlie.

"If he did, I couldn't tell you," said Mrs McGwiggan.

"So there is a librarian's code of secrecy," said Charlie, then blushed when he realised he'd said it out loud.

"Not as such," said Mrs McGwiggan, "but he asked me not to tell anyone."

Which was as good as admitting that he'd been here after all. Charlie was about to point that out when her eyes twinkled at him. Mrs McGwiggan knew exactly what she was up to.

"Could you include us in your code of secrecy?" asked Charlie humbly.

"I'm not in the habit of talking out of school," said Mrs McGwiggan. "Come this way."

She led them between stacks of old papers and ledgers that looked ready to collapse on them at any moment.

They stopped in the far corner of the room. A narrow window near the ceiling illuminated the dust and cast barred shadows on an old desk with a leather insert.

"This is where you can read through what you've found," said the librarian. "And that," her cardigan-clad arm gestured at an ancient Victorian bureau, "is where you'll find all the documents from the mid-1800s. The microfiche has a catalogue of our newspaper articles, but it's not complete."

"Thank you," said Charlie.

Dante crossed his arms, staring towards the double doors. Charlie thought he looked uneasy.

"I'll be back at my desk," said Mrs McGwiggan. "Call if you need anything." She vanished back into the main library.

"Dante," said Charlie, "are you alright?"

"I don't like... libraries," said Dante.

"Why's that?" Charlie felt a sense of tragedy.

"I was once trapped under a mountain of books," said Dante. "I don't want to talk about it."

"Perhaps..." Charlie searched for a side quest Dante could go on. "Do you think you could go and see whether Fran has kumara and chicken pies at the RSA? We'll need some to keep our energy up. Though we won't eat them in here." He raised his voice slightly, just in case Mrs McGwiggan was listening.

"Ok," said Dante. "I'll be back."

Alone in the records room, Charlie stretched his fingers and, with a sigh of satisfaction, began the search.

There was a microfiche machine in one corner, and he began by creating a list of likely sources. Forty minutes later, he'd covered the desk with an assortment of scanned and reprinted newspaper articles, harbour master reports, tide tables, and a book written fifty years ago by local historian Eric P. Weatherby. It covered the history of Te Kohe from the early settler days until the book's publication in the 70s, but there was an entire chapter dedicated to the wreck of the *Whitby*.

He was moving on to check the harbour master's reports when Charlie came across a small article published in 'The Moanahe Bugler.' It detailed one Austin Carrall, who had been a rigger on the *Whitby*.

A year after the shipwreck, Carrall had journeyed to Auckland and returned with a deed of purchase for ten hectares of land in the hills behind Te Kohe.

"That's interesting," said Charlie aloud. And the name: Austin Carrall. A shipwrecked sailor who'd come into enough money to buy a block of land. What had he taken with him from the *Whitby* to get all that money? Could he be an ancestor of August Carroll?

A shadow fell across the desk. Dante must be back from the RSA. Charlie hoped he'd brought some of Fran's pies. His stomach rumbled, reminding him he hadn't had breakfast yet.

"Hey, I think I've found something," he said. When there was no reply, he turned around.

"And the thing that you've found would be?" asked Inspector Avery.

"Erm... local history project," managed Charlie. "Very boring. That's why Dante left. I thought he was you... What are you doing here?"

"There was a talk on soil management." Avery's dark brown eyes scanned the documents spread on the desk. "It was boring, even by my standards, and you cannot imagine how boring some police work can get."

"Er... how come you're here?"

"A happy coincidence," said Avery. "I wanted to browse some books. The bookstore is closed today, and when I came into the library, this door was open, and I wandered through. You're looking into an ancient shipwreck and a lost shipment of orchids from Florida. Hardly boring, I'd say."

Charlie wished he had Eleanor's gift for invention and distraction. However, he felt even Eleanor's imagination might fail her here. All the evidence was in plain sight.

"There's no law against—" he started to say when Dante's form appeared in the doorway.

He was moving quickly, though he paused for a moment when he saw Avery.

"Fairfax is here," he said in a low voice to Charlie. "He's asking the librarian about records from the 1850s."

Avery gave a low whistle, followed by a grin that made him look forty years younger. "Coincidence? I think not."

"We can't let him see all this," said Charlie. "Can we lock the door?"

"I'm not getting locked in with a whole lot of books," said Dante, and Avery raised an eyebrow.

Fairfax's voice, smooth and cultured, issued from the main library.

"I would so appreciate having a look at the old records. I love local history — so fascinating, don't you think?"

"That's our cue." Avery hurriedly shoved all the documents spread across the desk into a pile and pushed them into Charlie's hands.

"What are you doing?" Charlie looked at him in confusion.

Avery shot a look over his shoulder. "His Lordship's ancestors ransacked half the Pacific for rare specimens. He is *not* getting his hands on a lost shipment of mind-blowingly rare orchid specimens if I have anything to do with it."

"O-kay," said Charlie.

The conversation was headed their way, with Fairfax making comments like 'I love these Art Deco flourishes,' and Mrs McGwiggan thanking him, and perhaps taking a little more time than necessary to cover the ground to the records room.

Dante scanned the space rapidly, then jerked his head towards the dustiest corner, an alcove where boxes stuffed full of books and old papers teetered dangerously.

They squeezed into the space a moment before Fairfax and Mrs McGwiggan walked past, his lordship turning on the charm. Charlie ended up with the sheaf of papers pressed to his chest, sandwiched between Avery and Dante, who seemed to want to stay as far away from the piled-up books as possible.

"We're sitting ducks if he comes this way," muttered Avery. "Not a situation I want to be caught in."

"If we leave now, he won't see us," whispered Charlie, peering over the bulk of Dante's shoulders.

"I'm going." Dante ghosted out of the alcove, a silent shadow, and Charlie suppressed a shiver. Dante had transformed before his eyes into a predator in full stealth mode.

"Move," whispered Avery.

Charlie took one step, then another, trying to be as silent as Dante. Fairfax and Mrs McGwiggan were behind a row of shelves, looking at 1850s documents. But at any moment, Fairfax could step out and see them.

Papers rustled behind the shelves, and Charlie froze. He wondered what Mrs McGwiggan and Fairfax were up to. Avery gave him a tiny push, and Charlie carried on, tiptoeing like a cat burglar.

"You look like something out of 'Carmen Sandiego,'" breathed Avery. "You couldn't look more suspicious if you were wearing a black and white striped jumper and a mask."

Chagrined, Charlie tried to walk normally but quietly. He almost made it to the door when a noise from the 1850s corner made him look up sharply.

One of his sneakers caught on the other, and he stumbled forward. He would have careened into the double doors and made an awful racket, but

Dante loomed up as a warning shadow. He took the stack of papers out of Charlie's hands and opened the doors to spin him out of the room in one swift, silent motion.

Charlie gulped. He gave Dante a thumbs-up and pointed towards the office. He, Avery, and Dante made their silent way there while Charlie waited for his heartbeat to return to normal.

A minute later, Mrs McGwiggan reappeared from the records room. Her eyes twinkled at Charlie behind their thick spectacles. She crossed to her office and motioned them inside.

"I'm afraid I rather took sides in your treasure hunt or whatever it is you're up to," she said as the three men shuffled in behind her. "Librarians are supposed to be neutral, but I decided to favour the home team." She held out one hand, and Dante dutifully laid the thin stack of papers in it. "I'll copy these for you, but it would be best if you came back in half an hour. I suspect Fairfax will have left disappointed by then."

"Thank you," said Charlie fervently.

"I will accept payment in beer, kawakawa gin, or you can hunt down anyone with overdue library books and make them pay," said Mrs McGwiggan. "That looks like a job for you." Her smile sharpened as she looked at Dante.

"I could do it," said Dante.

Charlie wondered if Mrs McGwiggan understood the forces she would unleash with this request.

Outside, the three of them blinked in the bright sunlight.

"Wow, Inspector," said Charlie. "I didn't know you could do things like that."

Avery looked sheepish for a moment, then remembered himself and put on his Inspector's face. "Tell Eleanor I want in. No ifs, buts, or maybes."

"Why would we want you?" said Dante. He folded his arms. He was a full step below the inspector, but he still looked down on him slightly as they eyed one another.

Avery considered. “I’ll stop Eleanor from going off the deep end and doing something regrettable. She has a tendency to go all in, especially if her friends are in danger.”

“I don’t think we are,” said Charlie. “In danger, I mean.”

“If there has been a murder,” said Avery, “then there will be a murderer. Also, it appears you’re on a treasure hunt, two steps ahead of a ruthless and moneyed aristocrat.”

“Erm,” said Charlie.

Avery patted his shoulder. “It was a guess, Charlie. But your face is an open book.”

“You will look after Eleanor, and I will look after Charlie,” said Dante.

“Deal,” said Avery. “Conspirator meeting adjourned.” A grin crept across his face. "And now, I want you to phone Eleanor.”

22

In which our sleuths delve into the past.

"You did what?" said Eleanor into her phone.

She had returned home and was preparing to go to another orchid lecture. Really, the lecture was a pretext. She planned to spend the time snooping around their suspects and trying to figure out what each of them was after.

"Avery caught me in the act." Charlie sounded uncomfortable.

Eleanor gave an exaggerated sigh. "Why didn't you make up some story, excuse, anything? The whole idea was to let him in on a bit of the action — enough to get the postmortem — but not the whole enchilada. I don't want a policeman breathing down my neck while we're unravelling this tangle of intrigue. It's distracting."

"He saw the papers I'd found on the *Whitby*," said Charlie. "He's a really fast reader."

"And you now have copies of the papers? And Fairfax doesn't?"

"That's right."

"An excellent result. Let's get together and go over everything so far."

Charlie sounded even more uncomfortable. "Avery's here, listening in. He wants to come along too."

Eleanor gave a rueful smile. "Well played, Inspector. Fine, you can come along. But I've had enough of refined culture for today. Let's meet at the shack."

The Beach Shack was Te Kohe's best fish 'n' chips shop. For a beach town that housed a lot of fishermen and fisherwomen, this was quite a claim.

Dante arrived to find Eleanor waiting at one of the trestle tables set between the road and the dunes. Ten metres away, the graffiti-covered concrete block shape of the Beach Shack squatted on the edge of the car park. Fifty metres away, blue rollers crested with white foam washed up the broad black sand beach.

"Hi," said Dante, sitting opposite Eleanor. In the middle of the table was a newspaper-wrapped parcel. The aroma of deep-fried potatoes rose from its depths.

"Dante," said Eleanor, "why did you vanish after lunch?"

"I had to make a call."

Stephanie's presence troubled Dante, but he didn't know exactly why. Usually, his instincts were more helpful. See a shape outlined against a window — sniper. Duck out of sight. See an armed opponent reach for their sidearm — quick draw. Shoot them before they shoot you. Simple.

What was up with Stephanie, the redhead who caught saltshakers like a professional cricketer? He didn't have clear intel. Yet.

Dante ran a mental finger down a list of his usual methods for dealing with a problem like Stephanie. Lethal force was out. Kidnapping, blackmail, and deep surveillance came with complications. Diplomacy?

Eleanor unwrapped the package, and the smell of fried food grew stronger. "I ended up going for a walk with Marcel Lucier, who warned me off further contact with Fiorelli and Fairfax."

Eleanor placed two small plastic containers on the scarred wooden table and opened them. One contained ketchup and the other, malt vinegar. The sea breeze blew over the dunes, ruffling the pīngao grasses and bringing the scent of salt and seaweed.

"I want to find out more about Lucier," said Eleanor. "He's currently number two on our suspect list." With deft hands, she unwrapped the final layer of newspaper. Inside was a plain greaseproof paper parcel with steam escaping from the folds.

Dante rubbed his forehead. Maybe he was losing his grip. He'd heard of this. Usually, it happened to senior agents who'd nearly died too many times. Their mental radars began to ping off everything and nothing. They woke a dozen times in the night to check that the front door was locked. They'd make voice memos of suspicious goings on in case they were murdered in their sleep.

Dante hoped he wasn't headed that way.

"Do you think gardening is a good hobby to help someone like me become a civilian?" he asked.

"Perhaps you need another one," said Eleanor. "In addition."

"Bowling?"

Eleanor considered, then shook her head. "I'm not sure the bowling club would survive. I wouldn't recommend lawn bowls either. Maybe fishing?"

"Hi, guys." Charlie came into view over the dunes. He was wearing a bucket hat that pushed his auburn curls down over his forehead. "I got some more chips, and Inspector Avery is ordering fish."

Eleanor unwrapped the greaseproof paper bundle to reveal golden potato chips, piping hot and deep-fried to perfection.

Charlie eyed the small container of malt vinegar. "I think we're going to need a bigger vessel. Also, I found a suspicious bottle of digitalis medicine at Carroll's house. It said 'cardiovascular support.' That means it's for the heart, right?"

"It does." Eleanor's gaze took in the rapidly approaching figure of Avery. "Let's discuss it later, when it's just you, Dante, and me."

"This is where you want to have a clandestine meeting?" asked Avery, sliding onto the seat next to Eleanor. "Not your usual style, Eleanor."

"It's perfect." Eleanor's wave encompassed the bowl of the sky, the bright sunlit ocean, the rolling dunes. The other picnic tables were distant enough for privacy, and there were no convenient buildings, bushes, or cars to eavesdrop from.

"It's also the best fish 'n' chips in town," said Charlie. "Please don't tell Fran I said that," he added hurriedly.

"She comes here every Monday when the RSA's closed," said Eleanor.

"Do I have to swear an oath of secrecy?" Avery flipped an electronic order counter onto the picnic table.

Dante eyed it suspiciously. It would be the easiest place imaginable to hide a recording device. He wondered if he should accidentally on purpose smash it into very small pieces.

"We are gathered here today," intoned Eleanor, "to reflect on the case thus far." Mischief crinkled the corner of her eyes. "Charlie, show us what you got."

Charlie took the photocopied documents from his satchel and laid them next to the parcel of chips. Then, he took out a Pelican Micro Case and clicked it open to reveal the notebook. "It's what boaties use to keep their phones dry," he explained. "I thought if the notebook's old and valuable, then we should protect it."

Dante approved. He'd used Pelican cases for storing gun suppressors, rangefinders, and signal jammers. They were a good choice.

"This belonged to Professor Carroll," said Eleanor, pointing to the notebook. She took some more pages out of her bag. "The originals of these are in the possession of Doctor Fiorelli. I know for a fact that Marcel Lucier is also criminally interested in them. And it seems Fairfax is also on the trail."

Eleanor put the coloured printouts in a neat pile on the table and weighed them down with the ketchup container.

Avery slipped on his reading glasses to study the photographed documents. He leafed through them once, frowned, and started studying them in detail.

"Fiorelli has a list of the goods the *Whitby* was carrying." Avery shook his head. "Amazing. Do you know about the ship in question?"

"Not really," said Eleanor. "I think it's related to what we're looking into. And I love a good shipwreck story."

"As a mystery fan and orchidist, I've always loved this legend." Avery took a chip from the pile and dipped it in ketchup. A boyish grin stole across his face, and Eleanor felt a brief flutter in the area of her heart. Focus on the case, she told herself sternly. "The wreck of the *Whitby* is like... the *Titanic*, for orchidists. It's El Dorado, the lost city of Atlantis, the great treasure that got away."

"I like it already," said Eleanor.

"In 1852, a three-masted barque left from Florida," said Avery. "It had on board many items wanted by those in the far-flung colonies — tobacco, cotton, sugar, and the all-important muskets. But it was also a smuggling ship, and it had a secret hold, hidden below the main hold. And that's why it didn't put into shore first at Auckland, where the customs agents waited. No, it had one stop first — in Te Kohe harbour — where the captain planned to unload his secret cargo of tobacco, rum, and muskets to be sold directly to settlers and the local tribes.

"There was a botanist on board the *Whitby* — one Giulio Albarelli. He was famous, but this was to be his last voyage. Albarelli had spent a season gathering specimens in the Florida Everglades. He'd harvested rare orchids, cycads, bromeliads, and lotuses. He had dry specimens for Kew Gardens and the Fairfax Estate. But he'd also packed some live plants into glass terrariums to transport back to England, where he had buyers waiting. It was the boom of the botanical collecting craze, and throughout Europe, wealthy families with glasshouses were ready to pay high prices for rare and beautiful plants."

Charlie bounced on his seat. "What about the Ghost Queen?"

"I was getting to that." Avery smiled faintly. "You know about ghost orchids, right?"

"Imagine I don't," said Eleanor.

"Ghost orchids are very rare. They're called this because they have no leaves - just a root system and a flower that's ghostly white. They live in symbiosis with a specific fungus — it's why they rarely survive out of the wild. And it's why they're hard to see unless they're flowering."

"And the Ghost Queen?" asked Eleanor.

"A mythically rare orchid. It was said to bloom only under the full moon. Over the years, other strange tales have grown up around it."

"Such as?" asked Eleanor.

"There's one legend that it lets people speak to the dead." Avery shrugged. "That's folklore for you."

Eleanor smiled demurely while Charlie flushed a delicate shade of pink.

"The point is," said Avery, "Albarelli's last mission was to obtain the Ghost Queen from the Florida Everglades. He was said to have succeeded. The *Whitby* was loaded with an amazing botanical haul."

"What went wrong?" asked Eleanor.

"The night the *Whitby* was due to enter Te Kohe harbour, a huge storm blew up. The harbour is treacherous in bad weather. There's a hidden sandbar that's shallow enough to founder a ship. The *Whitby* struck it in the early hours of the morning. They launched the longboats, and most of the crew reached safety. But not Albarelli. It wasn't recorded whether he died in the initial crash or whether he failed to board a longboat. The *Whitby* was grounded, but didn't sink. It stayed on the bar all the next day, with the waves smashing it and the wind wrenching at the sails. There was talk of mounting a mission to rescue the cargo, but the harbour master forbade it.

"The following night, the storm grew stronger, and by morning, the ship had broken apart and sunk. However..." Avery nodded towards the thin stack of photocopied pages they'd taken from the records room. "Charlie discovered that Austin Carrall was a sailor on the *Whitby*. Despite being shipwrecked with just the clothes he was wearing, he returned a year later and bought land in Te Kohe."

"It's a telling name," said Eleanor. "Carrall... Carroll?"

"Quite likely," said Avery.

"Fairfax, Fiorelli, or Lucier might have enough pull to get the Orchid Symposium held here," suggested Eleanor. "It's a nice cover story for them to search for this lost shipment."

"Any of them could swing it." Avery tapped the papers. "All three of them are obviously interested in this shipment. And this notebook of Carroll's — have you read it?"

"Briefly. We haven't discovered if it's hiding any secrets," said Eleanor. "Things have been a little busy."

"Do you mind?" murmured Avery. He carefully wiped his fingers free of chip grease on a paper napkin, but Eleanor shook her head and fished in her handbag.

"Here." Eleanor passed Avery a pair of white cotton gloves. "We don't need grease stains on this pristine relic, even if it's from Te Kohe's finest chips."

Avery slipped the gloves on and picked up the notebook, his fingers deft on its battered leather binding. He made a humming noise and smiled. "It's beautiful."

The pages were filled with an elegant copperplate cursive script, but what really drew the eye was the art. The drawings were done in black ink with delicate washes added in watercolour.

Every page was filled with flowers, leaves, beetles, moths and butterflies. They were vibrant with life and drawn with a detail that spoke of an artist who loved their subject.

A third of the way into the book, the content changed. Now, it was all orchids.

Orchids hung down from trees, they sprouted from fallen branches, they appeared amidst forest foliage or in solitary splendour. And then, near the end, the artist began to draw just one orchid.

The plant had delicate white flowers, twisted brown roots, and no leaves. It appeared first on a brown branch, then by itself, the same plant, again and again and again.

"It's definitely a ghost orchid. But different from any I've seen." Avery pulled his phone out of his pocket and keyed in a quick search query.

The sea breeze stilled, and the air became utterly calm. Avery set his phone down on the table next to the notebook.

"You think it could be a Ghost Queen?" asked Charlie.

Avery held up his phone, where an image shone. It was an old-fashioned botanical drawing of a flower with delicate petals. "That's the only known drawing of the Ghost Queen. Declared extinct in 1880."

Charlie's eyes widened. "That looks like the same flower. Do you think the professor might have done the last drawings? Do you think he might have owned — in secret — a Ghost Queen orchid?"

Eleanor leaned over and studied the notebook. "I'm not completely certain, but this looks like it was sketched from life. It has that feeling."

"If Carroll had a Ghost Queen," said Charlie, "then..."

"It would be worth a lot of money," said Eleanor.

"Worth killing for," said Dante.

Eleanor smiled. "I love a good mystery. So, Inspector, are you still in?"

"I'm interested in this." Avery tapped the notebook and the ship's papers. "And the *Whitby* cargo. But I don't want to wade in, assuming murder, because a healthy, but decidedly elderly gentleman had a heart attack."

Charlie started forward, a protest on his lips, then hesitated. He took an agitated handful of chips instead.

"So you're all care, no responsibility," said Eleanor.

"If you want my help," said Avery, "then I can help you as an orchid enthusiast. Not a policeman."

"May all our boundaries be so clearly defined," said Eleanor.

"If you gather enough evidence to prove it's murder, then I'll be obligated to do something about it," said Avery. "Until then, I'm on holiday. With a bit of botanical treasure hunting on the side."

"I can work with that," said Eleanor. "On to our next step. We should try to find the Professor's Ghost Queen, if it exists. And work out which of our suspects is responsible for his death. You can skip that part, Avery."

"Deal. This," Avery pointed at the ship's manifest, "intrigues me. I would love to find that the *Whitby's* cargo survived." He looked up at Eleanor, trying and failing to suppress a smile. "This is going to be fun."

"Finally, something we can agree on." Eleanor turned to Dante and Charlie. "Now, it's time to go on an evidence hunt."

23

In which certain artefacts come to light.

Dante stalked into the covered car park adjacent to the Pepper Tree Hotel, Eleanor beside him. Charlie's mother, Delia, was the new owner of the hotel, and she had directed them to the guest room rubbish bins and given them permission to do whatever was necessary, no questions asked.

Dante carefully checked the sight lines before zeroing in on their target. Carparks were good places for ambushes, and his radar had not settled since meeting Stephanie.

Charlie had gone into the hotel to see if any ghosts had seen their suspects leaving in the middle of the night to rob Carroll's house.

"If we're thinking poison, it's possible the murderer brought along their own handy supply," said Eleanor. "Or, they may have made the poison from crushing pills or emptying medication capsules. If that's the case, they may have thrown the capsules out in their hotel room rubbish bin, and we'll be able to find them."

"Or they used the bottle Charlie found," said Dante.

Eleanor sighed. "True. Poison is tricky stuff to pin down."

The hotel staff emptied the room wastebaskets every day, and unfortunately, they'd already done so. But there were the large wheelie bins in the garage, and Eleanor had commandeered a tarpaulin. At her request, Dante emptied the bins, one by one, onto the tarpaulin for closer examination.

Bin one yielded nothing but the usual: tissues, food wrappers, cotton buds and toothpicks. Bin two was similar, except someone had thrown away what looked like a toupee.

"Odd, but not obviously criminal," said Eleanor, snapping a photo of it lying in a slightly macabre heap on the blue tarp. Dante thought it ought to have a chalk outline around it. It looked ready to crawl away by itself.

"Done?" he asked, and Eleanor nodded. He gathered the rubbish up on the tarp and fed it back into its tall green bin.

"Lucky last. I have a good feeling about this bin," said Eleanor.

"Do you enjoy detecting?" asked Dante.

Eleanor raised her eyebrows. "Many years ago, I wanted to be a police officer. It was a different time, though — especially in New York. In the end, a life of crime seemed to be the cleaner path."

Dante felt there was a whole world of ups and downs behind that simple statement, but he didn't ask for more. He kept a strict 'don't tell, don't ask' policy toward people with interesting pasts, including himself.

He tipped the contents of the last bin onto the tarpaulin, then spread them out with his shoe. Tissues, cotton buds... what did people do with all these tissues and cotton buds? It was better not to ask.

Something was bugging Dante, and he felt now was the time to verbalise it. "What if it turns out to be death from natural causes?"

"For Carroll?" asked Eleanor, poking through the rubbish with an umbrella she'd found leaning by the stairs. "Then I suppose I'll have to find something else to occupy myself for the next week or so. I might even learn about orchids. Would you mind opening that?" Eleanor pointed at a black plastic bag, knotted shut.

Dante slid the knife out of his wrist sheath and advanced on his target. The last time he'd done something like this, the bag in question had contained a large quantity of expensive white powder. Luckily, he hadn't breathed it in.

With one shoe, he pinned the bag down and skewered it with the knife point, drawing upwards to slit the bag. A twist of the blade and the contents lay revealed.

"Interesting," said Eleanor. She took a photo.

"What is it?"

"I have no idea. But I want to find out."

Dante studied their find. Lying in a tangle on the black plastic was a white muslin cloth with flakes of green plant matter stuck to it, an eyedropper, a plastic menu with a piece of sticky tape attached, a small hotel bar bottle of vodka, and a larger glass jar.

"It's unusual to tie things up in a black bag before disposing of them, don't you think?" Eleanor gently turned over the bag's contents. "That larger glass jar has bits of leaf matter on it too - as if it was being used as an improvised rolling pin. And the menu — if we re-attached the tape, it would form the shape of a funnel. It might have been used to pour liquid or powder into a container. An impromptu chemistry set. Very poison-y."

"So it might have been murder." Dante sniffed the air. It was ripe with the smell of garbage, but there was something else. Subtle. Tropical.

"It's a bit of a leap. But this is suggestive." Eleanor straightened. "I'd like to get the residue analysed to find out what it is."

Again, if Dante had his usual contacts, this would be easy. "Charlie might know someone."

"I might, too." Eleanor took a clean rubbish bag, courtesy of Delia, from her handbag and carefully put the black bag and its contents inside. "While you were at the library, I talked to Greg, the Symposium MC. According to him, Carroll arrived at the Symposium shortly after we did. He said that Carroll refused all offers of a drink, and though he said he was fine, he was already looking unwell."

"So if someone poisoned Carroll, they must have done it that afternoon. Most likely one of the three orchidists who visited him."

"It fits," said Eleanor. "If someone local killed Carroll, they could have been quite circumspect. They could arrange things so that nobody would discover him for several days. For it to happen now, when we have famous orchidists coming from overseas... probability points toward one of them having done it."

"All of them had the opportunity."

"Marcel Lucier admitted to visiting Carroll yesterday afternoon, and he said Fiorelli went there too," said Eleanor. "The clay on her shoes supports this story. Fairfax might have gone as well. He could have gone straight from Carroll's house to Majorie's tea party. Soon after Fairfax appears, Fiorelli leaves, possibly to go see Carroll. We left while Lucier was still there, but I can find out at what time he left the tea party."

"What's the motive?"

"Lucier and Fairfax are supposedly both wealthy. Maybe they found out Carroll had Albarelli's journals, or this Ghost Queen. They offer to buy it, but Carroll refuses. What's next? Poison him, and perhaps buy his estate from his heirs? That plan could also apply to Fiorelli, except I doubt she'd be able to offer as much money as Lucier or Fairfax."

"Murder seems extreme. Burglary would be simpler."

"Someone did burgle him," said Eleanor. "Though we don't know if they were successful or not. It's a good point, though. Why go straight to murder? I suppose someone under the grip of orchidelirium could snap. If any of our three suspects had been on the trail of this rare orchid for years, and were being denied it at this late stage... they might decide a small dose of poison was the easiest way to remove this last obstacle. After all, no one would suspect murder. It's only because of Charlie that we're considering it at all."

"What's next?" asked Dante.

"We figure out what this is." Eleanor swung the bag gently. "And we try to work out which hotel room it came from. I hope Charlie's ghost interviews are going well, because I suspect solving this is going to be tricky."

24

In which 80s slang comes in handy.

Charlie slipped into the hotel through the kitchen. It was nice to roam through the hotel, knowing that it belonged to his mother, and Ted Andrews wouldn't pop up like an ill-willed goblin. If Charlie was in luck, Milo would know which guest had left in the night to burgle Carroll's house.

Years ago, when Charlie and Milo had been the same age, they'd watched '*The Shining*' together. Charlie had regretted it for two reasons.

Firstly, it had terrified him. For several months, Charlie had fallen asleep watching the wooden door of his bedroom to make sure a madman didn't chop his way through it. This was no problem for Milo, as he didn't need to sleep.

Secondly, Milo had decided the boy hero of the film was his new role model.

Eight-year-old Charlie had rather enjoyed running alongside Milo as he pedalled his bike up and down the corridors of the Pepper Tree Hotel. Twelve years later, the shine had worn off.

He listened for the telltale squeak of pedals as he climbed the hotel stairs. On the third floor, the corridor narrowed, then widened as a thin window took in a sliver of sea view.

'Squeak....creak...squeak.' The sound came from further down the corridor, and Charlie quickly checked for staff and guests. He wasn't yet immune to the embarrassment of people looking at him like he was crazy when he talked to ghosts. He hoped that one day, perhaps when he was eighty, he wouldn't care.

A small boy came around the corner. He had a BMX bike with spokies and a lowrider seat.

"Hey," said Charlie.

Milo skidded to a stop and gave Charlie a look full of attitude.

"Hey, yourself." Milo wore a red baseball cap on backwards, Converse sneakers, and jeans with holes in the knees. "What's up?"

Charlie glanced down the corridor again. "I was wondering if you could help me with something."

"Yeah?" Milo folded his skinny arms across his chest.

"Last night," said Charlie, "did you see anyone sneak out? Probably late, after midnight?"

"Maybe." Milo grinned, revealing a chipped front tooth. "What's it to you?"

"It's pretty important. Could be a case of murder."

"Cool!" Milo's eyes lit up. Then he checked himself and resumed his offhand posture. "If it's worth all that much, then you have to do a dare."

Charlie groaned inwardly. That was the problem with childhood friends who were ghosts. You grew up, they didn't. Games that were fun when you were a kid were painful as an adult.

"Can we skip it, just for once?" he asked.

Milo frowned. "Don't be an egg. If you don't do a dare, I might forget who I saw. If I even did see anyone," he added hastily.

Charlie studied the set of Milo's narrow shoulders. "Fine. What do you want me to do?"

Milo's slow grin did not help Charlie's nerves. "I've got just the thing. You're gonna love this. Follow me!" He pedalled his bike towards the stairway and Charlie followed, feeling apprehensive.

Downstairs in the foyer, a few staff members hovered around, doing the myriad tasks necessary to keep a hotel running.

Milo pushed his ghostly BMX bike backwards and forwards as he considered. "I dare you to go up to the first guest you see and tell them that..." he drummed his fingers on the brightly painted handlebars of the bike, "that they suck!" He finished triumphantly.

"Hey," protested Charlie. "That's not even funny. It's just rude."

"Then you have to say: 'Yo, babe, you're bodacious.'"

"What if they're a guy?" asked Charlie.

"They're not." Milo's dimpled grin reappeared as he looked past Charlie's shoulder.

Charlie followed his gaze and groaned. Coming down the stairs into the lobby was a gorgeous redhead. She looked like she'd just stepped off the cover of a surf magazine, with a green sundress and strappy sandals.

"I only have to say it once," he told Milo. "If she says 'What?!' I'm not repeating myself."

"You have to say it so she hears," said Milo.

"Fine. And then you tell me what you saw." From experience, Charlie knew it was best to get this type of thing out of the way as quickly as possible. He strode forward, and as the young woman reached the bottom of the stairs, he stepped quickly in front of her and said: "Yo, babe, you're bodacious."

There was a moment of stunned silence, and Charlie braced himself. The woman gave him a frost-laden stare.

"Is this your idea of a joke?" she said.

"Er..." said Charlie.

"Gotcha." Her face broke into a stunning smile. "You look like you just saw a ghost." She stuck out a tanned hand. "I'm Stephanie."

"Charlie." He shook her hand on autopilot. "Charlie Wilson. Umm... pleased to meet you."

Behind him, Milo was rolling on the floor, laughing.

"I'm glad '80s lingo is still around here. I reckon that was the best time for gnarly phrases." Stephanie's Aussie accent gave the words a beachside lilt.

"Uh, yeah." Charlie wondered if he should try to explain his actions, then gave up. Any explanation would make him sound even more like a crazy person.

"Are you a local?" asked Stephanie.

Milo propped himself up on one elbow and gave Charlie a thumbs-up. "Killing it," he mouthed.

"I was born here," said Charlie. "It's a nice place to grow up. Are you here for the Symposium?"

"Orchids," Stephanie grinned. "Are they amazing, or what?"

"Ask her out!" loud-whispered Milo. He'd gotten off the floor and was sitting on his bike again. "Say you'd like to show her the sights."

This was amazingly sound advice from an eight-year-old, and Charlie surprised himself by following it. "Would you like me to show you around? When you're not busy with the orchids, that is," he added. "There's this great ice cream place down the coast and some lovely bush walks." God, he thought. She'll think I'm a psycho-killer. Who invites someone they've just met on a bush walk?

"That'd be lovely. Thanks." Stephanie fished her phone out of her handbag and held it up expectantly. "Give me your number, and I'll call you this afternoon. Let's go out!"

Charlie did a double-take at her last statement, then decided she probably meant it literally. He told her his number and was about to say his name when she cut him off.

"Charlie Wilson. I remember. And I've got to go, but it's been great meeting you." She waltzed out of the hotel foyer, giving him a cheery wave over her shoulder.

Charlie watched her go, feeling baffled, but pleased. Milo gave a long, slow whistle.

"Charlie and Stephanie, up a tree, k-i-s-s-i-n-g."

"Shut up," said Charlie absently, then smiled in apology as the puzzled maitre'd hurried past. "Sorry, not you. Talking to myself." He rounded on Milo. "Now it's your turn." He climbed the stairs to the landing, where the two of them could talk out of sight from the foyer. "What did you see?"

"Last night," said Milo, "I was riding down the stairs. It was, like, about midnight. It was totally spooky, y'know? Witching hour. I got a chill feeling in my bones." He rubbed his upper arms. "Like brrrrr." He shot Charlie a sideways look.

Charlie sighed. "C'mon, give. I did the dare."

"Fine." Milo flounced against the wall in a classic '80s pop group pose. "Someone went past me on the stairs. I was doing a wheelie on the landing, so I only saw them for a moment."

"What did they look like?"

"They were about your height."

"Man or woman?"

"Dunno."

"What were they wearing?"

"They had on a big coat."

"What colour?" Charlie wondered if Milo was even telling the truth or making up a story because he wanted Charlie to stick around.

"A boring colour."

"Like?"

Milo shrugged. "Brown, I guess. Yeah. That was it. A boring brown coat."

"Did you see their face?"

The boy shook his head, looking innocent. "They had a scarf around their face. Like this." He covered the lower half of his face with his hand.

"What colour was the scarf?"

Milo traced a circle on the carpet with the toe of his Converse sneakers. "Dunno."

"Think about it," pleaded Charlie.

Milo squeezed his eyes shut and tilted his head up to the ceiling. "It... was... green!" he said triumphantly, opening his eyes.

Charlie sighed. Once again, he wondered whether Milo was actually remembering or, in the way of some eight-year-olds, imagining that he remembered. At that age, it was hard to separate the two.

"Was there anything else?"

"Yeah." Milo gave him a broad grin. "They were wearing a hat. Like Michael Jackson in 'Smooth Criminal.' Except it was black, not white."

Charlie thought this detail might be true. He could ask the cleaning staff which of the guests had a hat like that. Or a hatbox. It would be hard to hide one in a hotel room. "Thanks, mate. That's really helpful."

"'S'fine." Milo traced another circle on the carpet. "Do you want to go do... stuff?"

"I'm sorry, but I'm busy today."

"Boring adult stuff," said Milo.

"Yeah."

"Because you're a boring adult now."

"I'm sorry."

A cord of sorrow tugged at Charlie's chest as Milo slowly carried his bike up the stairs, thump, thump, thump, the wheels leaving no mark as they dragged across the carpet.

25

In which Eleanor is reminded of Rule Number One.

Eleanor set up her tablet on the kitchen counter and tried to remember how the damned thing worked. The power was on, the appropriate app had been deployed. So why was it not calling her friend?

She remembered not being indifferent to computers when they emerged in the nineties. If she'd known they were going to invade every corner of her life, she'd have made an effort to get up to speed with how they worked.

Of course, back in nineties New York, she'd been having far too much fun riding the wave of gentrification and the East Village art scene, going to the same parties as Jeff Koons and Lou Reed, and working cons to relieve the Manhattan elite of some of their excess wealth.

It had been a fun time, and she'd almost (but not quite) left before the party crashed.

She tapped the screen again, hoping it would do something useful. Her ignorance was beginning to annoy her. Even her four-year-old grandson would do a better job.

She cast that thought out of her mind, along with the accompanying pang of sorrow. It wouldn't do to think such things. She'd made the best choices she could with the hand she'd been dealt, and now she was living with the consequences.

At last, a small green icon appeared, bobbing up and down as the call connected. The black view screen was abruptly filled with the familiar face of Hannah, her oldest friend, fellow conspirator, grifter, forger, and one of the foremost society ladies of New York.

"Let's get a good look at you." Hannah was sitting on a black and white sofa in a beautifully appointed flat with high ceilings and arched windows. Through them, Eleanor saw the green of Central Park and the sparkle of the lake's waters. Hannah's perfectly made-up lips pursed as she studied Eleanor's face. She shook her head sadly. "That shade of lipstick with your hair colour? Ellie, darling. We have to fix this."

"Good to see you too," said Eleanor. "It's been too long."

"It has. Now, is this call business or pleasure?"

"Mostly business," admitted Eleanor.

Hannah rolled her eyes skyward. "Oy va voy, the chutzpah of this woman. Says she's retired, shoots off to hell and gone with no forwarding address, and now she pops up, saying it's business." She leaned back and folded her arms, a smile playing around the corners of her mouth. "Well, go on, darling, spill the beans. Who is he?"

"Who is who?"

"The man, darling."

"There is no man."

"Bubbeleh, I know you too well. There's always a man."

"Fine," said Eleanor. "There is a man, but there is absolutely nothing going on. Thank goodness."

"Oo, do tell." Hannah leaned forward. "Is he a looker?"

"No one says 'looker' any more. Not even my mother, god rest her soul."

"He must be, or you wouldn't be so evasive." Hannah watched Eleanor closely. "Doctor? Lawyer? He isn't in the trade, is he?"

"God no."

"That's a relief. Nothing more likely to drag you back into our world than a good looking no-goodnik. So what's the biz, sweetheart? What's got you so uptight you need to call your friend so early?"

"It's eleven a.m."

"Nu? You never used to get up before two." Hannah sighed. "You've become respectable, darling, and it's horribly disappointing."

"I need to figure out whether this thing I found is a poison and what kind of poison it is."

"Ah." Hannah's eyes lit up. "So that's what you're up to. Playing cops and robbers from the other side!"

Eleanor didn't see any point in denying it. The truth will set you free, she thought. After it tries to put you in jail for twenty years. "It's a hobby."

"Show me the goods," commanded Hannah.

Eleanor put the tray containing the items they'd found in the rubbish onto the table and aimed the tablet at it. Back in the day, Hannah had been an expert at cooking up whatever inks and chemicals they needed to fake everything from passports to bearer bonds. It was a useful skill set, and she hoped it would help her now.

"Hold it higher," said Hannah. "That's it. Now, hold still."

As the silence stretched, Eleanor wondered if her friend had gone off for a mid-morning cocktail. Hannah was both capricious and fiercely loyal, traits that had made working with her a ride indeed.

At last, there were sounds of rustling from the tablet speakers. Eleanor righted the tablet and was rewarded with the sight of Hannah's cleavage retreating from the camera. Her friend grinned and blew her a kiss.

"So?" asked Eleanor. "What do you think?"

"What do I think?" Hannah shrugged. "I think you waited all this time to contact me because there was nothing going on in your life, and you didn't want to admit it. I think you should come back to New York. You know they've started a shadow auction house just off East Seventy-Second? It's wonderful, darling. You walk two blocks from my place, and you're there. Can you imagine?"

Eleanor sighed. She felt like an alcoholic walking past her favourite watering hole, catching the scent of fine red wine and hearing the clink of glasses. "I can also imagine Vince or his sons, their cigar cutters ready to use on some unsuspecting schmuck, and the Feds never far away."

"Oh, old times." Hannah waved this away. "That's all cleaned up now. City Hall goons got on top of things and now everybody's too busy making money off real estate to get their hands dirty." She stopped and peered into the camera, her face concerned. "Is this about Daniel? Because darling, there was nothing you could have done."

"No, no." Eleanor concentrated on keeping her game face. "I just wanted to make a clean break of things. So, what do you think?"

Hannah made a see-saw motion with her hand. "It looks like an improvised rig to make an infusion. What are you thinking? Belladonna? Aconite?"

"Foxglove, actually."

"How very English." Hannah's lips curved up. "Who are your suspects? The village gossip? The butler? The vicar? Please tell me it's the vicar."

"An English lord, an American collector, and an Italian scientist."

Hannah sniffed. "My money's on the lord. Aristocracy can't help overreaching."

"Spoken like a true populist, but the lord is currently last in the running."

"Hmph. He could take the inside lane on the last corner and come from behind. And this man of yours..." Hannah trailed off and waited, her eyebrows raised suggestively.

"First, you have to tell me how I'll know it's foxglove."

"Look who's come up all high and mighty," said Hannah. "Lady Eleanor of New Zealand."

"I never said where I was."

"Darling, I traced your call back to its source five minutes ago. My nephew - such a dear boy - set me up with all the latest greatest. Please tell me you haven't called anyone else with this setup?"

"No..." Eleanor quelled the sudden spike of adrenaline. She added 'get latest encryption' to her to-do list.

"Just as well, darling. So... you want answers." Hannah tapped gold-painted fingernails on the countertop as she thought. "Here's what you do." She reeled off a set of instructions, which Eleanor wrote down in shorthand.

See? she thought. That's a useful skill they don't teach nowadays. And it's faster than typing.

"How accurate is the test?"

"Maybe eighty percent? You'd need to take it to a fancy lab to be sure," said Hannah. "Or feed it to someone's pet. I'm joking! You're always taking things too seriously."

"My friend has a cat. I don't think I'd survive testing foxglove on it."

"So this man," said Hannah. "What's his deal? Has he asked you out?"

"Certainly not."

"Your words say no, but your voice says yes," observed Hannah.

"Fine," huffed Eleanor. "We went dancing. One time." After he threatened to arrest me.

Hannah tilted her head up, her eyes fluttering. "I'm sensing... an attraction, yes. But also conflict. A fraught destiny, a star-crossed fate." It was a throwback to her psychic act — one she'd used back in the early days when they'd needed a way to access high society.

Eleanor snorted. "Keep your star-crossed baloney. I'm perfectly fine, thank you. And not in danger of losing my heart to anyone."

"So tell me what he does," said Hannah in a normal tone.

Eleanor winced internally. It would take a while to live this down. "He's a cop."

She waited while Hannah fell dramatically back onto the sofa cushions, hooting with laughter. "No conflict? Oy vey. Ariadne would turn in her grave. What's rule number one of the grift?"

"Leave your heart at home," said Eleanor. "But, like I said, I'm not in any danger of anything. This is purely a hobby."

"Sure." Hannah sat up and smoothed her hair. "I'll believe that when I believe the one about the innocent having nothing to fear." She grew serious. "You do know you could come home in a heartbeat, darling. There's a loft here for you, and most of the old crew are still around. It'd be fun."

"I do know. Thank you." Eleanor fought to keep the sudden rush of emotion from showing on her face.

"Take care, darling," said Hannah. "And remember rule number one."

26

In which Dante plays bad cop.

Dante found Eleanor, Charlie and Avery talking animatedly about orchids in the Saturday evening Symposium crowd.

He stepped in to loom over Eleanor, who smiled up at him, then turned to Avery.

"Excuse us," she said. "I understand you only want to be involved in the orchid treasure hunt, not our investigation. The conversation Charlie, Dante, and I are about to have would totally ruin things for you."

Avery hesitated, and for a moment, Dante thought he was going to disagree. Then he gave a curt nod. "Fine. Good night."

"Right," said Eleanor, her gaze following Avery as he vanished into the crowd.

They were standing in the foyer outside the lecture hall, in a space that had been turned into an exhibition gallery. Tall plinths, each crowned with an orchid. were scattered throughout the space. Black and white photos of past orchid society members dating back to the early 1900s were set at intervals along the walls.

"How did your ghost interview go?" asked Eleanor.

"Someone wearing a scarf and a fedora left the hotel late last night," said Charlie. "I've asked the staff to look out for a hat or hatbox in the guest rooms."

"Dante and I found a poison-making kit," said Eleanor. "It could have belonged to anyone in the hotel, but I'm betting it'll belong to Dr Isabella Fiorelli, Lord Martin Fairfax, or Marcel Lucier."

Charlie looked glum. "You do realise that you've just named three extremely influential people in the orchid world?"

Eleanor shrugged. "Justice trumps fame."

"There's no proof or anything," said Charlie, "but everyone knows Marcel Lucier has ties to the orchid black market."

They had drifted down the exhibition hall, going with the general flow of people.

Dante's neck prickled. Out of the corner of his eye, he saw the glamorous redhead — Stephanie — looking at an orchid. She turned and smiled.

For a moment, Dante thought she was smiling at him, but no, she was smiling at Charlie, standing next to him. Charlie had gone bright red and was smiling back. Dante's heart thudded in his chest, and it was all he could do to keep his composure.

Did Charlie somehow know Stephanie? Charlie blushed a lot. Was he just smiling at a stranger? He looked back to see if Stephanie was blushing, but she'd disappeared into the crowd.

"That's gorgeous," said Charlie with feeling. "I've never seen a real one before."

Dante did a double-take, then realised Charlie was talking about the display in front of them. On a tall white plinth was an elegant glass and steel structure, like a miniature greenhouse or an oversized lantern.

Dante studied the plaque. It said: "A Victorian-era terrarium, donated by the Fairfax estate. Botanists used terrariums to transport live plants from distant corners of the globe back to important collectors like Kew Gardens and the Fairfax Botanical Collection."

The terrarium was empty, but Charlie assured them it would have housed rare plants from the Andes, the Cape of Good Hope, and even New Zealand.

"It's probably been around the world in a tall ship," he said, looking wistful.

"I see you're appreciating the terrarium." The well-modulated tones of Lord Martin Fairfax intruded into their conversation.

"It's a lovely piece," said Eleanor, smiling graciously. "Lord Martin, I believe you've met Charlie, and this is my friend Dante."

Dante stuck out his hand. "Hi."

"A pleasure." Fairfax shook his hand enthusiastically.

In the handshake, Dante felt a tension that belied the lord's sunny exterior.

"Nice to see you again," said Charlie.

"You met Charlie the other morning at Carroll's house, didn't you?" asked Eleanor.

"Unfortunate circumstances, that." Fairfax frowned.

"Did you find the letters you were looking for?" asked Eleanor.

"Unfortunately not," said Fairfax. "To think someone would burgle a place just after the owner has passed. Unbelievable."

"Quite," agreed Eleanor. "Grace was just saying to me how her nephew — Sergeant Hemi Henare — is looking into it. He's sure it's some of the local kids."

"Shameful," said Fairfax.

"Was that your first visit to Carroll's place?" asked Eleanor. "It's usually so tidy."

"I'm sure it is," said Fairfax.

Eleanor caught Dante's eye, and he realised what she was up to. It was conversational tennis — except this time, she'd set up a lob ball, and she wanted him to smash it past Fairfax before he had a chance to react.

"You arrived late to Marjorie's tea party, because you had just come from Carroll's house," said Dante.

"I, uh..." Fairfax spluttered. "I say, that's a bit much."

"We all want to know what you and Carroll talked about that afternoon," said Eleanor pleasantly. "And whether you had tea with him. You see, we're quite certain that Carroll's death was not from natural causes."

"Now, look here." Fairfax's golden complexion darkened. "Just what are you trying to insinuate?"

"We want to know where you were yesterday afternoon." Dante gave the dead-eyed look he'd used on people whose time had come.

"I say..." Fairfax's cheeks went from flushed to pale.

"Just a simple explanation," said Eleanor. "That's all we want."

Fairfax looked around the crowded room, clearly debating whether to bolt.

"The truth," said Dante. "Now."

"Fine!" bit out Fairfax. "Carroll and I were corresponding. That's true. The old gent wanted to talk with me. But I didn't go there that afternoon. I was... busy."

"With what?" asked Eleanor.

Fairfax flushed. "None of your damn business. The point is, I didn't go. I did plan to visit him during the Symposium, though. That's why I went up there with Grace. I wanted to see if there were any letters about the matter we had been discussing."

"Which was?" asked Eleanor.

"Also, none of your business." Fairfax's jaw clenched as he bit off the last word.

"We'll find out," said Eleanor. "You'd just be saving us some time."

“If that’s all you wanted to know,” said Fairfax, "then this conversation is over.”

“Not quite,” said Eleanor. “You spent some time studying the lawn behind Carroll’s house. What did you see?”

Fairfax shifted gear, regaining control. He looked pointedly down at Eleanor and Dante’s shoes. “You were both there. You must have gone out the back when I arrived. Your shoe sizes fit the prints I saw, clear as anything, on the muddy lawn. But yours weren’t the only ones. Someone else had been there and was probably still up in the trees, watching us. Someone with size eight shoes, small tread. It looked like a bespoke brand.”

“A woman’s shoe?” asked Eleanor.

Fairfax shrugged again. “Or a narrow-footed man. Now, if you’ll excuse me.” He turned and stalked off into the crowd.

“That’s not exactly an alibi,” said Eleanor. “Do you believe him?”

“His pupils didn’t dilate when he was talking,” said Dante.

“That’s an indication, but not infallible,” said Eleanor. “Still, it’d be nice to know if he was our late-night burglar. Well played, Dante. I think you’re getting the hang of the bad cop schtick.”

Dante had no desire to be any kind of cop. But he reckoned if he had to, he could out-bad any bad cop who’d ever lived. After all, cops, good or bad, usually had to apprehend their suspects alive. In his past career, that had almost never been the case.

“Do you think someone saw us find the notebook?” asked Charlie.

“Someone with binoculars could see through the study window,” said Dante.

“So it’s possible,” said Eleanor. “This is both good and bad. Bad, because we don’t know who they are, and they’ll likely want to steal it. Good, because we could use the notebook as bait if we need to. What’s next on the program?”

"A lecture on New Zealand native orchids," said Charlie.

"Excellent," said Eleanor. "And after that, let's ambush the good inspector. I have an idea he could help us with."

27

In which Avery helps concerned citizens with their inquiries.

"Huh. Well, this is a should-have-been-expected surprise." Avery peered through his half-open hotel door to eye the delegation outside.

It was late, and he looked unusually casual in a blue dressing gown, reading glasses pushed up on his head, and, Eleanor was delighted to see, fluffy brown slippers.

"You're on holiday," said Eleanor. "So it's not a school night. Now, be a good host and let us in."

Behind her, Charlie bounced on his toes, looking keyed up, while Dante checked both ends of the corridor outside.

"Fine." Avery swung the door open, revealing the interior of his hotel room. "Make yourself at home."

"Wonderful." Eleanor strolled in, followed by her entourage.

The room was spacious, with high ceilings, a king-sized bed, two couches, a coffee table, and a sideboard cabinet. This was common in old hotels, built when good manners demanded enough space to swing a medium-sized possum.

French doors opened onto a small balcony, and the ever-present fire stairs gave an escape path to the ground. The dark blue velvet curtains were half open, revealing a strip of sea and the lights of ships in the harbour.

"Nice view," observed Eleanor.

"I was enjoying the tranquillity," said Avery drily.

Eleanor seated herself on the plush couch. "Charlie, would you display the loot, please?"

"Wait," said Dante. "I want to sweep this room for bugs."

"Oh, come on." Avery folded his arms. "Are you serious?"

Eleanor shrugged. "Why not? All our suspects are here in the hotel. Who knows what antics they'll get up to?"

"Very well." Avery rolled his eyes.

Dante reached into his sports bag and withdrew a shiny black device. Working quickly, he made his way around the room, pointing it at corners, light fittings, under the bed, and other likely places for a small listening device to hide. Satisfied, he returned the device to the bag and took up a post by the door.

"Ok, James Bond." Avery sat on the couch opposite Eleanor and Charlie. "Why are you lot here?"

"I feel like we need a whiteboard," said Eleanor. "And Charlie wants to do a murder wall with the red string. Have you ever found one in a suspect's house?"

"They're more of an American thing," said Avery. "Here in New Zealand, there's just two degrees of separation. A murder wall would contain your primary school teacher, your second cousin, and one of your drinking buddies. Too close for comfort. And you haven't answered my question."

"I'm helping you maintain plausible deniability," said Eleanor. "Apropos of nothing in particular, how hard is it to order a postmortem?"

Avery scratched his jaw. "It's too late at night for this conversation."

"Perhaps some coffee?" asked Eleanor.

"Someone's coming." Dante took two steps away from the door, his hand slipping under his jacket.

"That'll be room service," said Eleanor. "Please don't disarm them before they deliver the desserts, Dante."

"You ordered room service?" Avery's voice hovered between amusement and outrage.

"I thought you'd be tired after a long day of botanical treasure hunts," said Eleanor.

A polite knock sounded at the door. "Room service for Mr Avery?"

"Come in," called Eleanor.

Dante opened the door, one hand still poised over his hidden holster. He backed slowly into the room ahead of a young man with a trolley and a cheery smile.

"Late night party, is it?" he asked.

"Regrettably," said Avery.

The young man laid a tray on the end of the coffee table and trundled out, genial manner undiminished.

Eleanor lifted the silver cover off the tray to reveal four neat desserts in bowls, a carafe of coffee, and four white ceramic espresso cups.

"It's too late for coffee," said Avery.

"Tiramisu," said Dante with approval. "But you said this place doesn't do it well."

"Ah, but Delia is in charge of the late night kitchen," said Eleanor. "Everything that lady touches is gold."

"Tiramisu has coffee in it." Avery reached for a bowl.

"And Kahlua," said Eleanor. "How much proof do you need before you can get a postmortem for a recently deceased person?"

Avery sampled his first spoonful of tiramisu. "You're right about the tiramisu."

"I'm right about a lot of things," said Eleanor.

"I'm going to regret this." Avery took another spoonful of tiramisu.

"It's really important," said Charlie.

"Alright then," said Avery. "Present to me your proof."

"Carroll dies, and that night, somebody turns his house upside down looking for something. Tell me that's not suspicious," said Eleanor.

"It's what you'd call circumstantial evidence," said Avery. "Not conclusive."

"Someone left the Pepper Tree Hotel that night wearing a black fedora and a scarf over their face," said Charlie. "I have an eyewitness report."

"That sounds like you." Eleanor raised an eyebrow at Avery.

"I didn't bring a fedora," said Avery. "It's summer. I brought my straw hat."

"We may need to see it," said Eleanor.

Avery snorted. "If that's all you've got, then it's time to call this a night."

"Show him the bottles, Charlie," said Eleanor.

Charlie drew a Ziploc bag out of the satchel and laid it on the table. Inside were two small bottles, corked and labelled, with coloured liquid inside.

"I went to Professor Carroll's house the morning after he passed and helped Billy and Grace clean up. There was a kettle and two cups on the drainer," said Charlie.

"Carroll had tea with a guest," said Eleanor.

"And there was a bottle full of digitalis medicine. I took it," Charlie looked a bit embarrassed, "and I was wondering if you could see whose fingerprints are on it. Because there's no foxglove in his garden."

"I fail to see the connection," said Avery.

"Digitalis is a medicine for the heart," said Charlie.

"I know that. In larger doses, it stops the heart."

"It's made from foxglove," said Charlie. "The professor made lots of remedies, but only from plants that he grew in his garden. If someone wanted it to look like he had heart troubles, they might plant a bottle of digitalis in his kitchen."

"And if the professor's fingerprints aren't on it... I see." Avery sat forward again. "You're starting to grow a nasty, suspicious mind, Charlie Wilson. Probably as a result of spending too much time with this one." He inclined his head towards Eleanor.

"Charlie took another bottle so we could compare fingerprints. However," Eleanor pointed to the digitalis bottle, "the labels are not written by the same person. It's not bad, as forgeries go. But not good enough."

"And you would know," murmured Avery.

"Can you dust for fingerprints?" asked Eleanor.

"I always take my fingerprint kit on holiday. No, I'm joking," said Avery as Charlie leaned forward eagerly. "Does no one believe I'm on holiday?"

"I never leave my tools behind," said Dante from near the door where he was eating tiramisu. "Even when I'm on holiday."

"You're invisible when you want to be — I'd forgotten you were there," said Avery. "I don't own a fingerprint kit. I haven't dusted for prints in years. When I want them, I get forensics to run them for me."

"I suppose we've hit a dead end, then," said Eleanor. "Have you finished your tiramisu, Dante? We'd better leave the inspector in peace."

Avery blew out a breath and scowled at all three of them. "Don't think I don't know what you're up to." He rummaged in the sideboard and pulled out a pencil and a hotel notepad. "Dante, can I borrow a knife, please?"

"What size?" asked Dante.

"Most people would apologise and say they don't have one," said Avery.

Dante shrugged and handed him the medium-sized knife from his wrist sheath.

Eleanor sat back and enjoyed her tiramisu as Avery got to work, scraping and crushing the pencil nib into graphite dust with the blade of Dante's knife. Soon, he had a small pile of dark grey powder in the middle of the white notepad.

"Bottles, please?" said Avery. "Hold them over here." He pointed to the placemat in the middle of the table.

Charlie carefully withdrew the two bottles, lifting them by the rubber bungs. Avery gently tapped the paper until the powder fell in a light shower, coating the bottles as Charlie rotated them.

Eleanor leaned forward as Avery turned on the sideboard lamp to cast a strong white light.

"Ah." Eleanor relaxed back in her seat. She had acted on enough hunches to know they weren't failsafe. Sometimes, you discovered your assumptions were wrong when the only exits available were bad ones.

In this case, however, Charlie had been right. As the graphite powder caught in the residual oil from fingertips, the bottle with Carroll's headache remedy darkened with several partial prints she assumed were Carroll's.

The second bottle was wonderfully free of any hint that anyone had handled it.

Avery sat back, regarding the digitalis bottle with a frown.

"Do you mind?" Eleanor held up her phone and, at Avery's wave, took a few photographs of the bottles.

"So that's enough proof?" Charlie's eyebrows were also lowered, and Eleanor wondered if he was thinking of his father and how long it had taken for him to get justice.

Avery crossed his arms over his chest. "An absence of fingerprints isn't enough to get a postmortem."

"Don't tell me that after forty years on the force, you can't pull a few strings," said Eleanor. "Because we have a time limit, and it's running out fast."

Avery shook his head, but his eyes kept straying back to the bottle and its clean surface.

"This is a real case," said Eleanor. "We have a lot of circumstantial evidence, but we can't do anything concrete without proof that Carroll was poisoned."

"What's your motive?" said Avery.

"Motive for the murder, or motive for solving this case?" asked Eleanor.

Avery sighed. "For the murder."

"There are dozens of rabid orchidists here, and our professor may have been hoarding the holy grail of orchids. Or some priceless historical documents. Surely that's enough."

"I've seen people kill for less," muttered Avery. "Now I'm wondering what your motive is."

"It's for Carroll," said Charlie. "We have to bring his killer to justice."

"That, I believe," said Avery. He eyed Dante. "What about you?"

"Suppose you thought someone was dangerous," said Dante, "but you weren't sure why. How would you make sure people kept away from them?"

"Hmmm," Avery cast an amused glance at Eleanor, and she sighed inwardly. Convincing someone as stubborn as Avery wasn't easy, especially if your conversational partners threw curveballs. "All good relationships are built on trust. And you build trust by telling the truth."

"This has been an illuminating visit." Eleanor settled her tiramisu bowl back on the tray. "Thank you for your expertise."

Avery rubbed his forehead. "I just wanted a nice, peaceful holiday, learning about orchids and catching up with my fellow orchidists."

"You can do that," said Eleanor. "I won't bother you with another post-mortem request."

"That's not as comforting as you may think," said Avery.

"Goodnight, Inspector." Charlie rose from the sofa.

"Thank you for the advice," said Dante.

The last thing Eleanor saw as she closed the door was Avery, frowning at where the medicine bottles had sat.

28

In which Dante is given advice through metaphors.

On Sunday morning, Dante exited his house and crossed the road to the small villa opposite.

He opened the white picket gate and paced up the neat box hedge-lined path to knock on Mrs Haddock's front door. Dante shifted his feet while he waited for signs of life from within. He was unaccountably edgy. Perhaps it was because he'd never asked anyone for a favour like this before.

In his old line of work, he'd sometimes had to pull in favours — forged papers at an hour's notice, rushed extraction from a remote drop zone, a quick upgrade in firepower. But those had been ordinary requests, and there was always the unspoken agreement that Dante would honour the exchange in the future by returning the favour when called upon.

This was not an ordinary request.

"Dante." Mrs Haddock opened the door and waved him inside. "Good to see you."

Dante followed her into the parlour, taking in the smells of furniture polish, old books, and overlaying it all like a benediction, fresh baking.

"Tea with milk and sugar?" asked Mrs Haddock. Like a conjurer, she had a tray with a bright red kettle, two cups and two saucers already on the table.

"Just milk."

"You're sweet enough." Mrs Haddock had a twinkle in her eye. "Young Charlie was here the other day," she said as she poured the tea. "Wanted to speak to one of my special guests."

"You mean a ghost."

"Quite right," said Mrs Haddock. "How that boy manages it all, I'm sure I don't know. I have nothing but respect for him and his mother. She did a good job raising him after her husband passed."

Dante wasn't sure if tea was the right beverage to acknowledge the dead, but he raised the cup to his lips in salute.

"Shortbread?" Mrs Haddock took a cake tin from the middle of the table and levered it open, her wrinkled fingers working at the metal seam.

"Thank you." The golden squares of biscuit still lingered in Dante's memory as the best shortbread he'd ever tasted. Better than her majesty's own pastry chef.

"What brings you here, Dante? We don't have to beat around the bush. You're not that kind of person, and I'm too old to waste time."

"It's my cat."

"The black one, with three white paws?"

"Yes." Dante wondered how best to phrase this. "I might be going away for some time. I was wondering if you could feed my cat while I'm away."

"Ah." Mrs Haddock leaned back in her chair and smoothed the tablecloth with both hands. "Is this an unexpected trip?"

"Yes."

"Trouble overseas?"

"No."

"Trouble at home." Mrs Haddock considered. "You don't seem the type to run from trouble."

Dante thought about this. It all came down to how you defined trouble. He was used to his trouble being dangerous but straightforward. There was never any doubt in his mind as to who needed to be dead. Similarly, there was never any doubt in his adversary's mind that Dante was the one who ought to be dead. It was simple.

"It's the kind of trouble," said Dante, "that I'm not sure how to deal with."

"That kind of trouble that comes from people being people," said Mrs Haddock. "I quite understand. I used to have that kind of trouble, too."

Dante's interest perked up. "Used to?"

"Yes." Mrs Haddock took a sip of tea. "I stopped having complicated people trouble at the same time as I stopped caring what other people thought and started saying exactly what was on my mind, and doing precisely what I wanted."

Dante tried to picture this. "What happened?"

"Oh, a lot of people were upset. I lost a few friends. But the ones who stayed more than made up for that."

Dante wondered whether telling Stephanie he planned to kill her if she stayed in Te Kohe would solve his problem. Probably not. Perhaps he could pay her to go away?

"What is the nature of your complicated people problem?" asked Mrs Haddock.

Dante ate a shortbread while he thought about what to say. Mrs Haddock already knew his former job, so she wouldn't be surprised by anything he said. It was the novelty of trusting someone with sensitive information that stopped him. Mrs Haddock didn't have any level of MI6 security clearance.

This was the problem with trusting people. Trust became easier, and eventually, he'd end up relying on them, and they on him. And where would that lead? Somewhere dreadful, Dante was certain.

"Someone showed up in Te Kohe," he said at last. "I think they might be dangerous. But I'm not sure. It's like there's an error signal that I can't decode." It was bothering Dante more and more. "I could find out, but I'm not supposed to deal with them like I usually would. Also, I need Charlie to stay away from them."

"Female, then," said Mrs Haddock. "So you're wondering how to get rid of someone without killing them. And you thought you'd just go away for a while and hope nothing bad happens."

Put like that, Dante could see why she didn't look convinced. He took another shortbread.

"I don't have any other ideas," he confessed. "Apart from kidnapping. But that wouldn't end well."

"I suppose not." Mrs Haddock dipped her shortbread in her tea. "I think the problem is one of perspective."

"How?"

"You're thinking this young lady (I'm assuming she's young) is a problem you need to solve. It's not."

"It isn't?" This was news to Dante.

"No. Do you have kids?"

"No." The thought frankly terrified Dante. How on earth would he keep them safe? They'd need at least eight years of training before he'd be willing to let them leave the house. Apparently, that kind of restriction was frowned upon in normal society.

"I thought not. It's like this: sometimes, with kids, you need to let them make a few mistakes on their own. Let them put their pants on backwards. Let them crash their bike into the ditch. It's the best way for them to learn."

Dante tried this thought on for size. "You're saying Charlie needs to find out about Stephanie by himself?"

"Stephanie, is it? Yes. He needs to grow up a bit. Learn about the world."

"But... you wouldn't let your kid take the car on the motorway. Because they could end up dead."

"Just how dangerous is this Stephanie person?" asked Mrs Haddock.

"I don't know. But I'm going to warn Charlie off her. Next time I see him."

Mrs Haddock nodded in sympathy. "You can certainly do that. But here's what I suggest."

Dante leaned forward, hopeful.

"I'll look after your cat. That's not a bother. Just drop around some cat food, and I'll take care of things for however long you end up being away."

"Oh." Dante leaned back. This was not what he had expected. Then he saw the twinkle in Mrs Haddock's eye. "You're doing that thing on me," he accused. "Letting me put my pants on backwards."

"It's the only way to learn," said Mrs Haddock. "I know you'll figure it out, Dante."

Dante took two more shortbread pieces as an annoyance tax on his way out. They really were very good.

29

In which Dante practices the delicate art of conversation.

Dante walked up to the Pepper Tree Hotel restaurant with the same feeling he'd had approaching an enemy hideout. The difference was that approaching an enemy hideout was something he'd done many times before. Taking a woman out to dinner was not.

The restaurant entrance had cheerful golden lamps and a wisteria vine that looked like it was trying to swallow the balustrade whole. Dante climbed the steps, wishing he'd brought more firepower, whatever that meant in terms of dinner conversation.

The concierge at the reception desk gave him a cheerful smile.

"Name of?" she asked.

"Dante Reid. Table for two." Dante scanned the foyer and the street outside for Andrea. Perhaps she would be fashionably late. He'd heard that was something dates did. He had arrived fifteen minutes early to scope out the site and check for any threats that might need to be neutralised.

So far, nothing had emerged, and Dante found himself wishing something would show up. That way, he could get on with doing something he was good at.

"There you are." Andrea bounced up the steps, a broad smile on her face. Her curly black hair was loose, and it waved in the slight breeze coming off the harbour. She wore a sparkly black and red dress with a matching black handbag and high-heeled shoes.

"Hi." Dante searched frantically in his memory bank for Eleanor's advice. "How was your day?"

"Good, thanks," said Andrea.

"So was mine."

There followed a brief, expectant pause. Dante's mind went completely blank on what to say next.

"I can show you to your table now if you'd like," said the concierge.

"Thank you," said Andrea.

Dante flanked Andrea as the concierge led them to a small table in the centre of the restaurant.

The table was lit softly by a candle in the centre, but it stood exposed on every side. There was no way Dante could keep an eye on the entry and the doors to the kitchen. Worse, there was nowhere to take cover in the event of crossfire. And anyone could sneak up behind him.

Dante prepared a mental checklist if he ever went on a date again. The first item was a table with clear sightlines and ready cover in case of emergencies.

"This is lovely, isn't it?" said Andrea, looking around. "Mostly, I just go to the RSA. I forget what a nice scene this is."

"Yes." Dante thought for a moment. "Thank you for coming."

"Well…" It was hard to tell under the mood lighting, but it looked like Andrea might be blushing. "Thank you for asking me."

"What would you like to drink?" Dante had brought a clean stack of New Zealand banknotes with him, folded in an inner pocket of his shirt. Scanning the wine list, it looked like Andrea could drink a glass from every choice on offer, and he'd easily be able to cover it.

"Ummm...." Andrea put the menu down with a bright smile. "What are you having?"

"I don't drink." Dante wanted to say that since he planned to remain sober, he would be able to guard Andrea in the event of any danger. But it seemed a complicated sentiment to convey. So he settled for: "You can if you want to."

"Ah, ok." Andrea scanned the wine list again.

A waiter came to hover near Dante's left shoulder, and he resisted the urge to reposition his chair for better surveillance of the space.

"Can I get you anything?" the young man asked.

"A glass of house Chardonnay, thanks," said Andrea.

"A bottle of water, unopened," said Dante.

"Sparkling, or still?" asked the waiter.

Dante considered. "Sparkling."

Andrea put the wine menu back on its stand. "So, what have you been up to this week?"

Dante thought about the murder investigation, hiding in the records room, breaking into Fiorelli's room, and the notebook they'd found under Carroll's chair. For an instant, he wondered what it would be like to date someone he could talk about this stuff with. Then the moment passed.

"I've been at the Symposium with Charlie. There's been lots of orchids." Dante remembered the conversational tennis match. "How was your week?"

"It was quite busy." Andrea launched into an account of the various animals she'd treated, and Dante listened closely, memorising the details in case he had to recount them later. The waiter arrived to pour Andrea's glass of wine and give Dante his unopened bottle of sparkling water.

"Oh, look." Andrea interrupted her own story to gaze over Dante's shoulder. "Charlie's here. And he has a date. I wonder who she is."

Even though it violated every surveillance rule in the book, Dante swivelled to look behind himself.

Charlie was indeed entering the restaurant. He looked slightly uncomfortable in formal wear - ironed slacks, a button-down shirt, and a light cotton jacket. Next to him was Stephanie Church, in a slinky tan dress that outlined her figure to perfection. Dressed to kill. The phrase floated through Dante's head, just audible over the sound of mental alarm bells ringing.

"So," said Andrea. "You're quite young to retire. What did you do before you settled in Te Kohe?"

Dante faced her, a prickling sensation gathering between his shoulder blades. Behind him, Stephanie and Charlie were sitting down at another table. "I was an accountant. In Kent."

"How interesting." Andrea seemed to be working a little to keep her smile in place. "Do you have any good accounting stories?"

"Er..." Dante tried to think of a story. Was it possible to kill someone with a paper cut? With the right paper, he thought he could manage it. "No. Sorry." He shifted his chair slightly so he could catch any movement from Charlie's table in his peripheral vision. "Do you? Have any vet stories?"

He knew this was not quite the way Eleanor said it should be done. But having Stephanie behind him, dining with fifty percent of his friends, made it hard to concentrate.

"Why did you want to become a vet?" Dante also knew it was wrong to double up on questions, but he remembered this question from his conversation with Eleanor. It looked to be a good one, as Andrea brightened up and launched into an explanation.

"...and so I thought maybe I could make it my job, and..." Andea's eyes narrowed. "Dante, is something bothering you?"

Dante turned to face Andrea. It was obvious Stephanie wasn't packing a firearm — there was no place for one in that dress. But that didn't rule out a sidearm in her handbag or a knife sheathed in her ankle boots. He needed to know where her concealed weaponry was and how she intended to use it. Of course, she might intend to use poison. That would make things difficult.

"No," he said into the slightly frosty silence. He reran Andrea's tale. "So you helped your uncle on his farm, and liked working with animals so much you decided to be a vet. That's..." he searched for the right word, "good." Questions. There must be more questions he could ask. "Do you like being a vet?"

"I love it." Andrea's eyes shone with feeling. "Although sometimes it's sad."

"Why is it sad?" It was the first time a question had come without having to think about it, and Dante felt a touch of pride.

"Sometimes, when an animal is very sick and in pain, you have to put it down."

"Put it down how?"

"Give it a lethal injection. And even though it's the right thing to end its suffering, it makes me sad."

Dante leaned back in his chair, absorbing this information. It sounded startlingly similar to his past job. Although his actions usually ended other people's suffering, not the target's. It hadn't made him sad, though. Should it have? It was something to think about.

"Does that worry you?" asked Andrea. "You've been silent quite a while."

"No. It doesn't." Dante caught a flash of movement out of the corner of his eye and twisted in his seat.

Stephanie was searching in her handbag for something. Dante's hand darted under his jacket. Her hand re-emerged with some lipstick, and Dante slowly relaxed as she applied it to her face. He knew agents who carried all manner of dangerous gear disguised as common objects, but this looked like a genuine article.

When he turned back, the temperature of the silence had fallen several degrees.

“Charlie’s date is very pretty, isn’t she?” Andrea’s eyebrows drew down.

“She is.” Dante knew how to evaluate these things. In some branches of MI6, it was an asset to be attractive. In other roles, it was better to blend in.

This may have been the wrong thing to say. Andrea’s mouth tightened. “I suppose you’ve met many women in your travels.”

Dante scanned this sentence as he would a corridor with potential tripwires.

"I...didn't..." he said, thinking furiously, "travel much. I had a very boring life as an accountant. But now I have a cat." He hoped this would be a better topic of conversation.

It appeared it was. Andrea asked several questions about his cat, and Dante was able to answer them without lying, which was nice.

“Although my cat is getting fat.” By now, Dante had slowly shifted his chair so he could keep half an eye on Charlie’s table without having to turn his head.

Andrea gave a real smile, not the tight-lipped one from before. “It’s not always a bad thing for a cat to put on a bit of weight. We can have a look at its diet if you like.”

Charlie and Stephanie’s food had arrived: two gourmet burgers with chips. Dante watched intently as Stephanie squirted tomato sauce on their shared chips. If she were their poisoner, this was where she could easily strike and make herself look like an innocent bystander.

“Is there something more important over there right now?” Andrea raised her eyebrows.

“Do you know her?” asked Dante.

“The redhead?”

“Yes.” Dante wondered if he could work Stephanie being a possible danger into the conversation. At least it would give him something to talk about.

"I'll tell you what." Andrea rose to her feet. "Since it seems she's already crashed our date, let's make it official." And she strode over to where Charlie and Stephanie were tucking into their burgers, a wine glass in her hand.

"That's not—" began Dante, but it was too late.

With a mixture of smiling charm and small talk that Dante didn't think he'd ever get the hang of, Andrea introduced herself.

Dante made his way over as she was saying: "—and I thought since we're both here, why not double date? As they say — two's company, three's a crowd, four is... company again, I suppose."

Stephanie was smiling and nodding enthusiastically. As far as Dante could make out, Charlie wasn't as happy about the situation, but he waved over the waiter, and in short order, their two tables were pushed together.

"Isn't this nice?" Andrea glanced from him to Stephanie. Her smile reminded Dante of a freshly sharpened knife. She turned as a waiter approached, notepad in hand. "I'll have what they're having. Dante?"

"Same." At least at this range, Dante could keep a close eye on Stephanie and the tomato sauce.

"Wonderful," said Andrea. "Now, how did you two meet?"

Charlie broke into an awkward story of bumping into Stephanie at the hotel, but Dante's attention was on something else entirely.

People fidgeted in different ways. Dante knew a man who used to carve tiny animals with his machete. He knew another guy who used to engrave names on bullets.

Stephanie was fidgeting by folding the paper specials menu. But it wasn't just fidgeting. Something in the shape was becoming horribly familiar.

She was folding the specials into a specific shape — one with a reinforced point at one end. Dante recognised it. When he'd thought of killing someone with paper cuts earlier, he hadn't been idly speculating.

Back in his MI6 training days, Andrei 'Fox' Șerban had trained him in the many ways you could kill a human. One of the Fox's favourite methods had been to improvise with the tools at hand. 'You never know,' he used to say. 'You might be at the table with your target and your weapons — somewhere else. What to do?'

And he'd shown Dante exactly what to do. With a folded piece of paper, you could make a dart to stab in someone's throat. When used precisely, it was highly effective.

Right now, Stephanie was folding that same design. Dante stared at her hands, then at her face. Was she MI6? Did she know who he was? Was she trying to warn him? Or was she preparing a handy weapon to try to kill him, or Charlie, or Andrea?

He didn't like any of these options.

Dante's mind raced along various scenarios. Each scenario ended with an inevitable outcome: death. If he was going to maintain his one hundred and thirty-nine-day record, Dante had an enormous handicap.

Stephanie reached for the tomato ketchup, then started as Dante's hand was already there, placing it by his plate. She reached for the salt, and this time, Dante's intercept was even faster.

She reached for her fork and stared to find it wasn't by her plate. Now Dante's plate had two forks and one knife.

"Er," said Charlie. "Stephanie, do you want the ketchup?"

"No," said Dante, at the same time as Stephanie said, "Yes, please."

Andrea was looking from Stephanie to Dante, her brows drawn together in a frown.

The waiter arrived and placed two gourmet burgers and two sides of chips in front of Dante and Andrea. Dante didn't take his eyes off Stephanie.

His left hand, out of sight under the table, edged towards the knife strapped to his calf. It was a small table. With his knife, he could easily reach under the table and pierce Stephanie's femoral artery. She'd bleed out in minutes. He forced himself to move his hand away from the knife.

"Would you like to order more drinks?" asked the waiter.

"Ah," said Charlie. "Another bottle of wine?"

"Yes, please." Andrea looked at Dante. "Cab sav?"

"Sure," said Dante, through gritted teeth.

Stephanie nodded, her right hand gripping the only utensil she had left: the butter knife. She made a grab for the ketchup with her left hand, but Dante had already shunted it over to the other side of his plate.

"Dante," said Andrea, "I think Stephanie wants some ketchup?"

Stephanie blinked wide green eyes at him, and Dante searched them for the spark of killer instinct he'd seen in every other assassin he'd squared off against. Stephanie must be good at hiding what she was.

"Dante?" said Charlie. "Can you pass Stephanie the—"

In a split second, Stephanie's hand shot out to grip the ketchup bottle. But Dante was faster. He knocked her hand away, and as her fingers slipped forward, he put her hand in a wrist lock. She flipped her wrist around to break the hold, and her other hand darted forward to try to catch his hand in her own wristlock.

There was a moment of lightning-fast tangled limbs, but Dante saw it in slow motion. He saw Charlie's eyes widen, saw him lean forward, saw Andrea flinch backwards at the same time.

Stephanie tried to grab his wrist and knocked the ketchup bottle forward. As Dante slammed her hand down to block her attempted wrist hold, the bottle exploded. The lid shot off, sending a spray of bright red tomato sauce over the table's other two occupants.

Andrea gave a little shriek as ketchup covered her dress and face. Charlie just sat there, blinking as tomato sauce dripped down the front of his smart shirt, like the blood from a fatal chest wound.

There was a stricken silence.

Andrea slammed her chair back and leapt to her feet.

"I don't know what the hell is going on." Andrea's eyes flashed as she met Dante's. "But I don't like it. I'm done."

She backed this statement by grabbing her handbag and storming out of the restaurant.

"Dante," Charlie said quietly, and somehow, this was even worse. "This isn't how a friend would act. I was hoping to have a nice dinner with Stephanie. And now," he looked down at the mess of the table and his crimson shirt, "that's not going to happen."

Dante let go of Stephanie's wrist. "I don't think your date is who she says she is."

Stephanie's eyes widened. "I have no idea what you mean," she declared with wounded innocence. "Charlie, can you take me away from here, please? I don't feel safe."

Charlie looked from Stephanie to Dante. Then, slowly and deliberately, he held his hand out to Stephanie. "Let's go."

Dante was left with four unfinished burgers, three piles of chips, and a massacre's worth of ketchup.

It was not the best first date, thought Dante. On the other hand, nobody had died. Yet.

30

In which the straight way is lost.

Dante walked around the waterfront, his stomach churning uneasily. His next step was unclear.

An MI6 agent had come here, to his turf, and they hadn't made formal contact. The only reason for this was that they planned to kill him.

Worse yet, Charlie was with Stephanie. That complicated things immensely. The last thing he wanted was a hostage situation.

This required careful handling. Dante wondered who he'd managed to annoy enough to want him dead.

On his wrist, his watch alarm made a small buzz against his skin. Dante smiled, a curl of his lip that contained no humour whatsoever. Sometimes it wasn't nice to be proven right.

In his back garden, Dante waited in the deep shadows under the weeping willow. Someone had deactivated his alarm - the obvious, consumer-grade one that he'd installed as a first defence. That had tripped the silent alarm his watch monitored.

The second security system was working perfectly well, and showed Dante that right now, someone was stealthily and methodically searching the wall at the back of his sitting room.

His weapons stash was hidden there behind a false panel. It looked like the searcher was using an infrared flashlight with goggles — a nice piece of kit that Dante almost preferred to self-contained infrared.

He ran over his options. He could trip the alarm himself and set off an ear-splitting siren. The searcher would flee, most likely out the back and right past Dante's hiding place.

He could call the police, who would arrive, sirens blaring, with much the same outcome.

Or, he could enter his house in absolute silence and confront the searcher himself. The hairs on the back of his neck rose as this option swam clearer in his mind, like a shark circling closer through murky waters.

On this path, death awaited. If not his, then certainly the intruder's.

It felt as inevitable as the pull of the tide. Dante was not a gardener who used to be an assassin. He was an assassin pretending to be a gardener.

Waiting in the darkest shadows in the dead hour of the night, it was harder and harder to deny this fact.

He tried to remember the AA motto, but it slipped from his mind. Instead, another phrase entered his thoughts. It had been spoken to him, quite recently, by a man who was now dead.

"I found myself in a dark wood, for the straight way was lost."

Without consciously choosing to, Dante glided out of the shadows, his Glock fitting perfectly into the palm of his hand. The back door lock clicked open as his fingerprint touched the sensor.

It was the witching hour of midnight as death entered the house.

Charlie paced his kitchen, thoughts in disarray. Why had Dante behaved so strangely? What was going on between him and Stephanie?

Dante was normally so polite. What did he mean 'she isn't who you think she is'?

Stephanie had retired soon after their disastrous dinner, saying she felt exhausted and needed to sleep. For some reason, Charlie hadn't believed her. He paced some more, and then, without really deciding to, found himself walking out his front door and down the street towards Dante's house.

Dante was his friend and deserved a chance to tell his side of things. Charlie was sure that once they'd sorted out whatever the misunderstanding was, he, Stephanie, Dante, and hopefully Andrea too, could all be friends.

It was all quite straightforward in Charlie's mind, and this thought carried him all the way to the darkened porch outside Dante's front door.

Dante slipped on the night vision goggles stored in the secret drawer under his kitchen bench. A tiny display in one corner showed the searcher was still in his front parlour, just two feet away from finding his weapons stash. That would not be a good thing.

The cat slipped out of the pantry and wound around his legs, slowing him. Dante lifted it with one hand onto the bench and ran his fingers down its sleek length.

"Stay here," he whispered.

The cat, of course, did no such thing, but followed him silently down the corridor as he ghosted towards the front of the house. Dante placed each foot precisely over the joists, so no creak of the aged timber floor would betray his presence.

The front parlour door was open. The sounds of a stealthy search broke the quiet as he waited outside the door, counting his heartbeats. Quietly, he wound a silencer onto the gun's muzzle. It wouldn't mask all noise, but it would be enough.

He stepped into the parlour, Glock in hand. Stephanie was there with her back to him. She wore fitted black combat gear. Her balaclava hung loose around her neck, her goggles were on, and she held an infrared light between her teeth as she knocked on the wall panels, listening for a hollow sound.

Dante's night vision world was monochrome. A shadow moved at the same time as he did, and for a moment, Dante thought Stephanie had an accomplice. Then he realised it was just his reflection in the sitting room mirror, moving as he shifted into a firing position.

As if in a dream, Dante saw his reflection raise its gun and aim at the back of Stephanie's head.

All it would take was a gentle pull of the trigger, and a small projectile would bury itself in the back of Stephanie's head.

A single action would return him to a familiar pattern, cutting off forever the strange offshoot that was Dante's new life.

It would be so easy.

Measure the distance. Steady pressure. Breathe out on the trigger pull. Dante heard the voice of his teacher repeat the instructions he'd memorised and followed a thousand times.

Stephanie ran gloved fingers over the wall, oblivious to the fact that these were the last seconds of her life.

Moral uncertainty weighed on Dante's limbs. A heaviness settled in his chest as he prepared to once again be the instrument of death.

I don't want to kill her. But...

His heart hammered in his chest, striving against the pull of the gun.

I don't want to kill her, but...

Blood rushed in his ears, tugging against the need to ensure the safety of his friends.

I don't want to...

Infinitesimally slowly, as if it weighed a thousand pounds, Dante lifted the muzzle of the gun towards the ceiling.

Glacially slowly, as if he were pushing against a mountain, he backed out of the parlour and into the hallway.

The cat waved its tail in a distracted curve as Dante edged down the corridor. It seemed utterly disinterested in the titanic struggle taking place inside his head.

And then the doorbell rang.

31

Which contains various standoffs, tiebreakers, and penalty shootouts.

Charlie pressed the round copper button of Dante's doorbell. It emitted a strident 'brrrrng' and he shivered. There was something ghostly about this summer's night.

Normally, Charlie kept good company with ghosts. But there were times — All Hallows Eve, the solstices, the equinoxes — when it was wiser to stay indoors and not open his spirit to the uncanny.

Tonight had the same air. The entry to Dante's house felt haunted, giving him the sense that death was closer than usual, near enough to reach out and touch with his fingertips...

Charlie pressed the cold metal dome of the buzzer again, then tried the door handle. It swung open soundlessly onto a darkened corridor.

"Hi, Dante?" Charlie stepped into the house, wondering why his friend wasn't there to meet him.

At the end of the corridor, a dark shape disappeared into the kitchen. Charlie frowned. Dante wasn't usually like this. Granted, they'd just had a very awkward dinner, but still...

"Dante?" Charlie tiptoed down the corridor after the retreating figure. It seemed shorter than Dante's six foot three, which didn't make sense. Who else would be here?

The house seemed to be holding its breath. Charlie looked for the telltale signs of ghosts, but there were none. Strange. He crept forward towards the kitchen.

In the back garden, Dante waited in the shadow of the lilac bushes as Stephanie exited his house. Her balaclava covered her face, and she gripped her gun in both hands. She glanced over her shoulder, back to the house where Charlie was presumably looking for Dante.

Dante steeled himself. If Charlie came through the back door and Stephanie attacked, Dante would kill her. His friend would not become a casualty.

Stephanie crept to the opposite corner of the yard from where Dante kept silent vigil. She peered down the side of the house, perhaps getting ready to make her escape.

The backyard light switched on, filling the garden with searing white light.

Dante froze. Stephanie whirled to see him standing just twenty feet from her. Both their weapons were up and aimed at each other in an instant.

Dante focused on her trigger finger. If she moved a fraction of an inch, he would fire first and fire faster.

Then Charlie stepped out of the house to stand between Dante and Stephanie, directly in their line of fire.

"Don't move." Stephanie's voice was harsh and gravelly, as if she were trying to disguise it.

Charlie blinked. His eyes flicked to Dante, then back to focus on Stephanie. He raised his hands, but not like someone surrendering to an armed assailant. They stretched forward, as if to soothe a wild animal.

"Stephanie?" said Charlie quietly. "It's you under that mask, isn't it?"

"Shut up," barked Stephanie. "And don't ask questions. You're going to go back inside, I'm going to deal with this... situation, and then you'll never see me again."

"Stephanie, I'm sure this is just a misunderstanding." Charlie took one step towards Stephanie, and she tensed, her shoulders tightening as she prepared to shoot.

Dante would have closed his eyes in horror, except that would have meant taking his eyes off the train wreck unfolding before him.

He ran through his options. He could still shoot Stephanie. There was an inch of sightline between her head and Charlie's. He was a good shot. She'd be dead before she hit the ground, and Charlie would be safe.

"Dammit, Charlie," said Stephanie. "Get out of the way. This man is dangerous. You're going to get shot."

"Stephanie." Charlie sounded like he was on a long-distance call to a far-off friend. "I'm not going anywhere."

Dante felt the wash of adrenaline sweep through him. He'd never felt scared in life-threatening situations before. But it had always been just his life on the line.

"Charlie," said Dante, "she's right. You need to get out of here."

Charlie shook his head. His mouth turned up in a wry smile. "I don't want to get shot. Believe it. But I'm not moving."

"Are you crazy?" yelled Stephanie. "Go!"

It occurred to Dante in a rush that Charlie was different from every civilian he'd met. Charlie had seen death many times, in ways nobody else had. He might be scared, but he wasn't scared of death.

It was strangely awe-inspiring, while at the same time, Dante wanted to wrestle Charlie back inside his house and never let him out again.

"I'm not leaving until you both put down your guns and talk this out like... like normal people," said Charlie.

"Charlie." Stephanie had a slightly hysterical edge to her voice. "Nothing about this is normal. I'm not normal, Dante's not normal, and you're nuts. I don't want you to get hurt, but I will shoot you before I let myself get shot by this... this criminal."

"I won't shoot you," said Dante. "If you back off."

"Right," said Stephanie. "Like I'm going to believe that."

"Who do you think Dante is?" asked Charlie.

"He's a black market fixer," said Stephanie. "He's brokering a deal with Fiorelli."

"Huh?" said Charlie and Dante at the same time.

"That's impossible," said Charlie. "He's not. Dante's a Brit. And Fiorelli's a... an orchid scientist."

Stephanie gave an unhappy laugh. "I don't know what lies he's fed you, but things are not as they seem."

"That's what Dante said about you," said Charlie.

"I'm one of the good guys," said Stephanie.

"Then put down your gun," said Charlie. "Dante? Will you put down yours?"

Dante eyed Charlie across the barrel of his gun. If he put down his gun, he wondered whether Stephanie would shoot him or Charlie first. Probably him. Then Charlie. That's how he'd do it.

"I will if she does," he said.

Stephanie's laugh was a breathless huff of disbelief. "I'm not messing around. This is not a negotiation. These are real guns, Charlie. One bullet, and you'll be dead."

"I know that," said Charlie. "But since you're a guest here, in my town, and Dante's back garden, I'm asking you to do the right thing. Stop pointing guns at people, and let's work this out."

Stephanie's throat bobbed as she swallowed. Her hand trembled with the tension of keeping absolutely focused on Dante.

“I will put my gun down if you do,” said Dante. “You have my word.”

“The word of an underworld broker,” said Stephanie.

“You’re from MI6,” said Dante. “Do you know who I am?”

“You’re Dante Reid, a person with a fake online history and false employment record. And you’re brokering a deal between Fiorelli and some shadow geneticist,” said Stephanie. “Bio weapons, engineered viruses, you don’t care what you’re selling, as long as it makes money.”

“Dante’s a retired... well, he’s retired,” said Charlie. “He doesn’t broker anything. He’s been gardening. With me.”

Dante watched Stephanie’s shoulders tighten. If we carry this on much longer, he thought, she’ll end up firing her gun from sheer nerves. “I promise that if you holster your gun, I will too. Hear me out. That’s all I’m asking.”

The moment stretched, taut as a highline, and then Stephanie gave a small jerk of her chin.

“Fine.” Her gun lowered a few inches. Dante mirrored it. It dropped another six inches, and he allowed his gun to drift downwards. The tension ebbed slowly, draining away into the shadows at the edge of the garden.

“Ok.” Charlie nodded like this was simply another more-awkward-than-usual introduction. “Cup of tea?”

Stephanie shook her head. “No tea. You wanted me to hear you out. So talk.”

“I’m not a fixer,” said Dante. “And there’s a good reason my online identity is fake. I’m a retired MI6 wetworks agent. My old employer built me a legend, but I guess it wasn’t good enough to fool you.”

“That’s it?” Stephanie’s eyebrows drew together. “Prove it.”

“My codename,” said Dante, “was Persephone.”

“Ha!” Stephanie’s bark of laughter was, if anything, more disbelieving than before. “And I’m the King of Sweden. Persephone’s dead. Everyone knows that.”

"Persephone?" said Charlie. "Like... the Goddess of Spring? Ate six pomegranate seeds and created the seasons?"

"He's not Persephone," said Stephanie, "because Persephone died. About five months ago."

"The same time as I retired. It seemed like the best way to make a clean break." Dante thought wistfully of how much fun it had been to fake his death. His handler and a few top brass had been in the know. No one else. Until now. "Have you ever seen a photo of Persephone?"

"They're all redacted," said Stephanie. "He's a myth — the best wetworks agent in the history of the bureau. A dark tale to scare foreign agents with. He's a ghost."

"He's not, actually," said Charlie. "I would know."

Stephanie shot him a brief, bewildered stare.

"Do you know any of Persephone's identifying marks?" asked Dante.

Stephanie shook her head slowly, then hesitated. "He didn't have any. He was the ultimate professional. Except... there was a rumour about a tattoo that could only be seen by moonlight?"

"I'm going to roll up my sleeve," said Dante. "Charlie, could you turn off the lights?"

"If you think I'm going to fall for that..." said Stephanie, but Charlie had already moved to put his finger on the backyard light switch, located just inside the back door.

"Still no shooting people," said Charlie. "Ok?"

"Here." Dante held out his forearm, the sleeve rolled up to show bare skin. In spite of herself, Stephanie stepped forward to see.

"I'm going to switch the light off," said Charlie, "now—"

But Dante had already moved. He dived low, shoving Charlie inside. He caught Stephanie's hands as she brought her gun up to fire. Then he was behind her, one arm locked around her neck, the other twisting her wrist backwards.

"Dante!" yelled Charlie. "I said no shooting people."

"I'm not," said Dante through gritted teeth, "shooting anyone."

Stephanie gave a hiss of pain, and the gun clattered on the brick patio.

"Turn on the light," said Dante.

Charlie switched the light on as Dante relaxed his stranglehold, just a fraction.

Stephanie sucked in a desperate lungful of air.

"This is what happens when you let people put their pants on backwards," said Dante.

"What?" Charlie's brow wrinkled.

"I have a tattoo that can only be seen under specific conditions. But you're never going to see it," said Dante. "As a sign of good faith, I haven't snapped your neck. Yet. Are you willing to talk?"

Stephanie gave the barest of nods. She hadn't stopped straining against his hold, but Dante had the advantage of reach, position, and strength.

"Good," said Dante. "Charlie, can you please put the kettle on? I think it's time for a cup of tea."

32

In which a temporary truce is negotiated.

Dante put Stephanie's gun and other assorted weapons by the kettle where she could see them, but not reach them.

Her gaze kept flicking over to the small pile, but she kept her hands wrapped tight around her cup of tea. Dante had sat her in the chair opposite him, while Charlie sat between them as a sort of neutral zone.

Dante preferred this to Charlie's previous role as a human shield. He wanted to get Charlie body armour for his birthday, whenever that was.

"Why Fiorelli?" asked Dante. "I thought she was into growing rare orchids."

Stephanie took a quick sip of tea. "She's a geneticist. A few months ago, we traced some messages on the dark web back to her lab. She's been contacting some bad actors. We couldn't make out whether she was recruiting or being recruited. Either way, we wanted to know more. Then, she suddenly takes off halfway around the globe for an obscure orchid conference. She had to have found what she was looking for. They sent me to get answers."

"So you broke into her rooms?" asked Dante.

"What do you think?" asked Stephanie.

"Just about everyone has," muttered Dante.

"Why do you think she's making a bioweapon?" asked Charlie.

"Her dark web messages," said Stephanie.

"And you broke into my place because?"

Stephanie arched an eyebrow at Dante. "I heard you at the Symposium. Talking about burning notebooks after reading them. Then I looked up your online history. Too perfect to be real. I reckoned you had to be Fiorelli's go-between."

Dante scowled. "You shouldn't wear distinctive sunscreen when you're surveilling someone."

Stephanie reddened slightly. "Then I saw you use the hotel trash as a dead drop."

"You got that wrong."

"And you were spying on me when I was having dinner with Charlie."

Dante shrugged. That part was true. "I'm not who you think I am."

"I think we agreed you were going to prove who you were," said Stephanie tightly. "Before you jumped me."

"You burgled my place first."

"You messed up my dinner."

"Guys," said Charlie. "Please." They both turned to glare at him. "You're both being very... high maintenance. Whatever it is assassins are when they haven't done their murder yoga."

"There's no such thing," snapped Stephanie.

"You don't do murder yoga?" Dante shook his head. Kids these days.

"As I was saying," said Charlie, "it's all a misunderstanding. Dante, Eleanor, and I are looking into Fiorelli because we think she may have killed Professor Carroll. She's one of three suspects. Dante was acting suspiciously because he thought you were some sort of agent-assassin.

Which you are. Now that's sorted, can we calm down and problem solve?"

"There's no problem." Dante hadn't broken gaze with Stephanie.

"I'm worried that if I go anywhere, you two will be at each other's throats," said Charlie. "Literally."

"I need proof that he is who he says he is," said Stephanie. "And then I need you both to back down so I can do my job."

"Not going to happen," said Dante.

"Why don't we work together?" asked Charlie. "Pool resources?"

Both Dante and Stephanie directed suspicious looks towards Charlie.

"I don't need help," said Stephanie.

Dante folded his arms over his chest. "It looks like you do."

"I don't need help from a retired gardener," snapped Stephanie.

"Who jumped you when you had a gun in your hand," said Dante.

"Whoa, whoa." Charlie held up his hands. "Can we stick to the current problem, please?"

"I will if she does," said Dante.

"Fine. I won't do... anything. But only because of Charlie." Stephanie's eyes flicked over to her gun, sitting next to Dante's shiny red kettle.

The cat vaulted into Dante's lap and rubbed the side of its head against his knuckles, chest vibrating as it purred. Dante relaxed just a fraction, and Charlie blew out a deep breath.

"Great. We have a truce. And," Charlie held up one finger, "we're going to start working together. Stephanie can help us solve this murder, and we'll help Stephanie figure out who Fiorelli is trying to sell dangerous viruses to."

There was a long silence. Neither of the assassins looked convinced.

"Fine," sighed Charlie. "How about I start by telling Stephanie what we've uncovered so far?"

"Why are we starting?" asked Dante. "She's the one who broke in here with a loaded gun and nearly shot you."

"I nearly got you, too," shot back Stephanie.

Dante levelled a cold look at Stephanie, and she stilled.

"I was this close," he held up thumb and forefinger a millimetre apart, "to plugging you in the back of the skull while you searched my front room. Don't fool yourself that you had the drop on me. You're lucky to be alive."

Charlie let out a long sigh. "Let's... put the past in the past, shall we? I'll start as a gesture of good faith. Here's what we've found out about Fiorelli so far..."

33

In which Dante debates the path forward.

Dante stared at the wall as it gradually lightened with the dawn. He hadn't slept for the remainder of the night. He had no faith that Stephanie wouldn't simply double back to finish what she'd started. The cat was curled comfortably under his arm, breathing gently in its slumber. At least somebody had gotten some rest.

In the old days — a few months ago — the problem of Stephanie would have been solved by now. Now, it was anything but. Apart from the not-going-to-kill-anyone-anymore issue, there was the factor of not killing fellow agents. And Charlie and Eleanor.

Charlie would be upset if Stephanie died. He was fairly certain of that. Dante wondered when 'Charlie being upset' had become a thing he took into account. In the past, he'd upset people all the time. Usually, they were only briefly upset, but still...

He watched daylight brighten the curtains and turn the room interior a delicate gold.

Charlie wanted to work with Stephanie, but Dante didn't trust her as far as he could throw her. Which was about three meters. Maybe four.

However, (and this was what had kept him awake all night) there was another course of action. It beckoned him, easily within reach.

He could leave.

It would be simple. He had cash and several passports. Dante could travel light - just the clothes he was wearing would do. He could lock up the house and be gone in under five minutes. Mrs Haddock would feed his cat. He could even leave some funds for Charlie to take care of the garden. (Though he suspected Charlie would do it anyway.)

In twelve hours, the dilemma he was facing would be half a world away.

The cat chose that moment to stretch luxuriously and sink its claws into his shoulder. Eyes shut, it displayed a smile of smug contentment with four white canines bared. Its back arched, then relaxed, and it began to purr.

Dante stared at the ceiling and pondered. Outside, the birds broke into their dawn chorus.

34

In which Eleanor conducts a date postmortem.

Eleanor ascended the steps to Dante's front door. She remembered the first time she'd done this, and how reluctant Dante had been to let her inside.

He might have been right, she thought ruefully. She was hardly a trouble free friend. But neither, in all fairness, was Dante. Or Charlie, despite the fact that he always meant well.

It was the Monday of a long weekend, and the last day of the Symposium. Eleanor had bumped into Andrea in the cafe that morning. Her account of last night's events had not been the most coherent, but one fact was clear: the date had not gone well.

Eleanor rapped sharply on the front door and waited. There was no sound from the interior, but that was not unusual. Dante moved as silently as a cat.

Even though it was nine o'clock, the blinds were down. The house had a closed feeling, as if it were already abandoned.

She knocked again. Nothing happened.

"Dante," Eleanor called through the keyhole. "Get used to seeing me on your doorstep. I'm not leaving until you answer the door." With some ceremony, she sat on the wooden chair on the narrow front balcony, and prepared to wait him out.

Several minutes passed. A pīwakawaka flitted through the air, chasing insects too tiny to see. A tui alighted on the flowering stem of a flax bush, bending it low. It looked askance at Eleanor, then got on with the business of sipping nectar from the yellow flowers. The morning sun warmed her. Two sparrows washed in the birdbath on the front lawn, their flurries sending sprays of water to sparkle in the sun.

Who knew an ex-assassin's doorstep would be so peaceful, thought Eleanor. If this carries on for much longer, I may end up taking a nap.

At last, the door cracked open, revealing a strip of kauri floorboards and the black-clad figure of Dante Reid.

"I don't want to talk about it," he said.

In Eleanor's experience, that usually meant the person did want to talk about it, but in a way that skirted the painful parts.

"That's fine," said Eleanor. "We can talk about something else. Your garden is looking particularly fine this morning."

"Yes."

"Was the birdbath already here? Or did you install it?"

"Already here."

"Have you heard the tuis yet? They're here for your flax flowers, and they have the most beautiful, varied song."

"I know."

"Your feijoa hedge is flowering beautifully. Come fall, you're going to have so many feijoas, you won't know what to do with them. I suggest you make feijoa crumble or feijoa jam. Do you know how to make jam?"

"No."

Eleanor possessed an extensive supply of words, and she could, if required, monologue for hours. Dante, however, was hard work.

“I take it your date didn’t go well?”

“I don’t want to talk about it.”

Back to the garden then, thought Eleanor. “Tuis love honey. If you put a little mānuka honey in the birdbath water—”

“You can come inside.”

“Thank you.” Eleanor followed Dante down the passage into the sitting room, where the cat opened one green eye to appraise her.

“Tea?” asked Dante.

“Yes, please. Gumboot, white, no sweetener.”

Dante hesitated. “Gumboot?”

“It’s what they call black tea around here. Any black tea is fine.”

Dante vanished to do tea related things, and Eleanor eyed the cat.

“I don’t suppose you know what your master’s up to, do you? Although it’s fair to say, cats don’t have masters. I suspect you’re doing more than any of us to stop him from disappearing into the wide world again.”

The cat, unimpressed with this conversation, laid its head back on the carpet and closed its eye.

Cats were, as a rule, unimpressible. That was why Eleanor liked them.

Dante reappeared, carrying two cups and saucers. He passed one to Eleanor, then sat on the couch, carefully balancing his own saucer on his knee.

“Can you at least tell me what happened last night?” asked Eleanor.

In short, choppy sentences, Dante related the night’s events. Eleanor, reading between the lines, could see exactly why both Andrea and Charlie were upset. It was almost funny, except that Dante had quite a lot of repair work to do with Andrea.

And there was the problem of Stephanie. Had she invented an elaborate cover story? Or was she telling the truth?

"—and then Stephanie left and Charlie went home," finished Dante.

Eleanor waited. Dante remained silent. So that was the end of the story.

Where to go from here? Maybe start with Andrea.

"Dante, if you were out on a date, and the woman you were with paid a lot of attention to a handsome younger man at another table, what would you think?"

Dante set the cup and saucer on the arm of the sofa and leaned back, crossing his arms. "I'd think that maybe the young man had been tailing her. Maybe she'd made him, and was trying to figure out what kind of threat he was."

Eleanor sighed. "Try to imagine you're an ordinary person. What would you think then?"

Dante sat in silence for a full minute. "I'd think..." he said slowly, "that maybe... maybe the woman noticed the guy was packing."

"Try again."

"He might be signalling to someone on the roof? Or in a car parked outside?"

"Think normal people. No guns. No signals."

"He swapped bags with someone, and did the handoff without a glance."

"No spy craft."

"Military posture? Ex-serviceman tattoos?"

"Normal people, Dante."

"I don't know!" Dante displayed the first signs of frustration Eleanor had ever seen on him.

"I can tell you if you like."

"Yes." Dante tightened his folded arms, and his brooding scowl intensified.

"Andrea was upset that you paid attention to Stephanie because she likes you, Dante."

"She does." The words were phrased uncertainly, half question, half statement.

"That's why she agreed to go on a date with you."

"What does that have to do with Stephanie?"

"She didn't like you paying attention to Stephanie because she thought you liked Stephanie."

"But I don't."

"She didn't know that. She thought you didn't like her, and that you were attracted to Stephanie instead of her."

"Oh." Light finally dawned on Dante's face. "Oh." The frown returned with interest. "That's not good."

"No," agreed Eleanor. "But it is fixable."

"You mean when I get rid of Stephanie, Andrea will stop being upset."

"That's not exactly what I had in mind," said Eleanor.

"But that might work."

"I have an alternative suggestion," said Eleanor, thinking: I had better put the kibosh on that idea right now. "You might try talking to her."

"Who?"

"Andrea."

"But I can't tell Andrea about Stephanie being connected with MI6. That could put her in danger."

God save me from literal minded ex-assassins, thought Eleanor. "You can tell Andrea that you like her, and that you don't like Stephanie."

"Will that work?"

"It might," said Eleanor. "At least, it's unlikely to make things worse." She mentally crossed that statement out. Knowing Dante, it could certainly make things worse. But there was only one way to learn the art of relationships, and that was via the path of glorious mistakes.

"Talk to her..." Dante's frown had not diminished.

"Giving her flowers is always a good idea," said Eleanor.

Dante flopped back on the couch, and the cat got to its feet, stretched luxuriously, and leapt onto his lap. Its belly sagged a bit, and Eleanor wondered how much Dante was feeding it.

"So Charlie told Stephanie about our case," said Eleanor. "And she said she'd help, and then went back to the hotel."

"Allegedly," said Dante.

"You didn't follow her?"

"I slipped a tracker into her jacket," said Dante. "Not as good as a tracker in her shoe, but she went back to the hotel. The tracker's still there, so maybe she is too."

"I think we should try working with her," said Eleanor. "Trust, but verify. Surely you have people you could contact to find out if she's legit. Because I have a few ideas on how she could help."

"I specifically don't want her hanging around with Charlie," said Dante.

"I'll talk to her." Eleanor knew she'd better manage this situation before it got too out of control. Dante looked about as relaxed as a fully wound crossbow. "In fact, I'll do that next."

"I'm coming with you."

"Dante, I'll be fine by myself."

Dante gave Eleanor a level look. It said: do not try to soothe me. I am not a person to be soothed.

"Ok, we'll go together," sighed Eleanor. "Just remember: tonight is the last night of the Symposium. Our last chance to catch Carroll's killer. I'm starting to think that the only way to do it is with a baited trap, one that either Fairfax, Fiorelli, or Lucier will fall into. Just... trust me on this one. Please?"

Dante's eyebrows lowered. One hand stroked restlessly down the cat's back. "Ok."

35

In which lamington cakes come in handy.

Eleanor knocked three times on the hotel door.

"Try to look a little less threatening," she said to Dante, hovering behind her shoulder.

Dante scowled. He didn't know how to look less threatening. Looking more threatening was doable, but right now, he'd set the threat level as low as he could.

"Hello?" called Eleanor. "It's Eleanor. And Dante. I've brought lamingtons."

The door opened to reveal Stephanie, one hand tucked in her pocket with affected ease.

"Hello, dear," said Eleanor. "Please refrain from drawing whatever weapon you're hiding while we're here. I'd hate for you - or me - to get shot."

Stephanie looked over her shoulder to where Dante stood, blocking out the light. Dante felt the magnetic pull of his Glock, easily reached in his underarm holster .

"That goes for both of us," she said.

"A fair deal," said Eleanor. "Let's agree on ground rules: no one shoots anyone else. Let's also agree that we help each other. You have fresh intel on Fiorelli, and we're investigating her as a potential murderer. Mutually beneficial, I'd say."

Stephanie waved a wary hand towards the two sofas and coffee table in her room. Unlike newer hotels, this room wasn't a replica or mirror image of Avery's. Instead, it took in a generous view of the harbour via a balcony large enough to house two chairs and a small round table.

"I don't know why you thought the professor's death was suspicious," said Stephanie.

"Oh, we have our sources," said Eleanor. She didn't feel this was the time to explain Charlie's ghost moth. "It's nice that MI6 would pay for all this." She gestured at the glittering harbour view.

"The pound's strong enough for them to foot the bill," said Stephanie. "And this mission has a high priority rating."

Dante decided not to list the ratholes he'd stayed in during his years of service. When he was junior, older agents had gone on about how tough they'd had it, and it had grated.

Stephanie settled onto the couch facing them. Eleanor delicately straightened her skirt as she sat down, angling her legs to the side to allow for Dante's broad frame.

"Let's start with something to eat," said Eleanor. She set her bag on the coffee table and withdrew an octagonal tin. Stephanie tensed as she levered off the lid. Then the young agent leant over, sniffing in appreciation.

"I've never eaten home-made lamingtons before," said Stephanie, as Eleanor lifted out the greaseproof paper and laid the coconut covered cakes on the table. "They look good."

"They are good," said Eleanor. "I was runner-up in last year's bake-off. It was a year of stiff competition, with both Grace and Joyce fielding strong entries."

Stephanie picked up a chocolate lamington. "Ok, I'll bite. What do you have that could help me nail Fiorelli?"

"How about you tell us what you know?" said Eleanor. "Apparently, the information flowed one way last night."

"Hmmm." Stephanie bit into the lamington and her face brightened as the flavour hit her taste buds. "It's still warm."

"Baked fresh this morning," said Eleanor, "as an enticement to full disclosure."

Stephanie eyed the two of them — Eleanor perched demurely, and Dante in a more hulking mode on her two seater sofa. "Fine. In confidence and the understanding that we'll aid each other."

"We want justice, same as you," said Eleanor. "Dante checked your credentials last night. We are nominally already on the same side."

"Hmmm..." Stephanie took another bite of her lamington.

The cake seemed to have quite a salutary effect on her. Dante reflected that some of his past interrogations might have gone better with fresh home baking.

Stephanie straightened and assumed a more formal tone. "We became aware of Fiorelli's possible involvement in some dirty schemes from her messages on the dark web. She was looking for geneticists, but not through the usual channels. Fiorelli put forward enquiries to genetic scientists from the less stable parts of Eastern Europe and the Middle East — people who were on various security lists around the world."

"What's an orchid scientist doing getting involved in that kind of thing?" asked Dante. "Are you sure you have the right person?"

Stephanie made a face. "As sure as our analysts can be."

"Odd..." Eleanor leaned back, looking contemplative.

"And so you were dispatched here to... what?" asked Dante. "Dispose of her? Smoke out her scheme?"

"A bit of both," said Stephanie.

"I'd like to see that," said Eleanor, raising her eyebrows. "A bit of smoking out, and a bit of… disposal? You half-kill someone?"

"It's not like that," said Stephanie primly. "Times have changed."

"I doubt that," muttered Dante.

"Do you mind if I make some tea?" asked Eleanor. "It helps me think."

"Go ahead." Stephanie took another lamington. While Eleanor waited for the kettle to boil, she regarded Dante with open curiosity. "So you're Persephone. I thought you'd be… I don't know."

"Taller?" asked Dante.

Stephanie snorted. "Meaner."

Dante shifted in his seat. "I did my duty. That's all."

"Anyone else for tea?" asked Eleanor.

Both Stephanie and Dante shook their heads.

"Well, this is nice." Eleanor sat back down and set the steaming cup and saucer on the table. "So our orchid scientist tries to contact some dodgy geneticists, and MI6 freaks out and suspects a bioweapon."

"It is odd," said Dante.

"Why would she develop a bioweapon to sell on the black market?" said Eleanor. "She's not short on money. Apparently, she has buckets of investor funds flooding in."

Stephanie shrugged. "Maybe she's been radicalised."

Eleanor snorted. "She's Italian, going back at least a hundred and fifty years. What would she want vengeance for? VE Day?"

"She might want it to create a hostage situation. It's a good bargaining chip." Dante decided it was time to try a lamington himself.

"I just don't see it. Fiorelli is an orchidist through and through. Focused like nothing else…" Eleanor's voice trailed off, and she gazed into space. The steam from her tea curled in a contemplative arc as she thought.

Dante sampled his lamington. It was delicious.

Stephanie polished off her second cake and eyed the others with calculation — deciding whether she could get away with a third cake and still stay within the bounds of politeness.

Eleanor's lips curved upwards in satisfaction. "We've been looking at this all wrong."

Stephanie took a third cake. "How's that?"

Eleanor sipped her tea. "Let's review the facts. Fiorelli has a breakthrough technology to revive extinct plant species — starting with the rare and extremely desirable Ghost Queen. She's attracted a stack of investors with that promise. Your analysts get spooked by her sudden interest in geneticists, whom they consider black market or tainted by hostile political regimes."

"Well, she is," said Stephanie. "Interested in them, I mean. There's a lot of money on the bioweapon black market."

"If you're willing to risk being disappeared into a secure offshore containment facility," said Dante.

"Fiorelli must be desperate indeed. But not in the way you're thinking." Eleanor gazed through the French doors at the azure harbour and distant shoreline. "At the heart of every good con is an assumption. Once your mark has bought into that, the con is yours to lose."

"For example?" Stephanie looked intrigued.

"There are dozens," Eleanor waved a hand. "If you have the right badge and uniform, you must be authorised to be here. If you know the museum curator's name and morning schedule, then you must be a friend of his. Simple stuff, but with the right attitude, it can carry you a surprising distance."

"So what's our assumption about Fiorelli?" asked Stephanie.

"Everyone assumes that she has this groundbreaking tech, and it works," said Eleanor.

Stephanie frowned. "She doesn't?"

"Think about her actions," said Eleanor. "Fiorelli has investors and orchid collectors lined up, waiting for her Ghost Queen to debut. She should be in her lab getting ready for this stellar launch. Instead, she changes her schedule and takes off across the globe to attend a small symposium of keen, but not especially high-powered orchidists. At the same time, she's trawling the dark web for geneticists whose silence can be bought."

"The second bit makes sense with what you're proposing," said Stephanie. "The first bit doesn't."

"That's because you don't know about the *Whitby*, and our murdered professor," said Eleanor. "Fiorelli has good reason to believe what she needs is right here in Te Kohe. It's a fine tale, and the person to tell it to you is Charlie."

"Oh." Stephanie looked at once chagrined and a touch wistful.

"It fits," said Eleanor. "Fiorelli is once more our frontrunner suspect."

"Who's next in line?" asked Dante.

"Lucier," said Eleanor. "Obvious motive, and a suspiciously dead brother. Fairfax bringing up the rear."

"So how can you help me?" Stephanie crossed her arms.

"How good are you at dark web stuff?" asked Eleanor.

"I'm good." Stephanie shot a look at Dante. "Up with the latest greatest."

"Give me a couple of hours," said Eleanor, "and I'll create a hook baited specially for Fiorelli. Then you can show us your latest and greatest."

On the stairs down to the hotel foyer, Eleanor and Dante paused to confer.

"Well done for not shooting her," said Eleanor. "Charlie was right — she's going to be useful."

Dante wondered how Charlie felt about Stephanie now that he knew she was a foreign agent. He hoped Charlie wasn't too upset. Dante probably should have checked in with him last night before he left.

"What's next?" he asked.

Eleanor brought out her phone. "Charlie's texted me. He says he has some fresh information. I'll go see him, but I wanted to ask you — do you have a fancy dress costume for the ball tonight? It's our last chance to entrap our suspects."

Dante looked down at her. "I could go in stealth mode."

"Meaning no one would see you?"

Dante nodded.

"That might be useful," she admitted, "But I think a conventional costume might be more useful. Perhaps you and Charlie could go shopping later today?"

Dante thought a moment. "I will do that. But first, I will get some flowers. For Andrea."

36

In which certain facts come to light.

Eleanor waited for Charlie at the Frog and Gumboot cafe. She wanted to hear his news firsthand, and also have another crack at the notebook that Charlie was bringing.

To this end, she'd secured a table in a small nook in the far corner of the cafe. It was private, though Eleanor wouldn't mind if one of their suspects saw them with the notebook.

Having their quarry know they had something of value could be useful if they needed to bait a trap.

Her phone buzzed with a message from Avery. 'Where is the Scooby Gang this morning?'

She smiled and replied, 'Frog & Gumboot. Bring your deerstalker hat.'

The cafe was already full of Te Kohe residents, and the air was redolent with the smells of coffee, fried eggs, and butter.

Eleanor had a moment of homesickness for Katz's Deli and the accents from home. She'd arrived in New York as a seventeen-year-old so green she shuddered to think how lucky she'd been. The city had captured her imagination from the moment she'd arrived at Grand Central Station and seen the crowds of people who didn't care what your story was as long as you didn't get in their way. There, you could be anyone you wanted.

Charlie entered the cafe looking excited, and Eleanor's interest piqued.

"I've found out a bunch of stuff!" Charlie flung himself into his seat, then bounced in place, unable to contain his excitement.

Eleanor raised her eyebrows. "Do tell."

"Remember my eyewitness saw someone leaving the hotel late on the night Carroll died?" said Charlie. "They were wearing a black fedora hat. Fiorelli doesn't have a hat. But Marcel Lucier has a hatbox in his room. Meredith, who works at the Pepper Tree, told me."

"Well done."

"That's not all. Fairfax isn't even staying at the hotel," said Charlie. "He'd booked the executive suite, but then he cancelled at the last moment. That's how Fiorelli ended up there."

"Intriguing," said Eleanor. "We need to find out where he's staying and what he was doing before he arrived at Marjorie's tea party. Excellent sleuth work."

Charlie beamed.

Eleanor had just finished bringing Charlie up to date on the Stephanie situation when Avery arrived, looking dapper in a pale linen suit and light blue button-down shirt.

"I thought we'd have another go at cracking the notebook," said Eleanor. "Fetch it out, would you, Charlie?"

Charlie retrieved the Pelican case from his satchel and placed it on the table.

"Gloves, please?" asked Avery.

"Sure."

As Eleanor fished in her bag, Avery leaned over. "Just as I thought," he said, peering into her handbag. "I do hope you have a license for that."

"This old thing?" Eleanor tucked her small ivory-handled pistol back into its inner pocket of her bag. "Purely ornamental. It hasn't been fired since the seventies."

Charlie opened his mouth to say something, but Eleanor caught his eye, and he took a swig of coffee instead.

"A likely story." Avery took the gloves Eleanor handed him and began leafing through the book, his face thoughtful. "It's beautiful artwork. I hope it ends up in a museum." Avery bent the book lightly and let the pages fly by at speed.

Eleanor was treated to a changing landscape of flowers. Near the end of the book, the drawings of individual plants merged to become a single orchid that undulated on the page as if alive.

"Do you think the Ghost Queen could be somewhere in Carroll's greenhouse?" asked Avery. "Remember, it's a ghost orchid, so if it's not in flower, all you'd see is the root system."

Charlie's eyes grew wide. "That's a good point. I hadn't looked for that."

"I suspect Fairfax did," said Eleanor. "But you're right. We should check again. And search for a secret greenhouse in the forest behind Carroll's house."

"Charlie and I could check," said Avery. "There's just enough time before the Symposium field trip."

"Great!" Charlie was still slightly in awe of the inspector, but the idea of more time with orchids and Carroll's garden seemed to cheer him considerably.

"What happens on an orchid field trip?" asked Eleanor.

"The usual," said Avery. "We go rambling around the countryside, looking for orchids. Someone spots a rare one, photographs it, and then refuses to tell anyone else where it is, just in case there's an orchid smuggler in our midst."

"Sounds like fun," said Eleanor. "I'd like to find out how the orchid black market works."

"I'm sure you would," said Avery.

"What about invisible ink?" Eleanor nodded towards the notebook in Avery's hands.

"That's more your department than mine," said Avery.

"I could check for the common ones," said Eleanor. "Charlie, do you know if Carroll went in for that sort of thing?"

"He liked puzzles and crosswords," said Charlie. "He was always quizzing me when I helped out in his garden. You know the sort of thing: what's a word with ten letters that means 'old and precious?'"

"Antiquated," said Avery.

"Nice one," said Charlie. "The professor was also an artist. He always does the artwork for the Te Kohe Amateur Theatrical Society's backdrops." He sighed. "I mean, the professor did the artwork."

Avery paged through the book more slowly. "There's almost no text. Just some dates on the early pages."

"So it's unlikely there'll be any anagrams or codes leading to our treasure," said Eleanor.

Their breakfast arrived, and the next few minutes went by in silence, broken only by the clink of cutlery and the occasional grind of pepper.

Finally, Avery pushed his plate back and placed his knife and fork neatly in the centre. "That was a fine breakfast. Thus fortified, I want to know — how's your murder case going?"

"Our case, is it?" Eleanor looked amused. "Still pretending you're not involved?"

"You have only one more day for your wild goose chase," said Avery. "All the guests leave tomorrow."

"We'll probably have to make a trap," said Eleanor. "Using bait that would catch a murderer. Since all our suspects appear to be after the *Whitby* cargo, that rules out the notebook."

"You don't have any conclusive evidence to use as bait, though," said Avery. "Nothing to spook a murderer."

"So we'll invent some," said Eleanor.

"This is why I'm here as an orchidist, not a policeman." Avery held his hands up. "I'm not getting involved in any entrapment schemes."

"And I don't want help from high-maintenance officers of the law," shot back Eleanor. "Charlie, Dante, and I have this handled." She pulled out her phone. "I have a call to make and some plotting to do. See you on the field trip."

37

In which Eleanor goes fishing.

The orchid foraging trip happened much as Avery predicted, except that Fiorelli pleaded a headache and declined to join the orchidists on their bush walk. Afterwards, they all met at the Camellia Tearooms for high tea, which was to be followed by a surprise event.

Eleanor, Avery, and Fiorelli arrived at the Camellia Tearooms late to find everyone tucked into a delicious-looking high tea.

The party was seated at outdoor tables next to a large pond crowded with violet waterlilies. Marjorie guarded an empty seat for Fiorelli and brightened as the Italian orchidist appeared. But Fiorelli chose the last table where Eleanor and Avery sat — a small, round, wrought iron affair, tucked away in a corner and half hidden by a dwarf magnolia tree.

"Inspector," said Fiorelli, lowering her eyes in a way Eleanor found she did not quite like, "I was wondering if you could assist me in something?"

"I'm not here in any official capacity," said Avery. "I'm really here on holiday, as a keen amateur orchidist."

"Prego." Fiorelli waved a hand. Eleanor wondered how she had discovered

Avery's profession. "It is not a crime-related question. This is about the history of Te Kohe."

Eleanor studied the cake stand occupying the middle of the table. There was a sumptuous array of pastries - everything from macaroons to mini crème brûlée puddings. She selected a small carrot cake topped with an equal amount of creamy icing and feigned disinterest in Fiorelli's question.

"I'm not really an expert on Te Kohe history either," said Avery.

'No, no," said Fiorelli. "But as an accomplished police officer, you must know how to find things out."

Eleanor resisted rolling her eyes. Surely the flattery would go on thicker if Fiorelli used a trowel.

"What is it you're trying to discover?" Avery leaned forward.

"It has to do with my ancestor," said Fiorelli, selecting a dark chocolate torte topped with a filigree of white chocolate. "The botanist Giulio Albarelli."

"That's quite an ancestor," said Avery.

"Albarelli's daughter married Ernesto Fiorelli, my six times great-grandfather, so we do not share a surname. Still, we share the lineage, and in me, a profession."

"You must be very proud." Eleanor put on her impressed face.

"Very." Fiorelli turned back to Avery. "Albarelli was an important man in the botanical world. Before his untimely end, he was about to make a contribution that would have shaken the orchid world to its foundations."

"Are you talking about the lost journals from his Florida expedition?" asked Avery. "The ones that were on board the *Whitby*?"

"Ah, you know about the *Whitby*." Fiorelli's eyes brightened. "The journals were on board when it foundered. Everyone thinks they were lost with the ship. But," Fiorelli held up one finger, "I believe they survived. Rowed ashore by one of the crew."

"Dr Fiorelli." Avery smiled indulgently. "I didn't think you were one to believe in conspiracy theories."

"This is not a conspiracy theory," said Fiorelli. "I have been researching this last expedition all my life."

"You're an expert on Albarelli's work?" asked Avery.

"I have studied his other journals," said Fiorelli. "He was a lover of cyphers and codes. Things he put in one journal would point to pages in other journals, and so on."

"Seems an odd thing for a botanist to do," said Eleanor.

"Ah, but you must understand," said Fiorelli, "Albarelli lived in the papal states, back when they were controlled by the Catholic Church. Darwin was just publishing his *'Origin of Species.'* It was a time of great change, and those who believed in evolution had to be careful about sharing their views."

Avery exchanged a glance with Eleanor. "You're familiar with the codes Albarelli used to hide messages in his journals?"

"It is one of my specialities," said Fiorelli.

Eleanor's curiosity stirred. Fiorelli might help in their treasure hunt, but it was a risky play. Fiorelli was no doubt fishing for clues to find the Ghost Queen, just as Eleanor was looking for pointers to Carroll's murderer.

The problem was, the Ghost Queen mystery felt too much like the hunt for a missing Renoir or Degas, and this sent her art thief's instincts spinning.

"Did you mention your interest in Albarelli's journals to Carroll?" asked Eleanor.

"Why would I do that?" Fiorelli's beautifully pencilled eyebrows drew together in a frown.

"He was a scholar of botanical history," said Eleanor. "And living here in Te Kohe, where the wreck happened."

"Ah, I see." Fiorelli laced her fingers together. "So sad. I did have tea with him the afternoon before the Symposium started."

"Oh, yes?" Avery sounded only politely interested.

"A professional courtesy," said Fiorelli. "Of course, I want to ask him about the journals, but I do not. We scholars are like journalists, yes? We like to get the scoop."

Eleanor contained a sigh of frustration. If Fiorelli had denied meeting Carroll that afternoon, it could have been a sign of guilt. She was either too smart or innocent.

"If I were researching Te Kohe history, I'd start by talking to the locals," said Avery. "Why the secrecy?"

"Ah, but you see," said Fiorelli, "I have been under observation since I came here. Someone is spying on me."

Avery gave Eleanor a loaded glance. "How do you know?"

"My rooms," said Fiorelli. "On the first day of the Symposium, someone was there. My papers — important records I sourced through extensive research — were not in the same order as when I left."

"Incredible," said Eleanor, shaking her head. "It's like a thriller novel."

"And for Carroll to succumb to the heart attack, just when certain other people are here in Te Kohe — it is not a coincidence," said Fiorelli.

"Do you suspect anyone in particular?" asked Avery.

Fiorelli shook her head. "I do not want to say."

"Marcel Lucier," suggested Eleanor, and was rewarded by Fiorelli's hand twitching.

"His brother was a scholar of history." Fiorelli glanced over her shoulder. "We corresponded recently. He also died of an unexpected heart attack."

Eleanor raised an eyebrow at Avery. The object of their conversation sat by himself at a small table near the waterlily pond. Oblivious to the rumours forming around him, Lucier sipped his tea, eyes hidden behind round dark glasses, face unreadable.

"I have come to believe," said Fiorelli, "that Professor Carroll meant to share with me some secret about the *Whitby* shipwreck. He knew I was a descendant, but tragically, he never had time to confide his knowledge."

"That's certainly possible," said Avery.

Eleanor thought fast. It was a gamble, but maybe... "If you were to have a look at, say, a notebook of Carroll's that might date back to the 1850s, would you know if it were Albarelli's?"

Fiorelli swung to face her like a bloodhound on a fresh scent. "I have studied my ancestor's life and work for years. I am the foremost authority on Albarelli. So the answer to that is yes."

Eleanor folded her hands in front of her and considered. Avery had the notebook with him. It might be a mistake to show it to Fiorelli. But they were running out of time.

If Fiorelli were an expert in these matters, she might find a clue in Carroll's notebook. Or she might let slip information that implicated her in Carroll's murder.

Nothing ventured, nothing gained, she thought. Of course, the flip side was true: when you ventured, sometimes you lost.

"We might have something for you to look at," she said, taking care to sound noncommittal.

Fiorelli leaned forward, dark eyes burning with intensity. "Lead me to it, and I will solve your mystery."

Eleanor's eyes met Avery's with an unspoken question. He raised his eyebrows as if to say: You've led her this far. Too late to back out now.

"Avery," said Eleanor, "do you have the notebook with you?"

"As a matter of fact, I do." Avery reached into the inner pocket of the coat hanging on his chair and brought out the black plastic case that housed the notebook. He placed it on the table and popped it open.

Eleanor, who'd had a brief frisson of unease that the case might be empty, relaxed.

Fiorelli's gaze intensified. Now, she looked like she wanted to snatch the notebook out of its padded case. Instead, she delved into her shiny black handbag and came out with a pair of fawn leather gloves. "An academic's habit. We must preserve the pages, yes?"

"We believe the notebook contains the key to something important," said Eleanor, "but we can't figure out if there's a hidden message — or not."

"May I?" Fiorelli's gloved fingers reached out towards the notebook.

"Please," said Avery.

Fiorelli ran her fingers over the notebook's cover, then gently picked it up. "Buckram binding, hand-stitched pages, silk headbands and inbuilt ribbon bookmark, rag paper, hand-cut edges. This notebook is old — it could easily date back to the 1850s."

"So you think it's..." Avery's voice trailed off.

Fiorelli opened the notebook. Her eyes narrowed as she saw the first beautiful drawing of an orchid. "It is Albarelli's penmanship. He used a steel nib dip pen, iron gall ink, and this is his distinct radial crosshatching. We have here one of his notebooks from the Florida expedition."

Avery gave a sigh of satisfaction.

Fiorelli paged through the book with a reverent air. "This should be in the Orto Botanico di Padova. Against all odds, it's beautifully preserved." She leafed through some more pages, then paused as she reached the drawings of single orchids. "It can't be," she breathed. "The Ghost Queen."

"It is?" said Avery. "I wasn't sure."

"It is," said Fiorelli. "The elongated spur, the twisted sepals, the upturned labellum. This drawing shows an orchid that hasn't been seen for over a hundred and fifty years."

"Do you see any of Albarelli's cyphers?" asked Eleanor.

Fiorelli shot her a sharp glance. "Not yet. Perhaps if I could take the book away for closer study." Her gloved fingers curled around the pages.

"I'm afraid that's out of the question," said Eleanor with a pleasant smile.

"Who does it belong to?" asked Fiorelli. "I can make a very generous offer on behalf of the Orto Botanico."

"It's part of Carroll's estate," said Eleanor. "Which has not yet been settled."

"The professor? Curious that he should have this." Fiorelli rapidly scanned the drawing, then turned the page.

Her eyes flickered as the second orchid appeared. It looked very similar to the first. To Eleanor, the only differences were a slightly different shading around the petals.

"We think this is a new artist," said Eleanor. "Perhaps someone who studied under Albarelli?"

"You have a good eye. Perhaps it was Moretti, his assistant, or another crew member who took up the work of documenting his finds." Fiorelli turned another page. A third orchid unfurled its flowers across the page, exquisite details inked into memory by an unknown artist.

Fiorelli leafed through more pages, and Eleanor became drawn to the micro-expressions that flitted across her face. The slight pursing of her lips, the minuscule tightening of the muscles around her eyes.

As Fiorelli reached the last few pages, it came to her in a rush: Fiorelli was furious. Something she had seen in these beautiful drawings of orchids had made her so angry that she was using every fibre of self-control to contain it.

I wonder what it is, thought Eleanor. Perhaps we can find out.

"Aren't they pretty pictures? I'm sure the orchid community will want to see them," said Eleanor. "We should show Greg next. He's on the NZ Orchid Society board. I'm sure he'd love to publish an article about it."

"That would be...unwise." Fiorelli's dark brows drew together. "I advise against it."

"Why would you do that?" asked Eleanor.

"Suppose this were a clever forgery?" said Fiorelli. "Perhaps Carroll came across it somewhere else? Before showing this to anyone else, we need to prove its provenance."

"But you just said you were sure it was Albarelli's." Eleanor injected innocent good humour into her voice. "And they're such lovely drawings. If you don't see any hidden codes, surely there's no harm in sharing them. The pictures would look lovely in the NZ Orchidist Quarterly."

Fiorelli's fingers tightened momentarily. "If there is a secret in this notebook," she said slowly, "then publishing it might mean someone else gets there first. Surely you don't want that?"

"I suppose..." Eleanor wrinkled her forehead. "I mean, we're just guessing at its importance, really."

"If the illustrations turned out to be fakes, they could destroy Carroll's reputation," said Fiorelli. "This notebook needs careful study. In my laboratory, I can accurately date it and check the illustrations against other works of Albarelli."

Eleanor knew when someone was thinking hard and making things up on the fly. Fiorelli was certainly doing this. Again, she wondered why. Had she already seen the key they'd been looking for, and now she hoped to capitalise on it before anyone else did?

"What do you think, Avery?" asked Eleanor. "I mean, we can't let Dr Fiorelli take the notebook now, but we can certainly put in a request to Carroll's lawyer for this notebook to be lent out to the good doctor."

"Certainly." Avery had on his Inspector poker face. "Of course, an heir of Carroll might pop out of the woodwork and have other ideas."

Fiorelli flicked through the pages, her movements clipped.

Whatever else it might hide, the notebook and its illustrations were beautiful. Eleanor could not work out why they had angered Fiorelli.

At last, Fiorelli came to the final drawing. The facing page contained a note written in Carroll's handwriting. It said:

"Talk to CryoBloom // secured layer re. original GQ seed revival."

Fiorelli froze for a long moment.

"Do you know what that is?" asked Eleanor. "We thought 'GQ' might stand for 'Ghost Queen' but that's as far as we got. Do you know?"

"No..." Fiorelli's voice was distant. "It is a mystery to me, too."

It's always nice, thought Eleanor, to see what someone looks like when you know they're lying through their teeth. Odd expression, that.

"Well, it's truly an honour to have you look through this," said Avery. "I just wish it'd been worth your time."

Fiorelli gave a quick jerk of her head. "The honour is mine. I must circulate now, before our next event."

"What do you reckon?" asked Eleanor as they watched Fiorelli's elegant retreating figure.

Avey frowned. "What was that CryoBloom note about? It wasn't there when I last looked at the notebook."

"It's in Professor Carroll's handwriting," said Eleanor.

"Sure." Avery narrowed his eyes. "Did you put it there as some elaborate bait?"

"We think the murderer forged Carroll's handwriting on that medicine bottle," said Eleanor. "So they should know it quite well. As to why it's there, you said you didn't want to be involved."

"If only," Avery sighed. "I promise to visit when you're in prison for whatever wild scheme you're cooking up."

"For that dig, I will eat the only macaron."

"And I will mourn that macaron the rest of the afternoon."

"Thus is justice served," said Eleanor. "Bon appétit."

38

In which Dante explores the novel act of dressing up.

"What if I stuck some feathers on my balaclava?" asked Dante, picking up a black feather boa.

"Erm..." Charlie stuck his tongue in his cheek. He looked like he was thinking of a diplomatic response.

They were in the second-hand store on the main street of Te Kohe. On Eleanor's instructions, Charlie had dragged Dante into town to buy a mask for the ball that night.

"I don't like the idea of a gathering where people are wearing masks," said Dante. "Anyone could get away with anything."

"Well, in a masque ball," said Charlie, "the masks are kind of decorative. They might only cover the person's eyes."

"So you can tell who's wearing the mask?" Dante scowled at a stack of skeleton masks. "Seems a bit pointless."

Dante had never been to a ball before. Or rather, he'd never been invited to a ball before. He didn't think that infiltrating as a waiter, abseiling down the building exterior, or crawling through the air ducts counted.

"A masque ball is about..." Charlie waved a hand, "Dressing up. Having fun. Pretending to be someone you're not."

"Hmmm." Dante had spent a lot of time pretending to be someone he wasn't. Usually, he was pretending not to be an assassin. He was good at it, right up to the point when he stopped pretending and got down to business.

"What about this one?" Charlie held up a black Zorro mask. "You could be like Wesley from the '*Princess Bride*'!" His face fell at Dante's blank stare. "You haven't watched the 'Princess Bride?'"

"No."

"Have you ever had a movie night?"

"No."

"Would you like to have a movie night?" Charlie's enthusiasm returned in a rush. "We could eat popcorn and pineapple lumps and chocolate fish and watch all the classics. Star Wars, Princess Bride, Gremlins..."

"Aren't those all 80s movies?" said Dante.

"Yeah, but my dad liked them," said Charlie. "So... I do too." He finished on a wistful note, and Dante felt a sudden urge to find whichever prison Ted was in and kill him for once and for all.

Hard on the heels of that, he remembered the AA code. *'Never seek to remove those you deem unworthy of life....'* He could think of so many exceptions to this rule.

"A masque ball is meant to be glamorous," said Charlie. "It's like Carnival in Venice, where everyone wears sequined costumes and fancy masks."

"I could put sequins on my balaclava," said Dante. Then he thought better of it. Sequins might sparkle and betray his position at night.

"If we can't find anything here, we could always try the Te Kohe Theatre." Charlie's face took on a happy glow. "It's a wonderful place, and they have loads of costumes in storage backstage."

Theatres were a foreign country to Dante. He wasn't sure he wanted to visit one anytime soon.

"I think this Zorro mask would be perfect for you." Charlie handed it to Dante. "It makes you look mysterious without being too menacing."

Reluctantly, Dante tried it on.

"Maybe with some gloves," said Charlie. There was a bin of them in the corner next to a shelving unit full of sunglasses. Charlie rummaged through them for half a minute. "Aha!" He drew out a pair of olive green leather gloves, checking for a price tag that wasn't there.

"They're too small," said Dante.

"I think I'll get them anyway." Charlie flushed. "Stephanie might like them for the ball."

Dante scowled. Even though they were working together, he wanted to keep contact with Stephanie to a minimum.

"How about a hat, then?" Charlie surveyed the hat rack, where a forest of hats grew like strange fruit. His hand hovered over a beret, then a fedora, to land on a black scarf shaped into a turban. "This would make you look like Douglas Fairbanks in *'The Thief of Bagdad.'* All you need now is a moustache." Charlie spun around to seize upon a display stand loaded with fake moustaches. "Here we go. Classic swashbuckling moustache."

"I don't swashbuckle." Dante wasn't sure what swashbuckling was, but he was sure he didn't do it.

Outside, the tree-lined main street of Te Kohe shone golden in the late afternoon sun.

"Sure you do." Charlie's smile was like the sun. "Let's buy this lot and then set up Eleanor's plan for the ball."

They headed for the counter, and Dante wondered if he'd ever become a person who did, in fact, swashbuckle. Perhaps it was time to find out.

39

In which Eleanor conducts an interrogation at 1500 feet.

Te Kohe Scenic Helicopter Flights was not a luxury outfit. In reality, Ed, the owner, had only tacked on the 'scenic flights' part of the business when a surge of tourists coincided with a quiet time in the sheep rescuing, crop spraying, and beekeeping parts of his business.

"This isn't usual for orchid conventions," murmured Avery in Eleanor's ear. "Looks like they pulled out all the stops for our guests."

They were standing in the waiting area Ed had created for would-be sightseers. The 'reception' was really a shed barely civilised by a swept concrete floor, plywood interior lining, and some plastic chairs. On a whiteboard, Ed had scrawled today's weather: 'sunny and a bit windy.' A hastily drawn arrow below the weather report pointed to a small kitchen bench, accompanied by the words 'Help yourself to tea and coffee. Back soon.'

The guests milled around, making small talk while they waited for the helicopter pilot. Eventually Ed arrived, beaming, his beard in all its glory flowing down his chest, and his thick-framed glasses held together by enthusiastic spot welding.

"Great you all could make it," he said. "I'm Ed, your pilot for today. It's lovely weather for a flight, and I'm looking forward to taking you all up."

Eleanor's gaze was drawn to the kitchen bench, where Fairfax had hastily turned his back to the proceedings and was making a cup of tea. She frowned. This was strange behaviour for the usually polite aristocrat. She wondered why, and an idea formed in her mind.

"Who's up first?" asked Ed.

It just so happened that Eleanor, Avery, Lucier and Fiorelli were standing closest to the door. Ed's gaze lit on them, and he waved an inviting arm towards the bright sunshine outside.

"You four? Great! Come this way, she's ready to go." Ed waved one hand towards a field where a dark blue helicopter rested on a patch of gravel, its rotor blades bending down like plant stems as it awaited flight.

"I... don't think I shall go." Fiorelli looked a little pale.

"Our hosts have kindly arranged this outing," said Lucier smoothly. His eyes glinted. "Surely you don't want to disappoint them?"

"I am not sure." Fiorelli's eyes darted around the room.

"It's a bona fide scenic event," said Ed. "Greg was chuffed I could fit you all in."

"It'll be spectacular." Eleanor jumped on Ed and Lucier's comments. It might be useful to have Fiorelli along. "It'd mean so much to organisers for you to join us."

"If you think... I would rather..." Fiorelli's voice trailed off, seeing the interested eyes of other guests on her. "Va bene. It is a short ride, yes?"

"You'll love it!" Ed grinned, revealing a gold-capped front tooth. "This way."

Ed led the four passengers through a broad cattle gate into a muddy paddock.

"We are going through that?" Fiorelli looked askance at the ploughed-up field, then down at her Gianvito Rossi pumps.

"The heifers came through just before," said Ed. "Makes it a bit muddy. Give your shoes a bit of a scrape as you're climbing into the helicopter, and she'll be right."

"There are no stairs?" Fiorelli eyed her pencil skirt with doubt.

"Er... I can fetch a beer crate from the shed if you like," said Ed. "Got a few in there." She returned his conspiratorial wink with an icy stare.

"A crate would be lovely." Eleanor bestowed a gracious smile on Ed. "Unless you'd like to lift me in like the gallant officer you are?" she asked Avery.

"I think it would play heck with my sciatica," said Avery.

"Chivalry." Eleanor shook her head. "Have you been on many flights, Mr Lucier?"

"Please, call me Marcel," said Lucier. He studied the chopper with a professional eye. "When my brother and I searched the Everglades for rare orchids, we often used a helicopter for drop-offs and pick-ups."

"How adventurous," said Eleanor. "I imagine you must miss him terribly."

"Yes," said Lucier shortly. Then he sighed. "It was his dream to come here and see the New Zealand native orchids. I feel like I must live for two now."

"Have you been out in the forest before today's field trip?" asked Avery.

Lucier shook his head. "The professor - Carroll - wanted to take me on a walk to see some of his favourite wetland orchids. Alas, he, too, is now unable."

Lucier spoke with a curious cadence, and Eleanor wondered if he spoke Cajun French more than English at home in New Orleans.

Ed arrived, wooden beer crate in hand, and laid it ceremoniously on the gravel below the helicopter door.

From the cockpit of the helicopter, a cattle dog with one ear flopping over its eye grinned out at them, its welcome echoing its master's.

Fiorelli accepted Avery's hand and ascended into the helicopter with a regal air.

Eleanor followed. She winked down at Avery as he stood, feet planted stoically in the gravel. "My knight in cotton armour."

Four passenger seats faced each other in the helicopter, where Fiorelli contrived to sit next to Avery. Eleanor adjusted the four-point harness and tried on her headphones, while Ed did unspecified helicopter things outside in preparation for their flight.

"All good?" Ed swung himself into the helicopter and dropped into the pilot's seat. With a happy 'woof', the cattle dog leaned against his seat, placing an adoring head on his knee. "Steady on, girl." Ed stroked her silky ears. Then he began flicking dials and switches, accompanied by various beeps and whirs.

"Can you all hear me?" Avery's voice sounded in Eleanor's ear via the headset.

"Loud and clear," came Lucier's calm tones.

Fiorelli crossed one elegant leg over the other and gazed out the window.

"Right, then." Ed put on his headset. "Who's flown in one of these before?"

All the passengers said 'yes.'

Eleanor's favourite helicopter flight had to be the one that conveyed her to the front lawn of a mansion on Capri. One billionaire, a dozen glittering guests, and one Fabergé egg that would soon go mysteriously missing.

"Great!" said Ed. "Just a few things before we go. Everyone stay in their seats while we're in the air. If you have any questions, let me know on the headset. And, ah, I'll be pointing out local attractions and so on as we go. Sweet as? Good. Ready for takeoff."

With a whoosh, the helicopter blades began to spin, and Eleanor felt the thrill of imminent flight.

She smiled in anticipation and looked up to find Avery's eyes on her, a strangely wistful expression on his face. She raised an eyebrow in inquiry, and he looked away.

"Oy, none of that. Down, girl. Sit." Eleanor frowned, then realised Ed was addressing his dog, who'd put her paws on the window frame to look out. The dog had a pair of pink earmuffs over her ears, and her tongue lolled out the side of her mouth in a happy grin.

Eleanor suppressed a smile at the horrified look on Fiorelli's face.

The helicopter engine roared, and the rotor blades blurred into invisibility as they sped up. Grass flattened in a circle around them, and the cows in the neighbouring field cantered away.

"Quel maledetto cane ci ucciderà tutti," muttered Fiorelli, and clasped her white-knuckled hands in her lap.

'That damned dog is going to kill us all,' translated Eleanor in her head. She always preferred to interrogate people with scattered attention and stressed emotions. Now seemed to be an appropriate time.

"Dr Fiorelli, you said you talked to Professor Carroll the afternoon before the Symposium. What did you discuss?"

Fiorelli closed her eyes as the helicopter rose, dipped, and then rose again.

"You went to the professor?" Lucier's grey eyes were cool as he regarded Fiorelli. "I was at his house that afternoon. I must have just missed you."

"Per l'amor di Dio!" gasped Fiorelli. "What is it you are asking?"

"I was wondering about Carroll. It was his last day of life — do you think you could share your memories of him? He was a dear friend." Eleanor had her best sincere face on, but both Avery and Fiorelli were giving her similar looks of scepticism.

"We talked about many things, as you can imagine." Fiorelli drew in a quick breath as the helicopter tilted, gaining height with increasing speed.

Dark green hillsides covered in lush native forest filled the windows on one side of the helicopter, blue sky on the other.

"Any specific topics?" asked Eleanor sweetly. "It's the details that bring the past to life." She became aware of Lucier, watching her with interest.

"He said... he said the New Zealand orchids are beautiful." Fiorelli's eyes widened as Ed banked the helicopter to the left, and a distant mountain range swung into view.

Eleanor watched closely, hoping to uncover some of Fiorelli's less obvious tells.

"On the right, you'll see the Tūwhenua ranges," came Ed's voice. "Lot of good manuka growing in the foothills. Dropped a bunch of beehives over there this spring."

"So you talked about New Zealand orchids? Fascinating," said Eleanor. "Anything else?"

"Ah... he was interested in my work." Fiorelli closed her eyes as the helicopter dipped again. "He loved my plan to revive the vanished orchid lines."

"That's interesting," said Lucier.

"How so?" asked Eleanor.

"I understand the Professor was a great admirer of hybridisation." Lucier leaned back in his chair, a small smile curving the corner of his mouth. "He had an interesting theory about Albarelli and his views on hybrids."

Fiorelli's eyes snapped open. "Albarelli was a purist, like me."

Lucier shrugged. "Carroll thought otherwise."

"Did he have proof of this? Evidence, perhaps?" asked Eleanor.

"A catalogue of his writings and collected books will no doubt bring it to light," said Lucier.

"If you'll all take a peek down below," came Ed's voice, "you'll see the Waimaru River. It starts at Lake Ashburn and runs into the Te Kohe harbour just up from town. Lots of trout in there. Good fishin'."

"I'm sure his heirs will want all his works published," said Eleanor.

"Do you think that will happen?" asked Fiorelli.

"It usually takes a year or so to sort out deceased estates," said Avery.

"They might offer his estate up for sale," said Lucier. "Unpublished works and all."

"On the open market." Eleanor wondered why Lucier was being more helpful than Avery in this particular conversation.

"I might be an interested buyer," said Lucier. "I've always been an admirer of Carroll's work."

Eleanor flashed a smile as Fiorelli literally squirmed in her seat. "If you acquired Carroll's estate, would you publish all the works you found?"

"Absolutely," said Lucier. "I have the connections to ensure it happened quickly."

"If you look down now," said Ed, "you'll see a stretch of railway we call 'the nutcracker.' Er... It's quite steep, you see. Engineers had a real time of it, back in the fifties."

"I find it fascinating that Albarelli might have been a secret hybridist," said Eleanor. "That wasn't his original position, was it?"

"It was not," said Lucier. "But Carroll believed the Florida expedition changed his mind. He thought—"

"Basta!" snapped Fiorelli. "Albarelli believed in the purity of form, the majesty of the originals, unsullied by what came after. He cherished the pure ideal of an orchid that is only found in the primary lineages. Always, people seek to pollute, to change, to corrupt that which is already perfect. The hybrids, they are the bastardi, the lesser species of the plant world. If I could, I would—" With an audible snap, Fiorelli shut her mouth, perhaps aware she had said more than she intended.

The roar of the helicopter engine sounded loud in the sudden conversational gap.

"My dog Lucy's a mutt," said Ed at last. "A right smart one, too. Mongrels — best dogs there are."

Fiorelli mouthed a curse in Italian and leaned back in her seat, her eyes shut fast. Her hand strayed onto Avery's knee and gripped it, as if for support. Eleanor found her eyes resting on the hand. She carefully smoothed her brow and looked out the window.

It seemed they had found the mute button for the in-flight conversation.

40

In which duplicity abounds.

The Bughouse hall was a hive of activity when Charlie and Dante arrived, with a crowd of volunteers redecorating for the evening ball. Since all the volunteers were there of their own free will, their activities also included debating, negotiating, disagreeing, and occasionally storming off to air their grievances in another part of the hall.

Charlie kept close to Dante, sure that if he wandered too far, some community member would press-gang him into helping out.

The plan Eleanor, Dante, and he were staging involved what she called a mousetrap. Their job right now was to install the bait and the cameras to capture their murderer that night.

Charlie's heart raced thinking about it. He didn't think he was a natural conspirator. Eleanor revelled in this sort of thing, Dante seemed unaffected. Charlie felt like he was about to shoplift a store - something he had never done, and hoped never to do.

"How do you want to do this?" he asked Dante in a low voice.

"First the cloakroom," said Dante. "Then the powder room."

They threaded their way through the crowd, stepping over vast lengths of red velvet fabric and strings of fairy lights.

Charlie sped up as he caught sight of Marjorie Everton. Fortunately, she was engaged in an arm-waving argument with Greg and thus was too busy to send him on an errand.

Dante ducked under the swinging beam of a speaker stand carried by a man unaware of anyone around him. With two quick strides, he was out of the hall, and Charlie darted after him.

The back entry anteroom was blessedly empty of volunteers. On the right-hand wall, the cloakroom lay behind a reception desk — a cave of a room with a few forgotten coats still hanging in its depths.

"Tell me if anyone comes," said Dante. He slung off his backpack and stepped behind the reception desk. He laid the pack on the desk and pulled a small white device that looked just like a smoke detector.

"What's that?" asked Charlie.

"Camera." Dante reached up and attached it to the ceiling above the reception desk, rotating it to point at the back shelves of the cloakroom.

Next, Dante took a small bottle from his bag and set it on the shelf, turning the label so it was clearly visible.

"That's the digitalis bottle from Carroll's house?" Charlie stole another glance out of the room towards the hall.

No one looked their way, although the noise level had risen as Marjorie and Greg settled their differences.

"Eleanor made a copy," said Dante. "I can't tell which is the original. Phone, please."

Charlie handed Dante his phone, and he booted up the app he'd installed. Dante's fingers were lightning fast on the screen, dispelling Charlie's theory that he didn't own a phone because he was bad at technology.

Dante gave a grunt of approval. "All hooked up." He slung the bag over his shoulder. "Let's go."

They crossed the hall again to get to the powder room, where their second bait would be set. The noise level had receded, and Charlie saw the reason why.

Fairfax had arrived with a golden smile and shirt sleeves rolled up, and everyone was now on their best behaviour. No fighting in front of the British aristocracy.

Fairfax glanced up, saw Charlie, and gave him a cheery wave. Ears burning, Charlie waved back. Dante was already vanishing down the corridor toward the powder room, and Charlie had to dodge around an antique side table to catch up.

Dante was busy picking the lock to the powder room door when Charlie turned the corner. Thirty seconds later, the door swung open, and he vanished inside.

"Dante?" Charlie hurried forward to peer into the room. It was dark until Dante flicked on the row of lights surrounding a stage mirror. The powder room was painted bright red and cast everything in a lurid hue.

"You need to keep watch in case somebody comes," said Dante.

Charlie ducked back into the corridor. "No one here."

Dante placed another digitalis bottle amongst the row of leftover stage makeup bottles below the mirror. He reached inside his bag for another camera disguised as a smoke detector.

The ceiling was low, and Dante could easily reach it to screw the device into the plasterboard ceiling.

"Do you think—" began Charlie, then stopped. Too late, he ducked outside the room to see the well-tailored figure of Fairfax making his way towards them, a swing in his step and a slight smile on his lips.

"Charlie," said Fairfax. "I was wondering if you could put me in touch with Grace— oh, hello." His smile slipped slightly as Dante shouldered his way out through the powder room door.

"Hi Lord Martin," said Charlie. "We were just...checking for a jumper I lost." He knew his face would be bright red by now. Definitely not a natural conspirator, he thought.

"Any luck?" asked Fairfax.

"'Fraid not," said Charlie. "Er, I can ask Grace to call you if you like. Billy's still got your number."

"What? Yes, thank you." Fairfax smiled breezily, but his eyes were sharp.

"We were just leaving," said Dante.

"See you." Fairfax gave a two-finger salute.

As soon as they were around the corner from the powder room, Dante stopped. He took Charlie's phone out of his pocket and thumbed on the camera app. In the grainy light, they saw the powder room door swing open, and Fairfax enter. He strolled along the rows of bottles, checked his hair in the mirror, and seemed to be what he appeared - a casual visitor, curious about an ageing town hall and its various disused rooms.

Dante's mouth turned down. "I don't like it."

"Do you think he knows we're up to something?" asked Charlie.

"Yes."

"Should we plant the bottle and the camera somewhere else?"

There was a long silence. "There aren't many easily accessible rooms here that aren't full of people right now."

On screen, Fairfax took one last look around the room, then disappeared out of the camera view. Dante passed the phone to Charlie and walked back into the hall.

"He hasn't found anything," said Charlie. "Maybe it's alright."

Dante checked this watch. "Moving operations will look more suspicious now. If there's time before the ball, I'll see about a new location. But I don't think there'll be time."

"Charlie, could you be a dear and run these over to the kitchens for me?" Greg's wife, Daphne held out a tray of something sweet and alcoholic.

"Sure." Charlie took the tray. Nobody looked likely to ask Dante to help.

"We meet at Eleanor's place in half an hour," said Dante. "See you there."

41

In which certain suspicions are confirmed.

Eleanor waited outside the shed until the last of the Symposium guests had been up in the helicopter, and then left in their various transports. She flicked through her phone, checking for what she thought she'd find, and smiled to herself when her guess proved to be correct.

She wanted to speak with Ed alone, but Avery had insisted on waiting with her. She hadn't decided whether she was gratified or annoyed. Maybe both.

Eventually, Ed finished seeing to his helicopter and crossed the field, his long strides eating up the ground and Lucy trotting obediently at his side.

"You two still here?" he asked as he neared the shed where Eleanor and Avery were waiting. "What can I do for you?"

"I'm a friend of Charlie Wilson," said Eleanor.

"Hmm," said Ed. "What's the boy got himself into now?"

"Nothing serious," said Eleanor. "I was just wondering, do you own an Airbnb around here?"

"That's right," said Ed, his gaze flicking curiously between Eleanor and Avery. "But I'd have thought it's a bit basic for you. Or your gentleman friend."

"A friend of Charlie's is coming to stay," Eleanor lied smoothly. "He won't mind basic. Is it available?"

"Well, not as such," said Ed, absently stroking his dog's ears. "Got someone staying there now, as a matter of fact."

"Lord Martin Fairfax?" asked Eleanor lightly, and watched Ed's eyes widen in surprise, then narrow.

"Now, how did you know that?"

"I won't spread the news," said Eleanor. "I imagine it's something Fairfax wants to remain private. But I have something important to ask you. It's for Charlie."

"Ask away." Ed crossed his arms and leaned against the side of the shed. His bushy eyebrows lowered as he prepared to listen.

"Do you know what time Fairfax left your place on Friday afternoon?" Eleanor kept her tone neutral. It would never do to betray the importance of the question and spook the interviewee. In her mind, she substituted 'interviewee' for 'mark' at the last moment. She tried not to think of the implications.

"Let's see..." Ed's eyes drifted up to the left as he thought. "He arrived at my place around mid-morning, and I showed him the setup. It's just a converted garage, and I wondered why someone dressed up so smart would stay there. Mind you, he was looking a bit rough. Said he'd been up the Skytower the night before. I took that to mean a night out on the casino. He gave me his details then disappeared for a couple of hours — probably to sleep it off. I got busy doing stuff in the shed. Noticed his car was gone around half three."

"When was the last time you saw his car?" asked Eleanor.

Ed scratched his beard. "Half two. I was listening to the cricket. Kane Williamson got bowled, and I went out of the shed to relieve the tension. We were down four wickets and only 114 runs on the board."

"Not good?" asked Eleanor sympathetically.

"Not good. But yeah, his car was still there. So he must have left sometime between half two and half three, I guess. Are you going to tell me what all this is about?"

"Charlie will tell you. I promise. Once the dust's settled."

"If you say so..." Ed eyed her speculatively. "You're the one whose house almost got bulldozed. And you helped Ted Andrews get a bit of what he had coming."

"That's right," said Eleanor cheerfully. "It was a pleasure."

Lucy whined and pawed the air with one elegant forepaw.

"Alright, girl. Tuckertime." Ed nodded at Eleanor. "I'll be hearing from Charlie later, then. Afternoon."

And with that, he loped off, Lucy at his side.

Eleanor watched him go, a warm feeling of satisfaction filling her.

"Want to tell me what that was all about?" asked Avery.

"We've successfully crossed one suspect off our list," said Eleanor. "With that timeline, Fairfax couldn't have visited Carroll the day he died. He left Ed's at two thirty, arrived at Marjorie's tea party at three, stayed till six, and then went to the Symposium. Ed didn't have any reason to lie, and I don't think he was lying."

"I'd agree with that assessment."

"I also think Lord Fairfax has a pretty serious gambling problem. It was enough to cause him to cancel his expensive hotel and book into a cheap crashpad for a few nights. I had noticed his suit was looking a little worse for wear."

Avery gave a world-weary sigh. "It's unnerving to see how much overlap there is between conwoman and detective."

"You should be glad," shot back Eleanor. "We're doing all the legwork."

"And what — I'm supposed to do an arrest and take the credit in the end?"

"That depends," said Eleanor.

"Because I'm not arresting anyone on trumped-up charges."

"Don't worry yourself on that account."

Avery followed her to her car. "By the way, that's a gorgeous Mark II Jag. Classic."

"Be my guest." Eleanor passed him the keys.

"Madame," Avery swung open the passenger door for her. "Now, as you were saying..."

"Your taking credit depends," said Eleanor, lowering herself into the car seat, "on what you bring to the party."

"The party that's tonight? Avery climbed into the driver's seat and turned the key in the ignition. The car roared into life, and he smiled. "I'll be bringing my A-game, my best dancing shoes, and a disguise I think you'll approve of."

"Please tell me it's not a monocle, spats, and Harris tweed?"

"Ellery Queen? No... Lord Peter Whimsey." Avery guided the car out of the gravelled parking lot. "If I were going in that style, I'd be more Sam Spade: trenchcoat, whisky, and a fedora."

"I see." Eleanor smiled, but the mention of a fedora sent a spike of unease through her. Did Avery own a fedora? How well did she really know the Inspector? Wouldn't joining their investigation be the perfect cover for a murderer?

Eleanor told herself it was only old wounds that were sending her thoughts in this direction. But still...

"I have a duty of care to see that justice is done, and also seen to be done." Avery changed gear smoothly, and the car accelerated.

Eleanor corralled her doubts into a far corner of her mind and gave Avery a disarming smile. "Working with appearances is what I do best."

"That's what worries me," muttered Avery.

The Jag took the first corner fast, but Avery held a tight line, keeping the ride smooth. Eleanor relaxed back into her seat and began to scheme.

42

In which hooks are baited.

Charlie sat between Eleanor and Dante at Eleanor's dining room table and watched as Stephanie fired up her sleek black laptop. Outside, the late afternoon sun turned Eleanor's garden golden.

Dante had insisted on a weapons check upon Stephanie's arrival. There'd been a brief standoff, and then Stephanie had produced a Glock, two knives, and a taser.

Eleanor had put them on the occasional table by her hatstand. "You can collect them on the way out, dear."

Now, Dante maintained a brooding presence at one end of the table while Charlie nibbled away at the cheese tray and Eleanor quizzed Stephanie on what she was doing.

Charlie wasn't sure if Eleanor was genuinely interested or simply making conversation. Either way, it relieved some of the tension hanging between them all.

As Charlie understood it, Eleanor had written a codename into Carroll's notebook and made sure Fiorelli saw it. Now, they were going to use the codename and Stephanie's dark web skills to bait Fiorelli into revealing her intentions.

It was a plan that reached far outside Charlie's experience. He occasionally used the hotel computers to look up specialist plant care. Aside from that, he felt everything he needed to know could be found in real life.

"So you fire up the Tor browser to access the dark web?" asked Eleanor.

"Yep." Stephanie clicked a few buttons, settling into the slightly hunched posture favoured by laptop users everywhere. "After your call, I spent the morning creating and backdating a legend for CryoBloom. Then I seeded a PGP link in some forums where we've seen Fiorelli before."

"I have no idea what you mean," said Eleanor, "but it sounds promising."

"Fiorelli will be looking for a biotechnician who has the username CryoBloom," said Stephanie. "I laid a breadcrumb trail for her to find my onion-link."

"Sounds appropriately botanical," said Eleanor. "How long before she makes contact?"

"You got back from your field trip about half an hour ago," said Stephanie. "I reckon it'll take Fiorelli at least that long to track us down."

"Excellent," said Eleanor. "Anything you'd like to drink while we wait? Tea? Coffee? Chardonnay? Something stronger?"

"I'd like a coffee, thanks." Stephanie eyed Dante. "I didn't sleep much last night."

Charlie followed Eleanor into the kitchen. She turned on the grinder, and the air filled with the aroma of freshly ground coffee beans.

"How're you holding up, Charlie?" Eleanor asked quietly.

"Erm, fine, I think."

"Last night, you found out the young lady you liked was a foreign spy. It sounded like a tense situation. Are you sure you're ok?"

"I guess?" said Charlie. "I mean, it could have turned out worse."

"I suspect it would have been if you hadn't shown up. But how do you feel about Stephanie now?"

"I don't know." Charlie glanced back to where Stephanie was typing rapidly, her gaze fixed on her screen. "I'm wondering if she ever liked me. I mean, she might be married with three kids at home. Do you think red is even her natural hair colour?"

"I'm not sure about the hair dye," said Eleanor, "but I highly doubt there are three kids." She locked the portafilter into the coffee machine, flicked a switch, and espresso ran into the cup beneath it.

Charlie slumped against the kitchen counter while Eleanor steamed the milk. "I just... I haven't been interested in anyone like that for a while."

Eleanor smiled sympathetically. "There aren't many people your age in Te Kohe, and most of them you've known all your life. Sometimes, you need an opportunity to reinvent yourself. Have you ever considered travelling? Living somewhere else for a time?"

"Hey!" came Stephanie's voice from the dining room. "We've got a bite."

Eleanor poured the frothed milk into the cup of espresso, finishing with a flourish that produced a fern leaf pattern. She and Charlie reentered the dining room to see Stephanie looking excited, and Dante looking exactly the same as before.

"What's happened?" Eleanor placed the coffee on Stephanie's right and studied the screen over her shoulder.

"Fiorelli's found my profile on BioCrypt," said Stephanie. "That's one of the message boards she contacted geneticists on before. She'll post us a message any moment now..."

Her screen displayed a black page with green text. Charlie scanned down confusing menu items like 'Cultivars' and 'Cryto-genesis' to 'Encrypted Messages.' A small status bar read: Users online: 14 (3 hidden.)

There was a small 'ding' and a message popped into the empty inbox. It read:

> [AlbaOrchid] — 23:47 — Seeking revival protocols re legacy orchid seed. Terms negotiable.

“What do you want me to say?” asked Stephanie.

“Tell her,” said Eleanor, “that we require payment upfront. But make it sound technical.”

> [CryoBloom] — 23:55 — Terms: 100% payment upfront. BTC or ETH. Dropzone: USA.

> [AlbaOrchid] — 24:20 — 50% upfront, 50% on delivery.

“Tell her ok,” said Eleanor. “But probe into what she wants done.”

> [CryoBloom] — 24:35 — 50% upfront accepted. Orchid type? Provenance? Seed age?

The little dots appeared, disappeared, reappeared.

“Fiorelli’s thinking about this one,” said Eleanor. “She probably doesn’t want to give away her secret - anyone asked to propagate a Ghost Queen seed might just take it and run. Hurry her along a bit.”

> [CryoBloom] — 24:57 — In or out? Time is money...

> [AlbaOrchid] — 25:05 — Require surety of sample return.

> [CryoBloom] — 24:57 — My reputation is my currency.

> [AlbaOrchid] — 25:05 — Ghost orchid. Provenance unknown. Seed age 1-2 years.

“She’s hedging,” said Eleanor. “Wild orchid seeds are notoriously hard to propagate, even when they’re fresh.”

Stephanie grinned. “Do you want me to get an upfront payment?”

“Tempting,” said Eleanor. “What’s a reasonable price to charge?”

“Lab propagation done anonymously?” Stephanie shrugged. “Ten thousand US dollars? Twenty?”

“Make it thirty,” said Eleanor. “CryoBloom being expensive will boost Fiorelli’s confidence.”

> [CryoBloom] — 25:14 — $15k USD up front, $15k on delivery.

> [AlbaOrchid] — 25:18 — OK

"That was speedy," said Eleanor. "Either she's desperate — spoiler alert, she is — or we weren't greedy enough. Maybe both. Tell her we'll confirm later."

> [CryoBloom] — will confirm details in 10:00 hours.

[Exit forum.]

"I wonder if Fiorelli already has a Ghost Queen seed, or if she expects to get her hands on one soon?" mused Eleanor. "And if so, how?"

"Do you think she found something at Carroll's house?" asked Charlie. "Maybe she was the burglar."

"Either that, or Carroll gave her some seeds when they met at his house. Which would make Fiorelli a fraud, but not a murderer. Her lecture is a good place to poke around — it's the last one of the Symposium, and it's starting soon." Eleanor resumed her seat, her face thoughtful. "Thank you for your help, Stephanie. It's answered some questions and created others. Most importantly, does Fiorelli already have a Ghost Queen seed that she needs propagated in secret?"

Stephanie sighed. "Looks like you were right about her. No bioweapons. I flew halfway across the world for nothing."

"Not for nothing," said Eleanor. "You got to drink some excellent coffee... and meet some interesting people."

"Hmmph." Stephanie sipped her coffee, and her face brightened. "This is good. Thanks." Her gaze wandered to Dante, then slid off Charlie. "I guess... an apology is in order?"

Dante folded his arms across his chest and said nothing.

"I'm sorry I broke into your house," said Stephanie.

"And nearly shot Charlie," said Dante.

Stephanie at last locked eyes with Charlie. "I... I'm sorry you were there, Charlie. I didn't want..." she flushed. "I really do..." Her flush deepened, and Charlie felt a stab of sympathy. Despite her cool poise when she was in spy mode, Stephanie was as bad as he was when it came to awkward conversations.

"Dante," said Eleanor, "let's look at the garden for a few minutes."

"But we're in the middle of—"

"Now, Dante."

Charlie waited while his friends left, closing the French doors behind them.

"What I meant to say," said Stephanie, "is that I'm sorry you found out about me. Like that."

"Do you think I'd have ever found out otherwise?" Charlie swallowed. "If we'd gotten to know each other like normal people?"

"Charlie." Stephanie's mouth curved into a lopsided grin. "You aren't normal. Not even close. And I mean that in a good way."

"Oh." Charlie felt his face flushing too. "Thanks. I guess."

43

Which contains a book signing and dropped hints.

"This is it." Charlie bounced lightly on his toes. "It's going to be weird listening to Fiorelli's lecture, knowing what we know."

"It's going to be fun." Eleanor gave an arch smile. "Let's get some good seats. I want to see this up close."

She led Dante and Charlie through the crowd milling around the auditorium doors. They opened, and she shepherded them expertly to three unoccupied chairs near the front of the hall.

Eleanor was reading Fiorelli's bio on the program when Avery slid into the seat next to her.

"Fancy meeting you here," he said.

"I couldn't miss the star act," said Eleanor.

"I hope," said Avery, "you're not planning a repeat of your performance during Lucier's lecture."

"Hmmm." Eleanor wanted to leave her options open on that front.

Avery checked his phone was off, then put an arm around the back of Eleanor's chair in order to look behind him. "It's a full house," he observed, facing forward again.

Eleanor felt the cool brush of his linen jacket against the back of her neck. He's a police officer, she reminded herself. Allegedly on holiday. An officer of the law who knows entirely too much about your alleged past. She concentrated on forming theories about their remaining two suspects.

The crowd hushed as Greg made his way onto the stage, flashing a winning smile.

"It's a rare honour to have a scientist of Dr Fiorelli's calibre travel all the way here, and a true privilege to hear her keynote speech. Please join me in giving her a warm welcome!" Greg started the applause, which swelled in volume as the crowd joined in.

As it reached its peak, Fiorelli swept onto the stage, tall and elegant in a dark pinstriped pantsuit that exactly matched the shade of her glossy black hair.

"Grazie, grazie." She stepped behind the podium and adjusted the mic. "It is truly my honour. Today, I will be sharing my groundbreaking research into reviving an orchid that we all believed lost forever."

A dramatic pause greeted this statement.

"I come from a long line of botanists." Fiorelli's red lipstick shone under the bright stage lights as she tapped long fingernails on the podium. "We understand the importance of genealogy, of legacy, of original species."

"I am also a scientist. For many years, I have worked with botanical institutions to create stunning hybrids. It is delicate work, and we have achieved amazing results."

Eleanor smiled wryly, knowing Fiorelli's true views on hybrids. She couldn't fault the lady on the smoothness of her lies.

"However, my greatest passion," said Fiorelli, "has always been our history. For example, the famous botanist, Giulio Albarelli, ended his final expedition in a shipwreck just a few miles from our gathering today.

"Albarelli was returning home with a specimen of the Ghost Queen, the rarest orchid of the Americas, now extinct for over one hundred and fifty years. He failed in that mission. But soon, I will complete this impossible task. I will succeed and bring the Ghost Queen back to life!"

An excited chorus of 'oohs' and 'ahs' greeted this statement. Something made Eleanor glance down the rows of spectators to her left. There, five seats along, was Marcel Lucier, his face set in an impassive mask as he listened to Fiorelli. She resisted the urge to cross her arms against a sudden chill.

"In my labs, we have made a technical breakthrough. With our proprietary tech, we have sequenced the Ghost Queen DNA from a fossil in the Fairfax Estate collection. With this, we will bring back to life one of the rarest, most beautiful and unique orchids known to humanity."

"And bringing this orchid back is only the beginning." Fiorelli abandoned the podium and strode across the stage, her fluid movements unhindered by the six-inch stilettos of her glossy black pumps.

"Albarelli was working on a new classification system, one that would tie together all the orchid species in a perfect hierarchy. It will be a return to the classical order, and will set the original orchids, the prime species, in their proper place."

"All hail the new world order," murmured Eleanor, and Avery frowned.

"Our launch date is not here yet." Fiorelli raised her hands to quell the sudden swell of applause. "But it is soon. With help from our investors," she nodded towards an invisible audience, "I will bring to life the Ghost Queen, and change the face of the orchid world."

Fiorelli paused and waited for the excited applause to die down. She stood there, poised and statuesque, looking more fashion icon than scientist. Eleanor could already see the press conferences, the magazine covers, the mainstream fame that awaited Fiorelli. It was a compelling vision.

Fiorelli continued to speak of order, purity, and placing every plant in a rigid hierarchy. Eleanor remembered the curling wildness of the drawings in the notebook they'd found and wondered how that squared with Fiorelli's concept of Albarelli.

She came out of her reverie to hear thunderous applause and to feel Avery's eyes on her. She turned, raising a questioning eyebrow at him.

"You were a million miles away," he murmured. "I had no idea you found orchids this riveting."

On stage, Fiorelli bestowed a glamorous smile upon the audience. "Grazie, all. It has been a pleasure."

"Dr Fiorelli will be in the foyer in five minutes to sign books," announced Greg, springing on stage. "I hope you've all brought your copies of *'The Definitive Guide to Orchid Collecting'* to be signed. If not, you can purchase your very own copy at the table to the right of the signing desk."

"You must have brought yours along," said Eleanor. "What an opportunity!"

"I have, actually," said Avery. "And I fully intend to get it signed. Perhaps you'd join me in the signing queue? It's the perfect cover to ask your leading questions."

"An excellent idea," said Eleanor.

"One I'm sure I'm going to regret," said Avery. He offered his arm to Eleanor, and they stood as the crowd flowed towards the back of the auditorium.

Avery and Eleanor waited in the line of orchidists, many of whom had Fiorelli's book clutched under one arm.

"Imagine a convention of art forgers," murmured Eleanor.

"Would you be the expert sitting at the table, ready to sign people's books?" asked Avery.

Eleanor snorted. "As if I'd sign my own name on anything. I could sign yours, though."

Avery mock grimaced. "Perish the thought."

Several minutes ticked by, until there was just one person in front of them. It seemed Fiorelli was a brisk and efficient book signer.

"Can you please stop looking so intelligent and inspector-ly?" murmured Eleanor in Avery's ear.

"Inspectorly?" asked Avery.

"You know what I mean."

"Intelligent?" Avery smiled faintly.

"Just... can you stop looking like you're building a profile on everyone you meet? I want Fiorelli to be relaxed, and it's hard to do with you being all on-the-job-ish."

The last signee in front of them left, and Eleanor took Avery's arm as they stepped up to the table. She put on her best limpid smile as Avery placed the book on the table in front of Fiorelli.

"Inspector," said Fiorelli. "What a pleasure. And your charming companion... Eleanor."

Her smile was like a picture of a fire — attractive, but with no warmth.

"It's an honour," said Avery gravely.

"Darling." Eleanor clutched Avery's arm. "This is such a thoughtful gift. Orchids are the floral symbols of love, are they not?"

"Actually, they're symbols of virility," murmured Avery.

Fiorelli's smile became sardonic as she opened the book to the title page and dipped her fountain pen in the inkwell. "What would you like me to write as an inscription?"

Eleanor lowered her eyelashes and spoke before Avery could. "Please put: 'to my dearest Eleanor. Partner in fighting crime... and so much more.'"

A single drop of black ink fell on the paper, unnoticed, as Fiorelli's eyes bored into Eleanor's.

"I see," Fiorelli said at last. "How...romantic."

Eleanor gave her an insufferably smug smile. “Isn’t it, though? Just like Nick and Nora.”

“That must be some Americanism I do not understand." Fiorelli scrawled her signature on the page, the pen going straight through the ink droplet to leave a jagged black line running through the signature. “Enjoy the Symposium.”

“Thank you,” said Avery, taking the book back. He blew on it lightly to dry the ink, then whirled Eleanor away, his grip on her arm a little tighter than necessary as he guided her to a quiet corner of the foyer.

“Was that wise?” he demanded as they reached their destination.

“Probably not, but it served a purpose,” said Eleanor absently. She was thinking about shipwrecks and baited traps. “What?” She asked as Avery continued to stare at her.

“You agreed with me. Are you ill?”

“I’m allowed to agree with you once every seven exchanges,” said Eleanor.

“Seems a high ratio. What do you intend to do with the target you’ve just painted on your back? Or are you just making things up as you go along?”

“I have a plan, but it’s currently a work in progress,” said Eleanor. “Don’t question the process.”

“Going back to work is going to feel like a holiday. And don’t say anything about my ‘alleged holiday.’”

Eleanor gave him a sceptical look. “You look like a man on holiday. You dress like a man on holiday. But you don’t act like a man on holiday.” She raised her hands in placation. “Fine, fine. I’m sure this is how you normally spend your holidays.”

“Shadowing art thieves while they attempt to wreak havoc on innocent orchidists?”

“Alleged art thieves, darling.” Eleanor linked her arm through his. “Alleged — just like your holiday.”

44

In which Charlie makes a discovery.

Charlie unlocked the door of his family home. His mother had recently moved out of the house and into the manager's quarters at the Pepper Tree Hotel.

She'd said she wanted to give him space, but Charlie couldn't help feeling that maybe she also wanted space. It was fair enough. Charlie and his ghosts could take up a lot of room.

Charlie vented a deep sigh. He'd left after Fiorelli's lecture to get ready for the ball. The house felt cold and lonely, and he wished now he'd asked Stephanie to...what? He wasn't even sure.

In his kitchen, the ghost moth roosted in the coffee plant next to the fridge. Charlie felt a pang of guilt. The moth's wings, which had been a brilliant green when it first arrived, were ragged. It stared at him, its eyes faceted black mirrors, and climbed onto his hand when Charlie held it out.

He felt the tiny hooks on its slender feet and the feathery soft stirring of its wings.

"I'm sorry," he whispered. "I'm working on it. We all are. But there's only one night left in the Symposium, and we still have two suspects." Charlie raised his hand, and the moth climbed onto his shoulder.

He bent down to retrieve the case that held Carroll's notebook. Eleanor had given it back to him that afternoon. She seemed to think he'd have better luck discovering its hidden message.

He opened the case and stared at the small notebook as it sat on its foam-padded bed, looking stubbornly secretive. What did Professor Carroll want him to find?

Charlie pulled on a pair of newly bought cotton gardening gloves and leafed through the book. There didn't seem to be any clue, cypher, or any other helpful pointers hidden in its pages.

"Maybe you're a dead end after all." He let the book fall shut and glared at it. The moth brushed against his neck, and his shoulder twitched, making the notebook pages splay out a little.

"Whoa!" Charlie gave an excited yelp. He seized the book in both hands, manipulating the covers so that the page edges fanned out like a deck of cards. "That's it!"

Across the fanned paper edges, faint lines linked together to form a map. A delicate secret drawing, visible only when the pages were angled just so. There, right in the upper corner of the map, was a red 'X.'

Charlie changed his grip, and the map disappeared into the paper grain as the pages shifted back to their normal position. He pressed the spine on a diagonal, and the drawing slid back into view, clear as day. Studying it, Charlie realised he knew the place the mapmaker had drawn.

"X marks the spot," breathed Charlie. A wide grin broke across his face. "It's only ten minutes from Carroll's house. Did you know about this?" he asked the moth.

In reply, the moth said absolutely nothing.

Charlie picked up his phone and called Eleanor.

The conversation was brief - they'd meet at Dante's place, and then go straight to the map location. He rang off and abandoned his smart dress shoes to don hiking boots.

"It's only an hour till sunset," Charlie told the moth. "Probably best to find Carroll's secret hiding place in the daytime. Do you want to come?"

The moth made no reply, but neither did it flutter off its perch on his shoulder when he made to leave the house. Charlie didn't object. Perhaps it was lonely. And it was dying. He didn't have the heart to leave it behind.

With the moth on his shoulder, he stepped onto the footpath that led to Dante's.

The hedgerows and picket fences that lined the street cast long evening shadows across his path.

It was strange, he thought, that everything in town seemed so peaceful. No one would guess that he and his friends were in a race against time to solve a murder and uncover a hidden treasure.

Perhaps there were other secret goings-on in Te Kohe of which he was blissfully ignorant. The idea lifted his spirits as he walked past sleepy front gardens and neatly trimmed hedges. At last, they were off to find a treasure.

45

In which the sleuths reach their destination.

Charlie walked through the bush, following Dante as best he could. The ex-assassin moved through the forest unlike anyone he'd ever seen. He moved with such economy, Charlie found it hard to believe Dante hadn't travelled this path a hundred times before.

Charlie turned to check on Eleanor's progress. Around them, the forest grew velvety with eventide. Shadows pooled under the thick tree canopy, waiting to spread out as night fell.

"We're nearly there," Charlie called softly.

Up ahead, a cliff rose, visible between the trees. The sound of flowing water caught Charlie's ears — they had reached the Waimaru River. He and Eleanor caught up with Dante at the base of the cliff.

"This is it?" asked Eleanor, a little out of breath. "X marks the spot?"

"I think it's there." Dante pointed.

Fifty feet away, the shallow bowl of a cave was carved into the limestone cliff.

Excitement surging, Charlie followed Dante to its mouth. The cave entry opened into an amphitheatre hollowed out of the rock. It reminded Charlie of the deep labellum of a lady's slipper orchid. Or the trap of a pitcher plant. He shivered and hoped it wasn't a premonition of danger.

At the back of the cave, the Waimaru stream flowed out of the grey rock face, a sparkling stream of water that had found its way through the limestone. The small fissure from which it issued was rich with thick green moss and tiny ferns.

"This is the spot." Charlie checked the photo he'd taken of Carroll's map. "But I don't see Albarelli's journals, or a Ghost Queen. You don't think Lucier, Fiorelli, or Fairfax could have gotten here first?"

"I like to think we would've noticed a marked increase in smugness in one of that trio," said Eleanor. "Also, how could they have known where to go?"

Dante paced around the edge of the rock wall. The bottom of the cave was coarse grey sand, stippled with water droplets falling from the rock ceiling fifty feet above them. "There are no fresh footprints. And no evidence of anyone erasing footprints. No one has been here since the last rain."

"Let's continue on the premise that our murderer hasn't found this spot," said Eleanor, "and search for Carroll's treasure."

Charlie scanned the grey rock walls, his heart sinking. "I don't see anything. If it's Albarelli's journals, maybe they're buried in an airtight container."

"It's possible," said Eleanor.

"I can get underground scanning equipment," said Dante. "But not for a week or so."

Charlie did another sweep of the cave. Nothing but bare rock, moss, and ferns. "Do you think it's at the top of the cliff?"

Dante stalked outside the cave and gazed up at the sheer cliff wall. "I can bring climbing gear. Next time."

"I was hoping we'd find a Ghost Queen," said Charlie. "A rare, believed-to-be-extinct orchid, hidden for nearly two centuries."

Eleanor sighed. "It's the stuff collectors' dreams are made of. I can almost feel the orchidelirium setting in." She grinned wryly. "I'm joking, Charlie. But I think we're running out of time to find anything today."

The sun's rays turned deep amber as it dipped close to the horizon, illuminating the back wall of the cave. Soon, it would be gone.

"Carroll must have hidden it really well," said Charlie. "If it exists at all."

"We don't need to find Carroll's treasure to catch the killer," said Eleanor. "We just need them to think we know what they did, and that they can stop us from proving it."

"You want to set a trap here?" Dante looked around the cave's grey walls.

"I think we could set an 'in the event of an emergency break glass' trap," said Eleanor. "You have surveillance gear, Dante?"

Dante shrugged. "Enough for a decent stakeout."

"Do you think..." Eleanor paused in thought. "Could you come back here straight away and set up a couple of cameras? And a floodlight? This is just a backup. Because our trap at the ball could settle the question of who our murderer is before it's time for dessert."

"Really?" Charlie perked up with renewed hope.

"Only if nothing goes wrong," said Eleanor drily. "That's far from a given."

"Ok," said Dante.

Charlie gave the cave a last, longing look as they left. Unexpectedly, the ghost moth fluttered from his shoulder to settle on the cave wall. Doubt filled him. Had the ghost moth given up on his quest? Or did it want them to keep looking?

"Don't worry, Charlie," said Eleanor. "We'll be back tomorrow to find Carroll's legacy. But this is our last chance to uncover his murderer."

Alright," sighed Charlie. "I'm coming."

46

In which Eleanor remembers rule number one.

Eleanor swirled a black shawl shot through with silver thread around her shoulders. She ran her mind over the plan for the coming evening, then stopped herself.

Right now, it was time to relax and get ready for the masque ball. No point getting worked up before the main event.

There was a knock at the door, and she checked the security camera on her phone. Avery was standing on her porch in a dark suit and fedora.

Her spirits gave a small lift. Either Avery had some important news, or he was here for a pre-event drink. Either possibility was pleasant.

Eleanor opened the door with a smile and gestured for Avery to enter. "Come on in."

"Thank you." Avery followed down the corridor to the open-plan living and dining area at the back. "Place looks nice."

"It's the same as last time you were here," said Eleanor, "when we were searching for evidence of money laundering. Fun times."

"Yes," said Avery, and this time Eleanor noticed how sombre he looked.

Her brows drew together. "Has someone died?"

"What? No!" Avery leaned on the kitchen counter, meeting her eyes. "I have the results of the postmortem."

"The one you've been denying you can get this whole time? Marcus, I'm impressed with your duplicity. Some wine to celebrate?"

Avery rubbed his forehead. "Eleanor, please be serious and listen."

"Very well." Eleanor set a wineglass down on the counter next to a bottle of New Zealand chardonnay. "The coroner found evidence of digitalis poisoning."

"Correct," said Avery, his voice heavy. "The postmortem was a favour I called in. Not official, but not exactly unofficial either. But now that the findings are confirmed, it has rapidly become official. And as the senior officer here with boots on the ground, I am on the case. Which means..."

Eleanor's smile didn't fade. Instead, it changed in tenor from bright and welcoming to ironic. "That you've once again donned the mantle of a staid officer of the law. That's fine by me." She tugged on a drawer that slid open with Swedish engineered precision. Taking time to gather her thoughts, she selected a corkscrew.

"No, I don't mean to say—" Avery paused and took in Eleanor's changed stance. He straightened, becoming formal. "It's been a pleasure working with you, but I need you to stop investigating Carroll's murder."

"Now that the grownups are here to handle things, it's time for the kids to pack up their toys and go home. It was fun while it lasted, and now it's over." With an expert twist, Eleanor popped the wine cork and poured herself a serving of pale wine. Her eyes never leaving his, she took a sip.

"It's not like that," growled Avery. "I don't at all regard you as... as... whatever it was you were insinuating."

Eleanor swirled her glass of wine. "We're from different sides of the tracks, Avery." Her tone was cool as autumn rain. "It's probably just as well we're ending things now, before they get any messier."

"I was Marcus a minute ago," said Avery.

"We'll always have Paris." Eleanor raised her glass in mock salute.

"That's it? You're just going to walk away?" Avery didn't bother hiding his disbelief.

"You are no longer privy to my decisions. What are you after, my permission?"

"I don't even know," muttered Avery.

"Well, have a wonderful time doing your police work, as per the manual. I have a ball to prepare for. Would you like a glass of wine before you go?"

"I think I'll just go." Avery jammed his fedora onto his head and strode out. The door didn't slam, but it was closed more firmly than necessary.

Eleanor finished her glass of wine, her coolly ironic smile fixed in place. She did her hair and then spent twenty minutes applying her makeup. Even though it would be hidden behind her mask, details mattered. It was only when she fastened the mask in place to check the fit that her shoulders slumped.

It was never a good idea to get attached to people who ultimately wanted to put you and your kind in jail. Even if they looked good in a fedora, and danced the tango very well. It almost always ended like this. And when it didn't, the results could be far worse.

"I wonder," she murmured to herself, "where you got that fedora, Avery?" There were several possibilities, and only one boded well for their investigation.

47

In which party preparations are disrupted.

A few streets over, Charlie was helping Dante with the novel task of donning fancy dress.

"The headscarf sits over your ears," said Charlie. "Like this."

Dante controlled his instincts and held still while Charlie adjusted his head wrapping.

"Better." Charlie grinned. "You're looking sharp."

They were standing in Dante's kitchen, trying on their costumes while the kettle boiled in the background. Behind them on the floor, the cat was lying in flagrante, its white belly showing as it wrestled with one of Charlie's secondhand store gloves.

It had already torn the top off one finger and was working on the thumb. The cat was clearly in heaven, and Dante wasn't sure he had the heart to stop it.

"There are just a few more items," said Charlie, "and we're done."

"I'm not sure I'm a dress-up person," said Dante.

"You never know until you try." Charlie turned to pick up some kohl, and his gaze fell on the cat. He frowned, narrowing his eyes.

"What is it?" Dante came on alert. This was Charlie's looking at ghosts face. In Dante's experience, it meant trouble.

"Dante, it's your cat. If we don't do something soon, it's going to lose a life."

"What do you mean?" Dante's chest went cold.

"It's..." Charlie darted forward and gently tugged the glove out of the cat's mouth. The cat seized his hand instead, its claws wrapping around his fingers. "Ouch! Can you take this?" Charlie passed the gnawed glove up to Dante. "Something's made the cat sick."

Dante studied the glove. It was olive green suede, and dark with cat saliva. But on the tip of one unchewed finger, a faint residue of white powder remained.

"These are from the second-hand shop, right?" Dante heard his voice coming from far away.

"They were in the glove bin without a price tag, remember?" Charlie held the cat gently, staring at the glove. "I was going to give them to Stephanie, but forgot all about them. Until now..."

"These belong to the poisoner," said Dante.

"Oh." Charlie's eyes were wide. "Do you think the op shop people will remember who dropped them in?"

"I doubt it. Pass it here." Dante studied the glove, his focus absolute. "I've seen this before."

"Where?"

Dante's mind cast back to a warm, damp greenhouse, and the roots of an orchid being gently pulled apart.

"This belongs to Fiorelli." Dante's voice was deathly calm. He carefully took the cat out of Charlie's arms. It blinked up at him, glassy-eyed. "Call Andrea now."

"Right! Yes!" Charlie yanked his phone out of his pocket. "We know what the poison is, so she'll be able to help. I hope." He gave the cat one of his vague stares as he waited for Andrea to pick up the call. "Your cat's still on its seventh life. Hang in there."

The seconds seemed to stretch out into eternity as Dante waited. On the fifth ring, someone picked up.

"Thank god! It's Charlie. I'm sorry it's so late. Dante's cat has eaten poison. We think it's digitalis. Yes. Ok. Right away." He cut the call. "We need to meet Andrea at her vet clinic. There's medicine there that might help — if we're in time."

Dante was already moving down the hallway, cat cradled in his arms. It gave a fretful meow.

"If my cat dies, I'm going to kill her," said Dante.

"We'll be in time." Charlie rushed ahead to open the front door. His phone buzzed, but he ignored it. "Do you want me to drive?"

"Yes," said Dante.

"It'll be alright," insisted Charlie. He pushed open the garage door and hopped into the driver's seat of the Buick, taking the keys Dante handed him. "It's going to be ok."

"No," said Dante. "It isn't."

48

In which traps are set.

Eleanor entered the ballroom, appreciating the effort everyone had gone to. The hardworking volunteers had managed to transport the main gallery of the Bughouse back to the 1930s.

A live band played swing jazz, and crimson velvet fabric draped artistically on the walls, giving the space a soft, glamorous look. Someone had raided their grandmother's house for period lamps and side tables, and strings of tiny golden lights spangled the ceiling, transporting the ballroom into the Gilded Age.

The old place certainly cleaned up well.

The crowd had turned out, too. She was pleased to see they'd risen to the occasion, with sequins, feathers, and silk making the assembled throng sparkle.

She skirted the dance floor, wondering if she could fit in a dance or two before sighting her quarry. But there, near the bar, was a circle of guests she recognised.

Her friend Bernard was there, his walrus moustache bushing out beneath his eye mask. Marjorie Everton was easily recognisable by the flowing green silk gown she wore — a repeat of her opening night outfit. And there was Fiorelli. She wore a scarlet feathered half-mask; her distinctive cupid's bow lips clearly visible beneath it.

"Bernard." Eleanor laid one hand lightly on his shoulder. "Wonderful costume, darling. What an evening."

"Quite," harrumphed Bernard. "Good to see everyone turned out in their glad rags."

"Tell me," said Eleanor, "have you seen Inspector Avery around tonight?"

"I ran into him a few minutes ago. He's here somewhere."

"Excellent." Eleanor shot him a conspiratorial glance. "I... if you see him, tell him I've found it."

"Found what?" asked Bernard.

Across the circle of guests, Fiorelli's eyes narrowed behind their scarlet mask as she listened to the exchange.

"The thing we've been looking for." Eleanor channelled Marjorie Everton and flushed with smug self-importance. "The proof. Tell him it's definitive. We can absolutely get a fingerprint from under the label. Can you do that for me? I'm going to find a key to secure the powder room, but Avery can go see it..." she trailed off, as if reconsidering what she was about to say. "Never mind. Just tell him, ok?"

"I certainly can," said Bernard. "Though it's a touch cloak and dagger, m'dear."

"You know me. Lots of cloak. Very little dagger." Eleanor's eyes flicked across the room to where Fairfax was keeping several female orchidists entertained. "Avery will want to know about this now."

"If you think it's so urgent, I'll keep an eye out," said Bernard.

"Wonderful, darling. I know I can rely on you. This is simply thrilling, I must say." Eleanor turned to find Fairfax standing behind her, drink in hand, a slight smile on his face.

He raised his glass in salute, and Eleanor curtsied in return, her smile hiding a stir of discomfort. She told herself sternly to focus.

The first bait was set. Now it was time to cast a lure in Lucier's direction.

A few minutes later, Eleanor waltzed across the dance floor with Marcel Lucier. For a time, she simply danced, enjoying the pull and sway of the music. As she'd imagined, Lucier was an excellent dancer. Almost as good as a certain staid police officer of her acquaintance.

She mentally squared her shoulders. Time to get to work.

"You said that orchids are masters of deception," she murmured. "I suspect you are too."

"A strange accusation to level at your dance partner," said Lucier, spinning her out of the path of an approaching dancer. "To what do you refer?"

"You appear to be here for this conference, and those other dealings about which I've heard so many dark rumours," said Eleanor. "But in truth, your purpose is quite different."

Lucier looked amused. "Am I supposed to 'spill the beans' as they say? A little innuendo, a veiled accusation, and I'm meant to come clean?"

"Not at all. How dreadfully boring."

"You're fishing. You're not even sure what fish you expect to bite."

Eleanor inclined her head, smiling faintly. "I'm looking for Carroll's murderer, and I suspect... everyone."

Lucier led her through a complicated turn. "Surely you've narrowed down the suspects by now. Am I on your shortlist?"

"I'm hardly going to tell you that." Eleanor's eyes narrowed as she spied someone over Lucier's shoulder. A few seconds later, Lucier swirled her around. His face gave nothing away as he saw Fairfax waltz by, an ecstatic orchidist in his expert embrace.

The song ended, and Eleanor said she wanted to sit out the next dance, saving her feet for a long night. Lucier escorted her to the bar.

Eleanor retrieved her handbag from the barman and checked her phone. Her eyebrows drew down.

"Excuse me one moment," she told Lucier. "I must reply to this."

She dialled the imaginary number, then glanced over her shoulder. The barman passed Lucier his fedora, followed by a drink which Lucier sipped with evident enjoyment. He was distant enough to give the illusion of privacy, but close enough to overhear. Perfect.

"Yes?" she said into the phone, ducking down as if the call was hard to hear. "The what?" Now, a keyword to draw a murderer's attention. "That's right, Digitalis. What's that? Yes, a fingerprint. No, he doesn't." She put one finger over her other ear as if to block out the ambient noise. That would make her speaking louder more believable. "The cloakroom. No, not that one. The one out back. Half an hour? Ok."

She dropped her phone back into her handbag and straightened. Lucier, drink in hand, faced away from her as if only interested in the people waltzing by.

That was fun, thought Eleanor. A memory rose of reading *'The Famous Five'* as a child. All those conveniently overhead conversations — did the industrious five detectives ever consider the robbers were setting them up?

"Another dance?" she asked Lucier. "I'm feeling quite recovered."

"I'm sorry. I have to pass. Duty calls." With that ambiguous statement, Lucier slipped away into the crowd.

Her two hooks baited, Eleanor smiled and ordered a Drambuie on ice. All she had to do now was wait for a fish to bite.

She became aware, with a little prickle down her neck, that she was being watched with some intensity. She swivelled on her bar stool, searching for the source of the regard. Her gaze found Fairfax on the other side of the bar.

He was murmuring in Fiorelli's ear as they both stared at her. Eleanor did not like the look on Fiorelli's face — eyes alight, lips parted in a smile that glittered with triumph. In contrast, Fairfax's demeanour was cool, his mouth set in a firm line.

Eleanor gave them an absent-minded wave and reached for her drink. Her face was smooth, but her stomach churned.

Something had gone wrong; she could feel it. Fairfax had told Fiorelli something to make her both malicious and elated. What did he know?

49

In which best-laid plans are put to the test.

The moon had set, and the countless stars of the Milky Way illuminated the night. The pet shop / outdoor store / veterinary clinic was a dark silhouette against the starry sky.

Dante contemplated breaking in before Andrea arrived. Perhaps he could find the right medication in time.

The cat dug its claws into his hand.

“It’s going to be alright,” Dante told it. He had never said that to anyone before, especially not someone recently poisoned. He wondered why he was saying it now. “I’ll kill Fiorelli as soon as you’re better.”

“Here she comes,” said Charlie, relief in his voice. He waved at the oncoming headlights.

Andrea pulled up to the kerb and jumped out. She was wearing a battered pink dressing gown over blue silk pyjamas, her curls squashed down on one side.

“How long has it been since your cat ingested the poison?” she asked as she fumbled the key in the front door lock.

"We don't know," said Charlie. "Dante, please don't break down the door."

With a twist, Andrea opened the lock, and they all tumbled inside. She flicked the lights on, keyed off the alarm, and led them into the back room.

"You think it's digitalis?" she said. "That's unusual."

"We're pretty sure," said Charlie.

"Put your cat on the table." Andrea did a quick examination, running her hands over the cat's body, checking its eyes, and feeling the rapid heartbeat in its narrow chest.

"I'm going to administer a medication that will make your cat throw up," she said. "A lot. If we're lucky, we'll have caught the poison in time. I don't have a digitalis antidote, so this is our best shot."

Dante forced his hold on the cat to remain calm. He could feel his murderous impulses like a ticking clock inside him, ready to explode at the right signal.

The code was one thing, his cat was another. If his cat died, the code could go to hell, along with the poisoner. The seconds ticked by, and Dante waited.

Eleanor retreated to the darkest corner at the end of the bar. She sipped her Drambuie and retrieved her phone from her clutch.

She dialled Charlie's number. No reply. She tried again. Still nothing.

Not ideal.

Eleanor schooled her face to a calm repose and opened the app Dante had installed on her phone.

A split screen came into view: two video feeds, two baited traps — the forked snare to separate the innocent from the guilty.

The first feed showed the powder room with its unlocked door. There were numerous tonics and bottles there - leftovers from the last production of the Te Kohe Amateur Theatrical Society. Staged among them was the bottle of digitalis with its forged label and mythical fingerprint.

The second feed showed the interior of the small cloakroom. She'd made a copy of the digitalis bottle for this scene — a forgery of a forgery. It was in keeping with this case, where no one was who they appeared to be.

Eleanor drummed her fingers on the bar. Her money was on Lucier, but she was rather hoping it would be Fiorelli. Something about the woman jarred her, a reminder of someone she didn't like.

She sipped the liqueur, savouring the flavours of her favourite Scottish distillery. Watching the action on screen wasn't as fun as seeing a con play out in person, but it was close.

Eleanor wondered again where on earth Charlie and Dante had gotten to. They were each meant to watch the approach to the two rooms. But Charlie wasn't picking up his phone, and Dante didn't have one.

She tapped a staccato rhythm on her knee. It was not best practice to set a trap without backup, but waiting for Charlie and Dante was not an option. After all, Eleanor didn't know how long Lucier and Fiorelli would remain at the ball, and they were officially out of time to solve the murder.

She scanned the ballroom — Lucier and Fiorelli were both missing. Of course, it was hard to locate anyone in this glittering crowd, but still... Eleanor focused on the split screen again. A tingle crept down her spine. Her sixth sense told her they were about to discover their murderer.

The door of the powder room creaked open.

The camera feed went black.

"Clever," whispered Eleanor. "So very clever. Well played."

The camera was still running — Eleanor could see the little red timer counting away in the top corner of her screen. Someone had opened the door. Suspicions on high alert, they'd seen the digitalis bottle, and then switched off the light to make the grab.

But who was it? Fairfax? Fiorelli? Lucier only knew about the bottle in the cloakroom, and that camera feed showed an empty room.

Eleanor took a moment to appreciate the wreck of their plan. The fish had removed the bait and left the hook dangling.

Charlie had told her that Fairfax had seen them setting up in the powder room. Had he guessed their plan and warned Fiorelli? Was this his play to get a piece of the Ghost Queen treasure? Or was he the murderer?

In the back of her mind, her old friend and mentor Ariadne gave an earthy chuckle. 'Rule two of the grift, my sweet: when things fall apart (and they will,) don't stop. If you fall, turn it into a dive.'

She dialled Charlie's number.

"Hi, Eleanor?" said Charlie.

Eleanor resisted the urge to yell, 'Why didn't you pick up the last five times I called?' It would have been unproductive. "We have a problem," she said instead.

"Same here," said Charlie.

50

In which Dante clears up several misunderstandings.

With expert hands, Andrea deposited a few drops of medicine into the cat's mouth.

The cat snapped its jaws shut and glared at her.

"Shh, shh." Andrea stroked the cat's head. She looked up at Dante's expressionless face, then down at the cat. "This'll help. Even though your cat will feel like hell for a while." She fetched a fresh towel and lined the inside of a box. "Things are going to get messy, fast. You might want to put your cat in here."

Dante's hands tightened over the cat.

Andrea's face softened. "I wouldn't normally give this medicine to a cat in this condition, but we don't have much time. If we're lucky, she'll pull through just fine."

"She?" Dante frowned.

"Your cat is a she," said Andrea carefully.

"She is?"

"And she's not fat. She's pregnant."

"Pregnant?" Dante felt his face freeze. "She's pregnant?"

"Yes." Andrea frowned, concerned. "If we got in early enough, her kittens will be ok too."

"Kittens?" Dante knew he shouldn't just be repeating Andrea's words, but his mind had gone blank — a pure arctic whiteness, like a snowstorm.

"She's looking better already," said Charlie.

The cat, with an elegant sense of occasion, threw up on Dante's lap.

"I'm going to kill her," said Dante.

"Who?" asked Andrea.

"The poisoner." Dante held the cat as she retched.

"This is a good sign — she's getting it out of her system," said Andrea. "I'll give her the reversal agent in about twenty minutes. I'd also like to keep her in the clinic overnight to monitor her."

"She hasn't lost her seventh life," murmured Charlie in Dante's ear. "That's a good sign. But I've just talked to Eleanor, and there's a problem —" His phone buzzed, and he frowned. "It's a message from Stephanie. She says she's at the ball."

"She's not wearing her jacket," said Dante. "So I can't verify her location."

"Stephanie?" The soft look on Andrea's face disappeared.

"She's helping us with some stuff," said Charlie.

"She is?" Andrea turned away to put the medicine back on its shelf.

"Er, Dante, I'd better go see what's going on." Charlie's voice vanished out the door.

Andrea whirled around to face Dante. "Why would you have Stephanie's jacket?"

"I don't," said Dante. "It's complicated."

"Explain."

"I'm trying to keep track of her," said Dante. "She's dangerous, and I don't trust her."

"You mean..." said Andrea slowly, "you don't like her?"

Dante looked at her. "Like her?"

Andrea gave a breathless half-laugh. "Let me see. She's young, fit, single, gorgeous..."

Dante stared at Andrea. It was just as Eleanor had said. "Gorgeous?"

"She is, Dante. You didn't notice?"

"I was suspicious of her," said Dante. "And it turns out I was right."

"You were..." Andrea fell silent, lips slightly parted. "You don't like her." This time, it was a statement.

Dante stroked the cat gently as it puked industriously over his shoes. "I like you," he offered.

Andrea tried and failed to suppress a radiant smile. "Why didn't you say so?"

"I did."

"Yes, but..." Andrea's smile widened, and she shook her head. "Dante, I like you too."

Dante blew out a breath. "That's good. I'd like to kiss you, but right now, my hands are covered in cat vomit."

"I think..." Andrea folded her arms and leaned against the bench to regard Dante. "I think you are one of a kind, Dante. And I would like to get to know you better."

"There are a lot of things I can't tell you," said Dante. "About me."

Andrea looked thoughtful. "I can see that."

"If you promise not to ask too much, I promise to only tell you the truth."

"Deal."

Andrea stuck out one hand, and after wiping his hand carefully on his trousers, Dante shook it.

The cat took a rest from retching to glare balefully at them both. Even though it contained more cat vomit than he would have liked, for Dante, it was a perfect moment.

51

In which the tangled web tightens.

Eleanor cut the call, her head buzzing. So Fiorelli was the murderer, proven on two counts: the raided powder room and the poisoned glove.

She remembered the olive green gloves from Marjorie's tea party. But a glove that had been handled by several people and chewed by a cat was not compelling evidence. Neither was a blacked-out camera feed.

Dante was caring for his sick cat, and Charlie was making sure his friend didn't decide to take drastic action against Fiorelli. It was a wash, and Eleanor struggled to see how they could convict a murderer from this mess.

An idea flashed through her mind. It was a terrible idea, but the more she turned it over in her mind, the more it began to look like the only way forward. Before she could think better of it, Eleanor took out her phone and called Charlie.

"Hi Eleanor." Charlie sounded tense.

"Is the cat still ok?"

"I hope so. Still touch and go."

"I had a thought. I reckon we'll be able to find the Ghost Queen under the full moon."

"Really?"

"Yes — remember those stories? They only bloom by moonlight. Here's what I think we should do. You go there now, and I'll follow as soon as I'm able. We'll find the Ghost Queen, and with it, I'm pretty sure I can work out another trap to catch Fiorelli."

"You reckon?" Charlie was sounding hopeful again.

"Tell Dante to stay where he is. I'll come by the vet's and we'll catch you up."

"Ok. Will do. See you soon." Charlie rang off, sounding almost cheerful.

A few minutes later, Eleanor swirled the last of her drink. It was time to go. She looked for Fiorelli in the crowd and instead caught sight of Avery, bearing down on her with a thunderous scowl.

"We need to talk," said Avery, grabbing Eleanor's arm.

"Four words that never inspire confidence," said Eleanor.

"In there." Avery jerked his head towards the bathroom.

"You sure know how to show a lady a good time," said Eleanor. "Is it even legal for a policeman to enter a female changing room?"

Avery didn't smile. "Now, Eleanor."

The small bathroom interior appeared empty of people, although the last stall door was ajar, a tiny scrap of scarlet feathers poking above the door.

Avery dropped her arm and paced in front of the bathroom mirror, his movements choppy with suppressed emotion.

"It's over." Avery's face was hard. "I know what you've been hiding."

"Which is?" Eleanor folded her arms across her chest, her betraying heart beating faster.

"The cave with the Ghost Queen. Charlie decoded the notebook, and you've all been there."

"You seem well informed. Tell me, Avery, where did you get that fedora?"

Avery gave a mirthless smile. "This old thing?" He tilted it just a fraction, giving him a rakish air.

"Someone with a fedora left the hotel the night Carroll died and burgled his house. So I'm a little curious." Eleanor tried to sound breezy, but fear crept around the edges of her voice.

"Some of us would do anything to get a Ghost Queen." Avery's voice dropped low and dangerous. "Some of us would risk everything."

"What exactly do you mean?" Eleanor clenched her hands into fists as Avery loomed over her.

"Where is the cave, Eleanor?"

Eleanor shook her head. "I can't tell you."

Avery stepped back. Like magic, he gripped a Glock 17 in his hand. "Tell me."

Eleanor froze, her eyes going wide.

"Do not test me." Avery's knuckles whitened around the pistol grip.

"You're too late," said Eleanor. "Charlie's already there. He'll find the Ghost Queen and be safely out before you can even get there."

"I think not. Give me your bag."

Reluctantly, Eleanor held it out. Avery took it and shook it upside down. The contents spilled across the floor, and her handgun skittered away into a dark corner. "I can easily book you for carrying a pistol around like that, but I've more important matters to attend to." He bent and picked up the notebook. "You're so predictable. I knew you'd bring this along. Tell me its secret."

"You can't just shoot me. You'll never get away with it," said Eleanor.

"Think again. I know of half a dozen ways to pin this on your friend with all the weaponry."

"Policemen," spat Eleanor. "You're the same, the world over."

"The location of the cave, Eleanor. To save your sorry skin."

Eleanor's shoulders tensed, and then she slumped, defeated. "You close the book and angle the spine, then a map appears on the page edges."

"That wasn't so hard, was it?" Avery stepped back and whistled as the map came into view. "Amazing. It's just ten minutes away - where the Waimaru River comes out of the Tāpoko cliffs. So. I go get a Ghost Queen, and I'm afraid Charlie is not going to have a good night. If you try and follow me," he tipped his gun toward her, "it won't go well."

The door swung shut behind Avery's departing form.

"Bastard." Eleanor beat her hand against the wall. "Bastard, bastard, bastard!"

She snatched up her phone from the scattered contents of her bag and started to gather the other items, then gave up, hurrying for the exit.

"Charlie, pick up!" she muttered as she pushed the bathroom door open.

Eleanor stumbled through the crowded ballroom, her vision blurring as her emotions caught up with her. Lucier crossed her path, his eyebrows lowered in concern, but she waved him away with a half-formed excuse.

Things were spiralling out of control, and if Eleanor didn't get hold of Charlie soon, it could go very badly indeed.

52

In which life and death hang in the balance.

Charlie hurried down the forest path. He switched off his cellphone light, and after a few minutes, his night vision adjusted. Inky black shadows and splashes of moonlight covered the path, and the quiet murmurs of the river did nothing to soothe his nerves.

Eleanor was working on a new trap to catch Fiorelli, but time was running out fast. Charlie couldn't stop thinking of the ghost moth, waiting silently in the cave. To him, it seemed quietly hopeful that they would deliver the promised justice. He didn't feel nearly as confident.

A light flickered on the path behind him. He guessed it was Eleanor and Dante coming to help him search. The river grew louder, and he stepped out from the canopy of trees to see the water shimmering in the moonlight.

The cliffs reared up against the star-strewn sky, painted silver by the rising moon. The cave was a black hollow, like the maw of some immense and ancient creature.

Charlie drew in a deep breath. "For Professor Carroll," he said, and marched across the clearing to enter the cave.

Inside the cave, moonlight lit a jagged semicircle of ground. It also reflected off the river, dancing on the rock ceiling. Perhaps this light would reveal the orchid flower.

Charlie ignored the floodlight Dante had left here earlier and began a slow circle of the rock wall, looking for any trick of the light which might reveal the Ghost Queen's hiding place. He was engrossed in studying a large boulder when a blaze of light illuminated the cave.

"Hello?" Charlie squinted against the glare. He couldn't make out the dark figure behind the light, but its posture seemed familiar. "Eleanor?"

The figure set the light on a boulder, keeping it pointed at Charlie.

"Could you turn the light off?" asked Charlie. "I'm trying to do what you suggested and use moonlight to find the Ghost Queen."

"How interesting." The figure stepped into the light, and a wash of cold fright swept through Charlie.

It wasn't Eleanor. It was Fiorelli.

"How... you shouldn't be here." Charlie's mouth seemed to work without his brain's input.

Fiorelli shrugged. "I overheard an interesting conversation. After that, it was easy to work out where you were headed. Unfortunately, I am pressed for time. Your police inspector is on his way, and I do not want to be here when he arrives."

Charlie tried to think through his shock. Fiorelli had murdered once already. He doubted she would let him remove the Ghost Queen if he found it.

"So... the Ghost Queen." Fiorelli watched Charlie with the avid interest a cat might employ on seeing a small flightless bird.

"What Ghost Queen?" It wasn't a great rejoinder, but it was all Charlie's jangled nerves would let him come up with.

"You have discovered its whereabouts." Fiorelli studied him, then shook her head lightly. "No. You know it's here somewhere, but you do not know exactly where."

"I'm not looking for it while you're here."

"You will." Fiorelli raised her right hand. Nestled in it was a small, ivory-handled pistol, pointed at Charlie's chest.

Charlie's heart lurched. "I, uh..."

"I suggest you focus on remembering any hints your professor gave during his final months with you." Fiorelli's voice was silky. "Anything that might reveal where he hid this orchid prize. It is your only hope."

Two thoughts crowded into Charlie's panicked mind — the cameras Dante had installed, and that both Dante and Eleanor were on their way. At least he hoped they were on their way.

He just had to survive until they got here. But maybe if he were really clever, he could get Fiorelli to confess to murdering Carroll. On that count, his mind was as empty as the cave.

"Er... what do you mean, 'my only hope?'" he asked.

Fiorelli's fingers tightened on the pistol grip. "Start searching."

"Ok..." Charlie examined the closest stretch of cave wall. He tried desperately to think of something to say to buy time. "The Professor talked about ghost orchids and moonlight."

"I heard that theory from your friend." Fiorelli sneered over the last word. "I want to know how your 'Professor' protected the things most valuable to him. How he guarded his treasures."

"I... er... Didn't he tell you anything when you had tea together? I heard you talked about ghost orchids."

Fiorelli sniffed. "He did not want to discuss them. He said he could only say more once he'd gotten to know me."

"He didn't trust you." With a wrench, Charlie abandoned his natural good manners. It was tough, but he felt the desperate situation warranted it. "He probably didn't think you were worthy."

Fiorelli's eyes narrowed. "Carroll was a backyard dabbler with zero degrees to his name. Who was he to judge my worthiness?"

Charlie felt himself becoming angry. It didn't happen often, but when it did, he tended to a smouldering slow burn. "Who was he? Carroll was the guardian who kept the Ghost Queen safe from unprincipled thieves."

"The Ghost Queen is my birthright," Fiorelli hissed.

"You killed him, and you still don't have it." The words echoed in the silence.

Charlie's gaze locked with Fiorelli's. Neither of them blinked.

A slow, wicked smile curved Fiorelli's perfect lips. "Che uomo impossibile. Here you are, my gun trained on you, and still you argue. Va bene — I poisoned the old fool with his own tea. And I will kill you too unless you get me what I want."

"That isn't your gun. It's Eleanor's." Part of Charlie was telling him frantically to back down and look for a way out. But the larger part (for now) wanted to fight.

Fiorelli had come to his town and killed his friend. She had been a guest in Carroll's house. Charlie couldn't even begin to describe how wrong that was.

"And with your friend's gun, I will put a bullet straight through your heart." Fiorelli waved the pistol. "Keep looking."

Charlie spun away, his cheeks burning with anger and his chest cold with fear. The rock wall of the cave was just as unrevealing as it had been that afternoon, except now the floodlight threw every hollow into sharp relief.

"What if I can't find it?" he asked.

"You know what will happen."

"And if I do find it?"

"I'll let you go, of course."

There was a mocking edge to Fiorelli's voice that told Charlie she was lying. Of course she was. She'd just admitted to murder. And she needed a Ghost Queen to fake her scientific breakthrough. She had no reason to keep Charlie alive.

"I think we need to see the cave by moonlight." Charlie edged closer to a large boulder that could perhaps cover his flight into the night.

"That is not going to happen." Fiorelli's tone was clipped. "In fact, I don't see why I should continue this farce any longer." Charlie turned to see her aiming the gun at his chest. He raised his hands, adrenaline flooding his system.

"I see you've progressed your scientific method." The voice was cool, with the soft drawl of the southern states. Lucier stepped out of the shadows to stand by the floodlight. "From poisoning to bullets. What an evolution."

"You." Fiorelli all but spat the word. Her gun swung to point at Lucier.

The American rested one hand casually on the boulder, but there was nothing casual about his eyes. They fixed on Fiorelli with a burning intensity.

"Yes, me." Lucier's lip curled. "You stole my brother's work and pretended it was yours. You murdered him to hide your theft. And now you're going to kill this young man to save your career."

"I will get away with all of it." Fiorelli licked her lips. "You can't stop me. No one can."

Like magic, a small and wickedly sharp throwing knife appeared in Lucier's left hand.

Fiorelli sneered. "You brought a knife to a gunfight."

Her shoulders tensed as she lined up the shot. Charlie crouched to spring forward and try to save Lucier's life. Time seemed to slow as several things happened at once.

The ghost moth fluttered down from the cave roof, wings beating wildly as it flew between Lucier and Fiorelli.

Charlie shouted 'No!' as both Lucier and Fiorelli took their shots.

Distracted by the moth, Lucier's knife throw went wide, clattering harmlessly on the rock wall by Fiorelli's head.

Fiorelli's gun went off, the 'bang' hitting Charlie's ears like a blow. And Lucier's hand hit the floodlight off switch.

The cave plunged into darkness. Scrabbling and footsteps sounded in the dark. Fiorelli's gun went off again.

"I think this has gone on quite long enough," said a calm voice. The cave flooded with light again as Avery turned the light on.

Charlie blinked, then froze.

A few paces away, Lucier loomed over Fiorelli, who crouched, backed up against the cave wall.

"Crepa, bastardo," she snarled and fired her gun at point-blank range.

The sound ricocheted off the cave walls. Lucier staggered back, clutching his chest. His brows drew together in puzzlement as he looked down.

"You missed."

Fiorelli hissed and fired again. Lucier flinched, then ran his hands over his chest. Again, he appeared unharmed.

Eleanor stepped out of the shadows to join Avery. "One thing you ought to know, Dr Fiorelli. My gun is loaded with blanks."

Fiorelli's hands spasmed around the gun. "You... you... bastardi!"

"I'm sure I am," said Eleanor cheerfully.

"Ah." Realisation dawned on Lucier's face. He gave Eleanor an appreciative nod.

"Dr Isabella Fiorelli," said Avery. "You are under arrest for murder and attempted murder."

"But..." Fiorelli waved her gun at Avery. "I heard him! He is after the Ghost Queen. He is going to kill us all!"

Avery raised an eyebrow. "I have no idea what you're talking about. Do you, Eleanor?"

Eleanor shrugged. "I think she's a little overheated. Attempted murder will do that to a person."

"Stronzo! I will—" Fiorelli's face twisted in rage as words failed her. Her face turned an unusual shade of red.

Eleanor's voice filled with false sympathy. "I await your vengeance with interest. For now, though, best not admit to anything more while you're on camera."

Fiorelli blanched and shut her mouth with a snap.

Eleanor turned to Charlie, wearing a curious expression he had never seen before. He took a moment to realise that this was Eleanor looking guilty.

She walked over and touched his arm. "I'm so sorry, Charlie. It was awful to set you up like this. But... we had to get a confession."

Charlie lowered himself onto a rock, feeling shaky. "I really, really don't like people pointing guns at me. Even when they're loaded with blanks."

"I am so very sorry," said Eleanor. "I would have loved to tell you in advance, but your face gives away everything. The trap would never have worked."

"But... he had a knife!" Charlie pointed at Lucier.

The orchid collector watched Avery read Fiorelli her rights with an impassive gaze, but Charlie wasn't fooled. He'd seen Lucier's eyes when he spoke of his brother. He wouldn't put it past Lucier to try and finish the job later tonight.

"I had to work really hard to stop Avery from intervening when Lucier appeared," said Eleanor. "Lucky I did, though. Now we have two murders to pin on Fiorelli. Also, Dante only agreed to this plan because he's somewhere in the treeline with a sniper rifle. If Fiorelli had looked to be a real danger, I don't think she'd have left the cave alive."

"Oh." Charlie swallowed. "Just as well it worked out then."

A darker shadow detached itself from the cave entry.

"Hi, Charlie," said Dante.

He didn't appear to be armed, but Charlie knew his friend would have a dozen weapons ready to hand if the occasion arose.

"Hi, Dante. And thanks." Charlie blew out a long breath, and his shoulders slowly unwound.

"How do you feel?" asked Dante.

Charlie gave him an uncertain look. "You want to know how I feel?"

"It's what people do," said Dante.

"Er, I suppose they do," said Charlie. "Then I'm ok, I guess. Glad this is all over."

"Cameras did their job?" asked Eleanor.

"Yes." Dante circled the cave, collecting several cameras and checking their footage.

Avery handcuffed a tight-lipped Fiorelli, her face set in a mask of anger.

"Do you need help taking her back to the station?" asked Dante.

"Hemi's on his way." Avery looked around the cave, clearly torn between desire and duty. "You think this is where Carroll hid..."

"We haven't found it yet," said Eleanor smoothly.

Chagrin chased regret across Avery's face. "Duty calls, I suppose."

They watched Avery guide Fiorelli out of the cave and into the darkness.

The moth flew around Charlie's head and then vanished from the floodlight beam. Charlie felt calm wash over him, as though he'd been immersed in cool water.

"Can you switch off the light, Dante?" asked Charlie. "I think it's time."

The cave plunged into darkness. The moonlight brightened, and the rocks and hollows of the cave took shape as Charlie's eyes adjusted to the night.

"What's happening?" asked Lucier.

"It's possible," said Eleanor, her voice gentle, "that tonight we may discover the secret Professor Carroll was protecting. The one your brother was murdered for."

Lucier's shoulders straightened. "I would like to see that, yes."

Charlie looked up, following the green-winged moth fluttering above them.

"Is that your moth?" asked Eleanor.

"It's circling, and it's just landed... there." Charlie pointed to where the stream flowed out of the rock wall.

There was no room for anyone to crawl up the river. Even the most determined cave diver would have no space to enter.

Dante stalked forward and knocked gently on the rock. It went 'thunk.'

Eleanor smiled. "You said Carroll used to paint the sets for the Te Kohe Theatrical Society, Charlie. I guess he adapted his skills."

Dante tapped until he found the edge of the panel, then dug his fingers into a small depression to find a catch. He pushed it, and a section of faux rock wall swung open with the faintest creak of hinges.

A ghostly blue glow issued from the small tunnel Dante had revealed.

"I think," said Charlie, "we've found Professor Carroll's treasure."

53

Which contains magic, mystery, and moths.

Dante stooped and peered into the tunnel.

It was as if the night sky had drifted underground. The rock ceiling leading back into the hill was covered with tiny points of blue light, a constellation under the earth.

"Is that normal?" asked Dante.

Charlie grinned. "They're glow worms. They love to hang out in caves. They'll light our way for us."

The Waimaru stream sang gently as Dante gazed into the star-spangled tunnel.

A river to wash away all sins. It seemed appropriate to the day. Dante started forward, treading carefully on the wet stones, hands in front of him to sense unseen obstacles.

He heard shufflings and the occasional splash as Eleanor, Charlie and Lucier followed.

The cave turned a corner. Someone behind Dante gasped as the vista opened up before them.

"It's like a dream," breathed Charlie.

The mouth of the cave opened to reveal a hidden valley. Steep rock walls of dark limestone shot with white reared up to the night sky, covered in lush foliage. The valley was so narrow, the trees arched to touch branches in the centre. Dante guessed that even from the air, the valley would be invisible.

Creepers and vines bridged the gorge like garlands from a forgotten festival, and thick moss covered with tiny white flowers covered the valley floor. The stream ran down the centre of the valley in a narrow thread, glinting silver.

But that wasn't what had stunned Charlie.

Everywhere Dante turned, there were orchids. Silver orchids clung to every tree branch and grew from every fissure in the limestone rock wall. Delicate filigree petals reached up to the moon, next to orchid stems bowed under the weight of their blooms.

And the flowers glowed.

Every orchid shone with a pale light, as if the moon itself had come down to rest on its petals.

"They're Ghost Queens," said Charlie. "This whole valley is full of Ghost Queen orchids."

"No." There was a smile in Lucier's voice. "They're not Ghost Queens. These are all hybrids."

Now that Dante looked closer, he could see what Lucier meant. There were tiny starlike orchids, but also flowers with ornate lacy blossoms, and larger blooms like lanterns.

"Fiorelli won't like that," said Charlie.

Lucier gave a sharp laugh. "She'll never come here."

"They're a new kind of Ghost Queen," said Charlie. "Cross-pollinated with the New Zealand native orchids. It's how they survived."

Lucier's teeth shone white in the moonlight as he smiled. "A fitting tribute to your professor."

"Hey." Charlie reached a hand out to something Dante couldn't see. "You guided us here. Thank you."

"Charlie," said Eleanor. "I can't see your moth."

"But he's right here on my hand." Charlie held up his right hand.

"Your hand is empty," said Eleanor.

Charlie's face fell, and he blinked rapidly. "I see. My ghost moth is really a ghost moth now." He sighed. "I suppose it was bound to happen."

"Charlie, look." Dante pointed, and Charlie's eyes widened.

A great pohutakawa tree leaned out from the cliff, its branches spreading from one side of the valley to the other. Dozens of glowing orchids clustered around its roots, their starry flowers reaching up to the sky. And fluttering in and out of the moonbeams was a cloud of pūriri moths.

Charlie's mouth made an 'o' of wonder. "That's where the moth came from! It's come home."

Dante caught a glint of light at the base of the giant tree.

Charlie gasped. "Those are the terrariums! From the *Whitby*! Carroll's ancestor must have brought them here."

Nestled in the roots of the pohutakawa were four intricate glass cases, each about the size of a birdcage. They reminded Dante of his own Victorian glasshouse, but in miniature. Only a few panes of glass were still intact, and the tree roots curled around their bases, reclaiming them.

"This is magical." Lucier gave a deep sigh. "My brother would have loved this so much. I wish," he spread his hands, "I wish a lot of things. But I'm glad to be here right now."

"I think that we should keep this valley secret." Charlie's face became serious. "It's what the Professor wanted."

Dante studied Lucier, looking for telltale signs of duplicity. He was a difficult man to read.

"If this valley became known," said Eleanor, "collectors would descend on it like locusts. They'll steal the orchids, and then..."

"I know. Most likely, none of the orchids would survive. They would only prosper with someone like Fiorelli's help." Lucier's voice grew bitter.

"You told me you weren't someone who knew the price of everything and the value of nothing," said Eleanor.

Lucier gave a quiet huff of laughter. "I did say that." He gazed around the moonlight valley, with its moss-covered ground, glowing orchids and giant moths flitting between the flowers. He shook his head in disbelief and then surrender. "Very well. I give my word, on my brother's grave, that I will keep this place secret."

"Thank you," said Charlie. "Very much."

Lucier's face split into a smile that quite transformed it. "I'm glad to be here tonight. Thank you all."

Dante's grip eased on his handgun. He didn't want to threaten Lucier, and he knew threats had a limited lifespan. He wasn't sure how far Lucier could be trusted, if at all.

However, in that quiet moment, with the river pouring a libation to the goddess of spring, and flowers that had hidden for over a century glowing in the moonlight, Dante thought that, just this once, he might trust that things would turn out all right.

54

In which Charlie's guest leaves.

The next day, Charlie rose with the dawn and walked back to the cave. He paced to where he remembered the moth roosting the night before. There, the pūriri moth's body lay, a faded green against the dark sand.

He sighed and gathered it gently in his hands. His breath stirred the down on its wings, now stiff and furled tightly to its body.

He entered the valley and dug a small hole under a young kauri tree. Burying the moth felt like a final goodbye to Professor Carroll, and a few tears fell from Charlie's cheeks onto the rich loam as he covered the moth.

Charlie pressed his hands over the soil, feeling the life there, sleeping, waiting to awaken next summer.

"Thank you for helping us," he whispered to the fallen moth. "I'm glad you made it home."

Charlie smiled through his tears. He was used to endings. He'd lived all his life half in one world, and half in another.

But every so often, he felt like the other side reached out to him to lend a helping hand. He was still figuring out the rules of his strange life, but on the rare times this happened, he felt blessed, and part of something bigger than himself.

It was enough to go on with, for now.

55

In which the sleuths help the police with their enquiries.

"So," said Avery, "I now have footage of Fiorelli admitting to two murders, then attempting to enact a third and a fourth."

"She was having a bad day," said Eleanor.

Avery sighed. "And you have her glove with digitalis traces on it."

"It nearly killed my cat," said Dante. "She's pregnant. The cat, not Fiorelli."

Charlie, Eleanor, and Dante were sitting at the interview room table across from Avery. It was the next morning, and Eleanor felt her lack of sleep keenly.

Avery was wearing an impassive expression that Eleanor labelled the standard 'policeman deciding what to charge you with,' look. They probably practised it in police school.

"Andrea said your cat was going to be ok, and the kittens too," said Charlie.

"How can she tell?" asked Dante.

"She's a vet. They know these things," said Charlie.

"If we can refocus on the issue at hand," said Avery, "this recording was made without knowledge of the suspect—"

"That might have put Fiorelli on her guard," said Eleanor.

"—and by private individuals," finished Avery. "That makes it 'improperly obtained' under New Zealand law. It's up to the judge's discretion whether it's admissible or not. Although the fact that we're looking at a double homicide will carry some weight."

"There's also the dark web conversations you'll find on Fiorelli's laptop," said Eleanor. "They provide clear motivation for her crimes. And I imagine Marcel Lucier will be a convincing witness for the prosecution."

Avery leaned back in his chair. "This case isn't over yet. And my part in setting Fiorelli up may complicate things quite a bit if she goes to trial."

"I'm sure you can make it work," said Eleanor. "That's why they pay you the big bucks."

"They don't pay me the big bucks," said Avery.

"Fiorelli's been rather clever, though," said Eleanor. "There was the disguise when she left to burgle Carroll's house. She knew Lucier had a fedora and wanted to direct attention towards him. Fiorelli left the fedora in the Te Kohe second-hand shop. She probably didn't expect it to be bought and worn so quickly. Blame that on the masque ball."

"You mean it really is..." Avery blinked. "It's rather a nice hat, but I don't think I can wear it again, knowing who it belonged to."

"You were briefly on the suspect list," said Eleanor. "Though I thought it unlikely."

"Oh, did you," murmured Avery.

"Fiorelli took the foxglove leaves from Everton's garden the afternoon of her tea party," said Eleanor. "She wanted to make sure she had the means to get rid of Carroll if their meeting didn't go well.

"Fiorelli's latex allergy meant she couldn't use normal, anonymous gloves to handle the foxglove leaves. So she used her own gloves and disposed of them separately from the incriminating poison gear we found in the hotel rubbish."

"Her gloves ended up in the glove bin of the second-hand shop. After all, where better to hide them than in a larger pile of gloves?" concluded Eleanor.

Dante made a small, deep growl in the back of his throat, and Eleanor felt a wave of gratitude that Andrea had treated his cat in time.

"We needed to confirm that Fiorelli couldn't propagate an extinct Ghost Queen. So I put a message in the notebook, seemingly in Carroll's handwriting, and let Fiorelli read it. Then Stephanie helped us contact her on the dark web. Our theory was right — Fiorelli needed to find a recent Ghost Orchid seed, and someone to propagate it in secret."

Avery drummed his fingers on the desk. "Go on."

"We needed a trap to find out whether Fiorelli or Lucier was the murderer. At the book signing, I seeded the idea to Fiorelli that I was working with you to solve Carroll's murder."

Avery smiled faintly. "That message is indelibly in my book now."

"This helped me set the trap at the ball. I let both Fiorelli and Lucier know that we had evidence to convict the murderer hidden in two locations. Being innocent, Lucier didn't act on this information. I still think it would have worked on Fiorelli, but Fairfax tipped her off," said Eleanor. "It was still quick work on her part. She stole the poison bottle under the cover of darkness to avoid being caught on camera. The second trap at the cave, however, proved irresistible."

Avery's face gave nothing away, but Eleanor was sure he was storing everything in his police inspector's memory.

"Do you have enough evidence to get justice for Professor Carroll?" asked Charlie.

"That's not the subject of this interview," said Avery.

"When we failed to film Fiorelli stealing the poison bottle, I knew we had to use the cave trap," said Eleanor. "Thank you for agreeing to stage the argument with me — you were exceptional."

"Flattery will get you nowhere," said Avery.

"You know the rest. We waited until Fiorelli went into the bathroom, and then put on our performance." Eleanor's tone became aggrieved. "My pistol has been impounded as evidence."

Avery pinched the bridge of his nose. "I can't believe you actually had a license for that antique."

"I'm a paid up member of the Te Kohe pistol club," said Eleanor. "And the blanks were for the upcoming harbour swim on Sunday."

"There will be a fine for carrying even a licensed gun around in your handbag," said Avery. "This isn't New York."

"I'm aware."

"Don't get me started on your friend here and his penchant for concealed weaponry." Avery nodded towards Dante.

Dante's expression altered not one bit.

"I wonder if Fiorelli would prefer a murder charge to the ignominy of being exposed as a fraud," said Eleanor. "If you want to cut a deal for a full confession, I'd use that as a lever."

"Good point." Avery looked thoughtful.

"I don't think we broke that many laws," said Charlie. "Did we?"

"Breaking and entering, entrapment, planting evidence, recording without consent," Avery ticked them off on his fingers. "Enough to seriously inconvenience your summer holidays."

"The cave was Carroll's property," said Eleanor. "Surely we're allowed to record on private property."

"Add trespass to the list," said Avery.

"If we had a bit more time, I'm sure we could have created a legal trap." Eleanor paused, then shook her head. "Actually, no, I don't think we could have. But you can't argue with the results."

Avery laced his fingers together on the desk. "I'll admit you have good intentions. But if you continue to play fast and loose like this, it will come back to bite you."

"You just want to know if we found a Ghost Queen," said Eleanor.

"I really, really do," sighed Avery.

"We all swore a solemn oath," said Eleanor. "I'm going to have to consult my colleagues before revealing anything."

Avery contemplated his knuckles for a moment, then appeared to come to a decision. "Thank you for sharing your information regarding this case. You can all vacate the premises now. Please don't darken my door again, etc. etc."

"Bowls on Wednesday if you're still here?" asked Eleanor.

"No comment," said Avery.

Eleanor was just out of the door when Avery called, 'Eleanor, wait.'

She turned and re-entered the office, giving Charlie and Dante a vague 'carry on' gesture.

"Yes?" she asked.

Avery came out from behind the table to stand in front of her, a little closer than social norms would allow.

"How are you really?" His eyes were a warm brown, and his voice no longer carried police inspector overtones.

Eleanor decided to give an honest answer. "Tired," she said simply.

Avery lifted one finger to trace it down her cheek. "Did seeing Charlie in danger have a sobering effect on you?"

Eleanor looked away. "I had a backup plan, but yes. It wasn't a pleasant feeling." She met his gaze. "It's hard not to fall back on old habits. Especially when playing for high stakes."

"You took a lot of risks." Avery was standing closer now, close enough for her to rest her hands on the smooth cotton of his dress shirt. "I don't know why you find it necessary to pursue justice with such disregard for the law, but it's..."

"Captivating?"

"Concerning." His hands slipped around her waist, and Eleanor's breath caught.

"I'm sure this isn't how you usually conclude police interviews," she said, playing for time.

"I'm sure it isn't." His voice was steady, and his eyes never left hers. "I want you to promise me..." He paused, frowning. "I'm not sure."

"Something about not taking excessive risks to catch murderers?"

He shook his head. "No, that would never work." He stepped back and placed his hands on her shoulders. "I can see I'll have to keep a closer eye on you in the future."

"That will be interesting," said Eleanor faintly.

"No doubt," he murmured. "Go home and get some rest, Eleanor."

56

Which comes to various conclusions.

After their police interview, Dante, Eleanor, and Charlie sat at the most secluded table of the Frog and Gumboot. It was ten o'clock on a Tuesday, and the cafe buzzed with caffeine, gossip, and speculation.

Fiorelli's arrest late last night was supposed to be a secret, so of course everybody in town knew.

Steam rose from Eleanor's Assam tea, and Charlie contemplated the mushroom cloud in the frothed milk of his latte. Dante beheaded his boiled egg with one swipe of his knife and lined his toast soldiers up, ready for battle.

"They're all going to hate me," said Charlie.

"Who?" asked Eleanor.

"The orchidists," said Charlie. "All of them."

"And why's that?" asked Eleanor.

"I helped bring down the eminent Doctor Fiorelli. They'll be so annoyed. They won't forgive me in a hurry."

"I think there's something you're failing to take into account," said Eleanor.

Charlie frowned. "And that is?"

"The flexibility of the human mind." Eleanor nodded towards the long communal table currently occupied by members of the Te Kohe Botanical Society.

Greg was holding court at one end, while a few seats down, Marjorie Everton bemoaned the harm Fiorelli had done when splitting her prize orchid.

"Come with me to listen and learn." Eleanor took Charlie's arm and led him over to stand in the coffee queue that ran alongside the communal table.

"That Fiorelli." Greg took a sip of his coffee. "Obviously a crook. Should have seen it coming."

"Oh, I did see it coming." Marjorie leaned forward with gusto. "I picked her as a wrong'un from the start. All that nonsense about pure orchid lineages. You could see she was cracked!"

Eleanor raised her eyebrows at Charlie.

"It's called retroactive brilliance," she murmured in Charlie's ear, as other society members chimed in with their opinions on Fiorelli's villainy. "Otherwise known as 'post hoc, ergo propter hoc' — 'after this, therefore because of this.' Humans are geniuses at justifying away anything we don't want to deal with. On that subject — are you going to check in on Stephanie before she goes?"

Charlie blushed. "I don't know."

"Dante's tracker says she's still at the Pepper Tree Hotel. You could go there after breakfast."

"I guess so."

"One chocolate brownie, please," said Eleanor, as they reached the front of the queue. "Heated, with whipped cream. It's for you, Charlie. To cheer you up."

"Thanks." Charlie tried to look more cheerful.

Back at their table, Dante was starting in on the hash browns and mushrooms. He looked up as Eleanor's friend Billy entered the cafe.

"Billy," Eleanor waved her over. "Tell us the latest on Carroll's estate, please. We're highly interested parties, and would love to know any developments."

Billy grinned and slid into a chair next to Charlie. "You'll never guess."

Dante looked up. "Carroll kept Albarelli's journals in a safe deposit box at the bank."

Billy stared at him. "Ah, yeah. There are these historic journals from an Italian botanist listed in Carroll's will. The bank confirmed it. How did you know?"

Dante shrugged. "It's what I'd do."

"What's going to happen to them?" asked Charlie.

"Carroll wanted them sold to a museum or botanical institute," said Billy. "Apparently, Carroll's great-great-grandfather rescued them from this sinking ship. He was a friend of the Italian botanist and wanted to protect his legacy. There's going to be a bidding war. And Carroll wanted the proceeds to go to a trust my boss is setting up. The trust will look after Carroll's house and land."

Eleanor leaned back with a smile. "Carroll wanted his land undisturbed, and Charlie to look after his garden?"

"Right again." Billy frowned. "You seem well informed."

"Interested parties," said Eleanor. "I think this is wrapping up rather nicely."

"Hi, Stephanie." Charlie looked around the hotel room door. Stephanie was in the throes of packing up, with clothes strewn around the room like confetti.

"Hi." Stephanie sat cross-legged in the middle of the bed, holding a shoe in each hand. She looked pensive.

"You're leaving," said Charlie.

"I guess."

"Why not stay?" asked Charlie.

He'd been affected, he realised, by both Eleanor and Dante. Eleanor came up with preposterous ideas and then expected the world to go along with them, which it somehow did. Dante operated in a separate reality from everyone else, and simply did whatever made sense to him at the time, even if it had no bearing on anyone else's expectations.

"I don't think my bosses would pay me to hang out in Te Kohe," said Stephanie. "I'm supposed to be back in London by Thursday."

"I think your job sounds dangerous. Why not quit while you're ahead?" Charlie hadn't read any spy novels. He preferred books that featured natural landscapes, and, if possible, well-maintained gardens. But he could picture people in trench coats with silencer-capped pistols waiting in dark alleyways. It worried him.

"It's an adventure," said Stephanie. "That's why I joined up. To have adventures and protect the peace."

Charlie crossed the room to sit on the edge of the bed. "Do you really want to end up killing people? That doesn't sound very peaceful to me."

"How do you know I haven't already? Killed people, I mean."

Charlie gave her a vague stare, and his senses shifted to the spirit world. Stephanie's aura was as fresh and sunny as a March morning.

"You haven't," he declared.

"How come you're so confident?" Stephanie's smile was crooked, and Charlie's heart gave an awkward 'thump.'

"I just know."

"Well, this trip has been memorable at least. I never dreamed I'd go up against Persephone."

"How was it?"

"He's fast." Stephanie fiddled with a shoelace. "I'll be sure never to make that mistake again. That could have been it for me."

"See what I mean? Dangerous."

"Hmmmm." Stephanie wound the shoelace around her finger. "Oh, — before I forget — please give Dante this." She held up a small black object: the tracker.

"Keep it," said Charlie. "In case I ever need to find you again."

Stephanie's lips parted in uncertainty, then resolved into a smile. "Ok, Charlie Wilson. I will."

"See you around." Charlie stood and headed for the door.

He felt strangely cheerful all the way down the stairs. He even managed not to jump as, with a yell, Milo rode his BMX bike through the wall and skidded to a stop on the last landing. It was that kind of day.

After an afternoon rest and leisurely Devonshire tea, Eleanor knocked on Avery's temporary office door in the Te Kohe police station. It was more of a cleared-out storage room than an office, but Avery made it look official.

"Come in," came Avery's voice, and Eleanor opened the door. "Oh. It's you." He looked wary.

Eleanor regarded the piles of paper on the desk and wondered how much of it was due to her actions. "Inspector, I've come to apologise."

"Really?" Avery did not look soothed. In fact, he looked more cautious than ever.

"Yes, apologise. But apologies only take one so far. So I thought of a way to make it up to you."

"Yes?" Avery's eyes flicked back to the paperwork, clearly wanting to get on with it.

"Only if you're willing to stay the night, though."

"The night?" Now, Avery had on his poker face, which meant he was buying time while thinking fast.

Eleanor leaned luxuriously against the door frame and circled her high-heeled foot in a tango adorno. "That's right, Avery, you need to stay the night. Although Charlie and Dante might join us."

Avery frowned. "Join us?"

Eleanor smiled secretively. "It'll be a night to remember."

Avery's expression wavered between wariness, curiosity, and amusement. "Dare I ask?"

"Relax — it's all your orchid dreams come true. Tonight, if you swear a solemn oath of secrecy, we'll go to the El Dorado of the orchid world. As a thank you for your assistance in capturing our murderer."

"Hmmm," said Avery. "I'll let you know. My calendar's packed at the moment."

"Full moon's not going to wait. Bye for now, Inspector." Eleanor sashayed down the corridor.

"My name's Marcus," called Avery, and Eleanor suppressed a smile.

"Yes, Inspector," she called back.

Mending bridges was easier when you had a moonlit valley full of luminous orchids as your calling card.

57

In which we say goodbye... for now.

Dante sat on the sofa in his front parlour and eyed the fluffy cat bed and its occupant like it was an unexploded IED. Andrea, Charlie, and Eleanor filled the other sofa as an informal support group as Dante came to terms with his new status.

"I don't think I can look after kittens," said Dante. "How many are we talking?"

"Usually between four and six," said Andrea.

Dante winced. The cat, unconcerned, stretched out to bite at a stray piece of fluff.

"You could give them away," said Andrea. "But they'll need to stay with their mother for at least eight weeks."

"If I give them away," said Dante, "I'm holding each person personally responsible for their safety."

"What do you mean?" asked Charlie.

"I will do background checks on all of them," said Dante. "And install trackers."

"On the kittens?" asked Andrea. "I don't know if you can do that until they're fully grown."

"On the people, and the kittens. They will," said Dante with finality, "be going to good homes."

"Dante's having kittens about having kittens," said Charlie. "Get it?"

"Yes, dear," said Eleanor. "But it's not really a joke if you have to explain it. Also, you're too young to be making dad jokes. Leave that to Dante."

"I never make dad jokes," said Dante.

"You never make any jokes," said Charlie.

Dante considered. "I can make jokes." He thought some more. "Have you heard the one about the murderer who ended up in jail?"

"No..." said Charlie.

"She did," said Dante. "And we put her there."

There was a brief silence.

"I had a thought about your garden, Dante," said Charlie. "Your willow tree died in that midsummer dry spell. It'll need to be taken out, and I know exactly what to plant there."

"Yes?"

Charlie bit his lip, trying to hide a grin.

"I think we should plant a pomegranate tree." Charlie beamed. "In honour of Persephone, goddess of the spring."

"I am not planting a pomegranate tree in my back garden," said Dante.

"They're beautiful trees," said Charlie. "And the seeds are great on breakfast cereal. Or salads."

"No."

"C'mon," said Charlie. "She's also a goddess of the underworld."

Dante muttered something about shooting the next agent who revealed his codename. "Fine. You can plant a pomegranate tree. But I'm not putting any seeds on my salad."

"I love salad," said Andrea. "I'll make some next time I'm here. Charlie tells me you have some wonderful greens in your veggie patch."

Dante leaned back, defeated. He was outnumbered, outmanoeuvred, and his cat was having kittens.

Part of him wanted to stage a tactical retreat. But sometimes, he reflected, defeat looked very similar to victory. The only difference was in how you kept score.

AUTHOR'S NOTE

Whether or not this story was a two pipe problem, I hope you enjoyed it.

For a free short story, and to be in the running to beta read my next books, join my email list at:

https://naomikuttner.com/join/

ACKNOWLEDGMENTS

Many thanks to the generous members of the New Zealand Orchid Society and the Orchid Council of New Zealand.

Any orchid-related errors or botanical acts that stretch the limits of believability are entirely mine — they did their best to get me up to speed.

I want to underline here (especially as this is a murder mystery) that any resemblance to real persons, living or dead, is purely coincidental.

Although... if someone puts a few drops of suspicious liquid in your tea, it might be better to pour the whole cup into the nearest pot plant. Not an orchid, though - they don't like their roots to sit in water for too long.

A huge thank you to my beta readers! You guys are amazing, awesome, and all other things superlative, grammatical, and good.

It's thanks to you that Dante and Co. haven't tripped over misplaced Oxford commas or fallen into bottomless plot holes. Much appreciated.

Lastly, thank you to my family. Ben, Mum and Dad provided invaluable insights and feedback.

Ariella and Joshua — you both distracted me as much as humanly possible :) And you both have made my life so much richer. I dreamed up all of this because of you.

Printed in Dunstable, United Kingdom

80774620R00181